THE COMPLICATED TRANE

A Novel

CHARLIE GIRARD

ISBN: 978-1-09838-786-0 Paperback
ISBN: 978-1-09838-787-7 eBook

CHAPTER 1

The door was a fine rich oak, it was as hard as a rock with grain that streamed horizontally across from one side of the frame to the other. About half-way up the door was a pane of frosted glass. On the glass was written the words "**JACK TRANE—PRIVATE INVESTIGATIONS**". Since his last case, Jack had made some upgrades. The letters on the door were now written in raised gold lettering as opposed to the plain black lettering that was replaced. In his office, there was a reception desk with a small waiting area. The three chairs with cracked leather coverings that had once graced the office, had also been replaced by three mahogany guest chairs with a pleasant tan fabric and a modern circular pattern woven in. His secretary Trudy also benefitted from Jack's recent success. She had the same desk that she had used for the past 8 years, but now she was sitting in an executive deluxe leather president's office chair. It had handrails that were 6 inches wide and had a beautiful, polished mahogany finish. The chair had leather padding that was about 4 inches thick. It was large enough to fit a small cow but comfortable enough to make Trudy happy. And for Jack, that's what counted. The $1,800.00 price tag didn't matter. Although he did make a mental note of it.

For Jack, the simple things were what he liked, because that's who he was. A simple private eye who made the most of his skills and abilities, who once in a while, scored the big case. Which is what he had just done, and now he was reaping the benefits. He had just gotten himself a new deluxe banker's chair for his office, with a brown leather padded seat, to replace the old banker's chair with the vinyl padded seat. He had made one more addition to his office that he felt would come in handy when vetting his clients. He had installed 2 hidden cameras in the wall just behind his desk. One had a standard 50mm lens, the other had a telephoto lens. He had a button placed on the floor underneath his desk, with a Bluetooth connection to the cameras. When a new client would sit at his desk, he could take their pictures without them knowing it, and the pictures would automatically download to his phone. Isn't technology grand. Indeed, things were looking up for Jack and you might say that he was on a roll. He about to score another major case that would dwarf the case that he had just solved.

The rain dripped heavily on the windowsill outside Jack's office. It was late in the day, and he was just thinking about a nice cold beer down at *Big Jim's Sports* bar. Trudy was filing her nails in the next office. It was about 4 o'clock and he was just about to tell Trudy to take the rest of the day off when the oak door creaked open, and in stepped a rather distinguished-looking gentleman.

He was about 6 feet tall with dark hair greying at the temples. He had on a brown wool, 3-piece suit. It looked to be a *Brooks Brothers* design. It made him look almost presidential. His shirt was white with light brown stripes and a button-down collar. He had on a red tie with a paisley pattern on it, and he had a pocket square to match. He closed the door and stood squarely in front of Trudy's desk. There was about a 5-second silence as Trudy slipped her nail file back into the top drawer of her desk. She snapped her gum, made a half-smile, and then in her home-grown New York accent, she asked, "Can I help you?" The man smiled back at Trudy and spoke with a reserved English accent "My name is Harold Chumley and I'm here to see Mr. Trane about a very urgent matter. Would you be kind enough to let Mr. Trane know that I'm here?"

Trudy raised her right eyebrow and responded, "Mr. Chumley, is Mr. Trane expecting you?" He replied, "My dear girl, Mr. Trane indeed is not expecting me, but once he hears that my case involves 20 million dollars, I'm quite sure that he will want to take the time to hear my proposition."

Now both of Trudy's eyebrows were raised. She stood up. She was wearing a grey plaid skirt with a tan belt and a turquoise top with a low-cut neck. She had Mr. Chumley's attention and asked him to take a seat and she would go in to speak with Mr. Trane. She walked directly into Jack's office and closed the door behind her.

Jack was sitting at his desk with a big smile. Trudy started to speak, but Jack held up his hands to stop her. He said, "Trudy, I heard everything this guy said. But mostly what I heard was 20 million dollars. Let's make him wait a few minutes so he doesn't think that this is the only case that I have to work on." Trudy said, "But Jack, this is the only case you have to work on." Jack laughed, yeah but he doesn't have to know that. Besides, what are the chances that he really has a 20-million-dollar case? He's probably just selling magazine subscriptions and he wanted an excuse to get in the door."

Trudy shot back, "No Jack, you should see the way this guy is dressed and the way he speaks, I think he's legit."

Jack smirked, "OK Trudy, send him in, let's see what a 20-million-dollar case looks like."

Trudy went back out to her office. Harold Chumley was sitting in one of the mahogany guest chairs and he was smiling in a peculiar way at Trudy. He said to her "Is everything all right dear?" Trudy quipped back, "Yeah everything is all right and I'm not your dear." Then she said sarcastically, "Mr. Trane will see you now." Harold Chumley rose from his chair and walked into Jack's office. Jack stood up to introduce himself and shake the client's hand. He noticed what this man was wearing and now he felt a little under-dressed. Jack was wearing a pair of dark blue dockers and a brown belt. However, he was also wearing an impeccable white shirt with a button-down collar, his trademark. He also had on a yellow stripe tie, worn loosely under an open top button of his shirt. Jack extended his hand, "Hello, I'm Jack Trane, how can I help you?"

Mr. Chumley smiled and extended his hand and shook Jack's hand. Then he said, "Hello Mr. Trane, so very pleased to make your acquaintance. My name is Harold Chumley. I work for the Amalgamated Insurance Company, and I believe that we have a case that if you are successful in solving, will be very profitable for both you and me."

Jack sat back down in his brand-new banker's chair and offered Mr. Chumley a seat in the age-worn green vinyl chair in front of his desk. The rain had stopped but you could still hear the rhythmic sound of the rain hitting the windowsill outside Jack's window. It was like it was keeping time with the old Pink Floyd song "*Money*" tap.. tap..tap.

Jack leaned back in his chair, squinted a little as he looked at Harold Chumley, and said," Ok Mr. Chumley, tell me about this case, you have my attention." Before Mr. Chumley had a chance to start speaking, Jack stepped on the button under his desk and took some candid pictures of him for future reference. Mr. Chumley became profoundly serious. He leaned on the desk as he addressed Jack, "Mr. Trane, a very expensive timepiece has been stolen and as a result, my employer is responsible for covering the loss to the tune of 20 million dollars." Jack coughed a little when he heard 20 million dollars, out loud, coming from Mr. Chumley's mouth in an English accent. Mr. Chumley continued, "Mr. Trane, the Amalgamated Insurance Company would like to hire you to retrieve this extremely valuable timepiece and return it to us, so we can avoid paying the 20-million-dollar insurance payment. But time is of the essence. We can stall for perhaps 30 days on the payment, but we would like to have this timepiece found before that. And Mr. Trane, did I mention that there would be a 1 % finder's fee in addition to your normal investigation fee?"

Quickly Jack was calculating in his head, 1% of 20 million equals 200,000 dollars! Inside, Jack was experiencing butterflies in his stomach, sweat on his forehead, and his stomach was rumbling as it was nearing 5 O'clock and he was hungry. But on the outside, he managed to remain calm and cool. He responded, "Mr. Chumley, no offense, but there are probably a thousand private eyes that you could have looked up, to offer this case to, why me?" He was still looking at Harold Chumley with squinted eyes.

Mr. Chumley took a deep breath and looked at Jack and said, "Mr. Trane, that's a particularly good question, and let me answer it in the same way that you asked it. No offense, but it appears that this case requires someone that's familiar with the underbelly of this city and a certain intimacy with the criminal element that presents itself therein. You were the logical choice." He smiled at Jack and sat back in his chair. Jack laughed, "So it looks like you did your homework. Ok Mr. Chumley, tell me about this case so I know what I'm getting into."

Mr. Chumley looked up at the ceiling and then back at Jack and calmly began relating to Jack all the details of the stolen timepiece. "Mr. Trane, have you ever heard of the *Henry Graves Supercomplication?*" Jack answered "Henry Graves, didn't he play for the White Sox?" Mr. Chumley was not amused by Jack's wisecrack. "Mr. Trane, the *Henry Graves Supercomplication* is perhaps the most complicated mechanical pocket watch ever created. It was made in 1932 by *Patek Philippe* for a well know banker Henry Graves. It took more than 10 master watchmakers to complete the watch. It is made of solid 18 karat gold. It has 70 jewels and has 24 functions. To this day it is considered the most complicated watch ever created. It is an open face watch and measures exactly 2.9 inches in diameter and 1.4 inches in thickness, it weighs 18.9 ounces."

Jack had a smug look on his face, "Sound like quite a watch Mr. Chumley, not exactly something you find in a Cracker Jack's box." Mr. Chumley was not amused, "Can I continue Mr. Trane?" Jack leaned on his desk towards Mr. Chumley, "Yeah, go ahead I'm still listening." Mr. Chumley continued, "The watch was sold at auction 6 years ago at a record price of just under 24 million dollars. The sale was made to a private buyer. Then just about a year ago the watch again changed hands in a private auction to a private 3rd party. Again, the buyer has remained anonymous. The price was not disclosed, but we are to assume that it was far greater than the 24 million of 6 years ago. We insured the timepiece for 20 million dollars and that is what we will have to pay if the watch is not recovered.

Jack put his hands behind his head and leaned way back in his chair. He thought for a moment and responded to Mr. Chumley. "So obviously someone lifted the watch from this 3rd party. It would seem that the police would be involved in the recovery. Why don't you just go to them?" Mr. Chumley took another deep breath, "Mr. Trane, my dear fellow, it has been our experience that when it comes to recovery of stolen items, the police force is really not very motivated to bring the perpetrator to justice. We have found that by offering the proper financial incentive, to the right person, there is a much greater chance of achieving the desired results. Do you understand?"

Jack was thinking to himself. "Yeah, I understand, you want the right chump to do the dirty work for you, and for 200 thousand dollars, I'm the right chump". He smiled at Mr. Chumley, "Ok Harold, give me some details, what happened to the watch?" Mr. Chumley leaned forward and put his hands on Jack's desk. "Well as it turned out, the watch had been loaned to the MET for a display on complicated timepieces. As it was about to be returned to the owner by an armored car, somehow the watch was stolen and both armored car guards were seriously injured, in fact, one is still recovering in the hospital, the other is recuperating at home." Jack's mind was working fast, he was taking all this in, and he was formulating a $200,000 plan in his mind. He took out a small notepad from the top drawer of his desk and handed it to Mr. Chumley. He said, "All right I want you to write down the name of both guards and their addresses. I also need to know when the watch was delivered to the MET and when it was to be returned. Also, I'd like to know who owns the watch, just in case I need some more information."

Mr. Chumley breathed in and responded, "Mr. Trane, the identity of the owner is secret, even my company does not know who owns the watch, we are dealing with a third party who also wishes to remain anonymous. Your dealing will be with me. And when the watch is recovered, you will deliver it to me, and then you will receive your compensation." He handed Jack what looked to be a pre-printed contract with all the details that they had just laid out.

Jack felt a little uneasy about the fact that Chumley already had a contract drawn up. He said to Chumley, "If you don't mind, I will have my assistant draw up a contract that will cover all these bases." Mr. Chumley made a sour face and said, "All right then. Very well, as long as we can do it presently." Jack called out to Trudy in the next office. She came into Jack's office with a contract drawn up in duplicate and dropped it on Jack's desk. She smiled at Mr. Chumley and walked back into her office.

Mr. Chumley said to Jack, "My, isn't she pertinacious." Jack smiled, he said, "You have no idea." They both signed the contract. Interestingly, Mr. Chumley didn't take a copy for his records. Jack handed Mr. Chumley a pad and asked him to write down the names and addresses of the armor car guards and the details of the watch's delivery. Chumley wrote down the information and handed the pad back to him. Jack took the pad and put it on the left side of his desk. Then he stood up and reached out to shake Mr. Chumley's hand and said, "Mr. Chumley, where can I get in touch with you?" He handed Jack his card and a 4x6 picture of the watch. "All the information is there Mr. Trane. I will expect to hear from you presently."

Jack slipped the card into his shirt pocket. He took a close look at the picture of the watch and put it into his top desk drawer. He shook Mr. Chumley's hand and Mr. Chumley turned and walked out of his office, past Trudy's desk, and directly out the door. Trudy got up and ran into Jack's office. "Jack, what's going on, did you take a $200,000 case?" Trudy was seeing dollar signs too. She knew that when Jack did well, so did she. Jack opened the pad that Mr. Chumley had just given to him with the names of the guards. On the top 2 lines of the pad were 2 names: Don Valley, and Billy Bardsley. He handed the pad to Trudy and said, "Ok Trudy, now I need you to do your thing. I need as much public information as I can get on these 2 guys. Trudy was a whiz when it came to finding information on people. She could find a pearl in a marble factory. If there was any dirt on Mr. Clean, she would find it. Jack pointed his index finger into the air and said, “I’ve got a good idea. Since this is such a big case, Trudy, why don’t you just take the rest of the day off and we’ll get a fresh start tomorrow.” Trudy groaned, “Jack it's after 5:00, what do you mean take the rest of the day off? I’m working on overtime right now!”

Jack was always telling Trudy to take the rest of the day off, when in fact he knew the day was over. The joke was getting old. “Ok Trudy, sorry, why don’t you go home and get a good night’s sleep and we’ll get started first thing in the morning. Trudy looked at Jack with one eye squinted, “I’ll be in at 9:00 Jack, I expect you to be there too!” Jack had his mouth open, “9:00, you’re killing me, Trudy, let’s make it 9:30, I have to get breakfast, you don’t want to see me without my morning latte.” Trudy responded, “I don’t know if I want to see you at all”. They both laughed. This was the normal banter that went on all day between Jack and Trudy.

She picked up her purse and put on the sweater that she had on the back of her chair, and she left the office. Jack started to reflect for a moment. He took the picture of the supercomplication pocket watch out of his desk drawer and looked at it closely for about 2 minutes, then he slipped it back into his desk drawer. He was a bit of a collector himself. He had started collecting pocket watches back in his early 30’s, now he was approaching 50 years old. His grandfather had given his father a 1912 gold open-face Waltham pocket watch.

His father had handed it down to Jack. Over the years he had collected more than 20 Waltham pocket watches of many different sizes and types. He was quite sure that none of his watches came anywhere close in value to the supercomplication watch. He tried to imagine how the *Henry Graves Supercomplication* watch would look on his dresser. He smiled for a moment, then shook his head back into reality. He still wanted to head down to *Big Jim's Sports* bar for a nice cold beer and one of their famous burgers. He also had another motivation for going down to *Big Jim's*. Jack was a big hockey fan, and his Boston Bruins were playing the New York Rangers tonight, and he loved to torment the Rangers fans because he knew his Bruins were better. He put on his hat and draped his trench coat over his shoulder. He walked towards the door and left the office. Before he closed the door, he placed a single match under the last hinge in the door jamb. It was a simple security measure that he always took. If he came back to the office and the match was on the floor, it meant that someone was either inside or had broken in overnight. It was a simple security move, but it has served him well. As he left, he looked down at his watch and wondered to himself, "*I wonder how much this Casio is worth?*

CHAPTER 2

Jack sat on the edge of his bed rubbing his eyes. He opened them a couple of times to see if they were clear. Each time he opened them he could see just a little bit more. He had stayed at *Big Jim's Sports* bar last night just a little longer than he had planned. But the Bruins were winning, the *Guinness's* kept coming, and now he's paying the price. But the Bruins had won 4-1 so it was worth it. The morning light was coming in through the window and creeping across the room and he wondered exactly what time it was. The alarm had gone off at 7:00 AM but he had pushed the snooze button a couple of times, then he just unplugged the clock alltogether. He picked up his wristwatch from the end table and brought it up to his face so he could see the hands. It was now 8:30 AM and he was running late. Trudy was expecting him in the office at 9:00. He knew that wasn't going to happen. Trudy probably figured that too. He stood up and felt the little pain in the joints of his knees reminding him that his next milestone was 50 years old. That wasn't a milestone that he was looking forward to, but he took it in stride. He made his way to the bathroom for his morning ritual. A quick shower and a shave and he was ready for the day.

When he came out of the bathroom he headed straight for his walk-in closet. As usual, it was so crammed with all the broken appliances that he never threw away, along with books, magazines, and a few other collectibles, that he really couldn't walk into his walk-in closet. He reached into the closet and pulled out a pair of pants. They were the ones closest to the door. They were a nice coffee brown pair of pleated dockers. He reached in again and pulled out an orange print tie. He reached in one more time and pulled out a brown tweed sports jacket. The trifecta, it seemed every morning he was able to pull out 3 separate items that all matched. He figured that it was a gift.

He walked over to his armoire, opened it up, and took out an impeccable clean and pressed white shirt with a button-down collar. He was certainly not the best dresser in town, but he always had a clean white shirt with a button-down collar in his ensemble. He got dressed and sat back down on the bed for a minute. He thought about the meeting that he had yesterday with Harold Chumley. He knew that finding the stolen pocket watch would not be easy, but for $200,000, he was determined to make it happen.

He grabbed one of his favorite hats. It was a *Flechet fedora*, gray with a black band and a red feather. It had seen better days, but it was his go-to hat. He slipped on a basic tan trench coat that was draped over a chair from the night before. It was an early November morning, so he was ready for the chill in the air. His first stop would be the *Coffee Café* because he needed some breakfast, and he needed a Latte. He was hooked on Lattes. He didn't like to share that with anyone, it kind of ruined his tough guy-image. But the fact is, you can only be so tough at 5 feet 7 inches and 150 pounds.

He walked out of his apartment and down the stairs and out the door onto the street. It was a typical November morning in the city. There were fewer people on the street but because of the cold air, they were all moving a little quicker. Jack always likes to say hello to as many people as he could in the morning. It didn't matter if they were a bum or worked on Wallstreet, they were all the same to him. Just people trying to get by in the big city. He saw an old man sitting on the steps of a building along the way. There was a brown paper bag next to the man's leg. The man was wearing a ragged coat and an old beat-up cap. Jack stopped for a moment and asked the old man how he was doing today. The old man said, "I'm doing better than I was yesterday." He patted the old man on the shoulder and slipped him $10 dollars. He hoped that he wouldn't use it to refill his bag.

Jack crossed the street and went into the local newsstand and picked up the morning paper. He knew the owner of the stand and yelled at him when he came in, "Hey Nicky, how did those Rangers do last night?" Nicky made a rude gesture and Jack laughed. He dropped a couple of dollars on the counter and headed down to the *Coffee Café.*

He had breakfast there almost every day of the week, so he knew everyone there. As he walked into the Café he yelled out to the waitress, "Betty, how's my girl today?" Betty was wearing the typical waitress uniform. It was blue with white piping around the collar and the sleeves, and it had large white buttons down the front. The skirt was short, and she had on a white apron over her skirt. She smiled at Jack and said, "Gee Jack, it's getting kind of late, I was getting a little nervous that you weren't coming in. I didn't know if I could make it through the day". He quipped back, "Well Betty, I wouldn't want to ruin your day." She laughed and hit him with her washcloth. She smiled and asked him, "What's it going to be today Jack? We have a really good special this morning." He looked up at her and said, "Betty I don't even know what the special is, but if you say it's special, that's good enough for me, that's what I'll have". Betty raised one of her eyebrows and said, "Ok Jack, I'll surprise you. Of course, you want the Vanilla Latte with one shot this morning?" He responded, "Without the Latte, it would just be breakfast." They both laughed and she went to get his order.

Jack opened his paper to read the headlines of the day. There was nothing in the paper about the stolen *Henry Graves Supercomplication* watch. It was obvious that the anonymous owner wanted to keep this out of the public eye. As he was reading, he noticed out of the corner of his eye 2 rather large men sitting directly across from him on the other side of the room. They both seemed to be well dressed, but just looked out of place for some reason and they appeared to be watching him. They both had a cup of coffee in front of them, but they weren't speaking. They were just looking in Jack's direction as they sipped their coffee. Maybe he was just imagining things, but he felt a little uneasy. Like when a cat knows that the 2 dogs on the other side of the fence are just waiting for an opening to pounce.

Betty came back with Jack's order. It was 2 eggs scrambled, 2 pieces of wheat toast, and a side of strawberry jam. There were also 4 strips of bacon and 3 sausages and a glass of orange juice. And then what Jack was waiting for, his Latte. He looked up at Betty and said, "everything looks awesome!" Betty smiled and said, "Thanks Jack, but what do you think about the meal?". They both laughed and Jack sipped his Latte and Betty went back behind the counter. He ate his meal while he lightly read the paper. He kept looking out of the corner of his eye towards the 2 men on the other side of the room. They didn't seem to move. They just sat staring in Jack's direction, not even seeming to have any conversation with each other. About 10 minutes passed and he finished his meal. He sat back and put his hand on his stomach as if that were going to help in the digesting process.

Betty came back to the table with a big smile, "How was everything, Jack?" He smiled back at Betty, "You were right Betty, it was pretty special". She hit him with her washcloth again and said, "Jack, you know I'd never steer you wrong". Jack laughed, "What would I do without all your culinary advice?" Betty had a crooked smile, "You'd probably be eating out of trash cans Jack". They both had a good laugh, in the back of his mind, he thought that she might be right. He put a $10 tip on the table for Betty and then he paid the bill. All this time the 2 men on the other side of the room sat still in silence watching Jack's every move.

As he left the *Coffee Café* Jack looked back and saw the 2 men get up from their table and walk toward the exit. He was now 75% sure that they were following him. He took note of their appearance.

Now that they stood up into the light, he could see that they were each about 6' 4" tall and each probably weighed about 250 pounds. It was quite obvious that he was outnumbered and at a huge disadvantage size-wise. He didn't believe in carrying a gun, he knew too many guys that carried guns and they were no longer around today. However, he was not totally defenseless. In the heel of each shoe, he had a 2 ½ inch concealed knife that he used when in tight situations. He kept this in mind in case things got sticky. One of the men had on a blue suit and the other had on a pair of black pants and a brown leather jacket. When Jack didn't know someone's name, he usually made up a fake name for reference. These two were Blue suit and Leather jacket.

Jack headed up the street towards the newsstand. The 2 men followed and looked like they were gaining ground. He entered the newsstand and asked Nicky if he could use the back exit. Nicky made a gesture towards the rear of the store and Jack made his way out the back exit out to the alley behind the newsstand. His plan was to run back to the street and hop in a taxi to get out of harm's way. But the alley was closed off to the street by a chain-link fence. Jack was going to have to make a stand. There was a dumpster on one side of the alley that smelled like something had died in it and there were a few trash cans on the other side. Jack was going to hide behind the dumpster, but he just couldn't take the smell. So, he waited, hoping that if Blue suit and Leather jacket went into the newsstand, Nicky would cover for him. He was thinking to himself, "I shouldn't have made that crack about the Rangers this morning."

Blue suit and Leather jacket entered the newsstand and Blue suit spoke to Nicky. It seemed like he was in charge. He spoke with a Brooklyn accent, "Hey buddy, did a guy just come in here wearing a hat and a tan trench coat?" Nicky didn't want any trouble. He just motioned with his head towards the exit door at the rear of the store. Blue suit and Leather jacket came through the back door and out to the alley. Jack was waiting there; he was slowly reaching down towards the heel of his shoe but thought twice. He could only use one blade at a time and there were 2 of them. And in reality, he still didn't know who they were or what they wanted. So, he just stood there looking at the 2 men. It was like a scene from the old west when gunslingers faced off. He could swear that he saw a tumbleweed blow across the alley. Blue suit and Leather jacket just stood there looking at Jack. You could see their breath in the cool morning air. Nobody said anything for what seemed to be about 3 minutes. Little beads of sweat were starting to appear around the brim of Jack's hat. The little hairs on the back of his neck were standing up. He was preparing for action. Then, all of a sudden, Blue suit looked at Leather jacket and motioned with his head towards the entrance to the store. Neither one said anything, they both just left. They went back into the store and disappeared back into the city. Jack was relieved that this stand-off had ended, but he still didn't know what it was about. Who were they? What did they want? Does it have anything to do with the case he was working on? He would find out soon enough.

Jack walked back into the newsstand and looked at Nicky and said, "Hey Nicky, remind me not to come in here if I'm being chased by a couple of gorillas". Nicky made a gesture towards Jack and went back to packing his shelves with 5-hour energy drinks. Jack thought to himself, I got to find another place to buy my papers.

Jack looked down at his watch and noticed that it was quarter to 10. He pictured Trudy in the office drumming her fingers on the desk waiting to give him a lecture about the finer points of being on time. The fact is, he hadn't been on time in 7 years, Trudy just liked to remind him every day. He pulled out his cell phone and called his office and Trudy answered. "Hello Trane Investigations, Trudy speaking". Jack smiled, "Hello Trudy it's me. Were you able to dig up any information on the security guards Don Valley and Billy Bardsley?" Trudy rolled her eyes, "Jack, you were supposed to be in by 9:30. I've been in for over an hour". Jack could hear her snapping her gum. She continued, "What about you bringing in some food when you show up, and hopefully it will be lunch and not dinner". Jack responded, "come on Trudy, cut me a little slack, I've already been chased by 2 gorillas, and I haven't even made it to my car yet. What about the 2 security guards, did you find anything?" Trudy put the phone down on her desk and put the speaker on and opened up the spreadsheet she was typing up on her laptop. "Yeah Jack, there was quite a bit of public information on these 2 birds. It appears that Billy Bardsley has been arrested for domestic abuse. He lives out in Hoboken. His address is 132 Garden street. He's been married 3 times, but presently divorced. And Don Valley is married and lives outside the city in White Plains. The address is 181 Church Street. And his wife's name is Paula. How is that for an hour's work Jack". Jack was shaking his head, "Trudy have I ever told you how unbelievable you are?"

Trudy flicked her blond hair, "Well Jack, some of us have it, and some of us just don't." Now Jack was rolling his eyes. He said, "Good thing I took that course on how to manage an overachiever." He laughed, Trudy didn't. He continued the conversation, "Look Trudy, I'm going down to the precinct and see if my friend Harry Soul can help me out with any information, I'll see you when I get in." Trudy rolled her eyes and responded in her most sarcastic voice, "Yeah, I figured as much Jack. Just remember the food." Jack knew that he would probably forget the food, but he appeased Trudy, "No problem Trudy, I'll surprise you." She responded, "If you bring any food, that will be a surprise." They both hung up the phone and Jack headed towards the parking garage.

He used to park his car just outside the city, but he had found a secure garage just a few blocks from his apartment just off 3rd Ave. He walked quickly and made it to the garage in about 5 minutes. As he entered the garage, he noticed a guy at the attendant station. He gave him a wave and the attendant waved back. Jack took out a card from his wallet and put it into the machine on the wall. After a couple of beeps and a password, his keys came down a chute. He picked up the keys and headed up the stairs to the second level. The stairway smelled of urine and old clothes. He held his breath and made it to the second level. His car was parked about 2 spaces up from the entrance of the stairs. This was Jack's pride and joy, really the only possession that he valued. A 1967 Mustang Shelby GT-500.

It was truly a classic. It had a beautiful olive-green finish with white striping. The black leather interior had just been upgraded this year. He unlocked the door and sat down in the driver's seat. It was like sitting on a fully padded body glove made just for Jack. He put the key in the ignition and started the engine. The Mustang came to life, it roared as the engine turned over and then came to a deep-throated idle. He sat back and enjoyed the experience. For the 10 years that he owned the car, this part never got old. Probably like every time the Lone Ranger mounted Silver.

He put the car in gear and made his way down the ramp to the exit. He waved to the attendant and the yellow bars at the entrance went up and Jack hit the street. The precinct was across town, so he was going to enjoy the ride. As he came up to the first set of traffic lights, it was red, so he came to a stop. He noticed in his rear-view mirror a black SUV pull up behind him with darkened windows. He made a mental note. The light changed; he took a right on the East 35th Street. He went up about 5 blocks and turned onto 5th Ave. and came up on another red traffic light at East 33rd Street. He happened to look in his rear-view mirror again and the black SUV was directly behind him again. Jack was having none of this. He got out of his car right there and started walking towards the SUV. Before he could get to the front of the SUV, it jammed on the gas pedal and flew past Jack as it sped away. Now horns were blaring as Jack's car was in the middle of the road and the traffic signal had turned green. He quickly got back in his car and proceeded down 5th Ave towards 29th street. He started wondering if this SUV was connected to run-in he just had with Blue suit and Leather jacket about 20 minutes earlier. In both cases, it looked like he was being followed, but when push came to shove, they just backed away like he was made of plutonium.

He made his way to the police station and parked in front of the precinct. He pulled out his cellphone and dialed up his good friend Detective Harry Soul. Harry answered, "This is Detective Harry Soul." Jack responded, "Hey Harry, that sounded really official, what are you doing, eating donuts by the coffee machine?" Harry knew it was Jack on the line, he knew the voice. "All right Jack, what is it this time? Whatever it is, forget it, I can't help, I'm under strict orders to keep you out of the precinct." Jack answered, "Harry, I'm hurt, I thought that we were friends." Harry was irritated, "Look, Jack, I don't work for you, I work for the city of New York, and I'm not even sure you pay your taxes." Jack used his smooth voice, "Harry, I'm working on a case that involves over 20 million dollars, you see there was this…" Harry broke in, "Hold it right there, Jack, I'm a homicide detective, I don't get involved in grand larceny. Unless somebody gets whacked, I'm not involved. Maybe you want to speak with the boys down at the 28th precinct. Remember your last case you got to meet detective Danny Watts? Well, he transferred out of here and now he handles all the high-profile theft and larceny cases. Why don't you go down to the 28th precinct and talk to him? I'll put in a good word for you." Jack remembered Danny Watts all too well. A young good-looking, young, punk of a detective. He had tried to finger Jack for a murder in his last case. As he recalled their relationship was not exactly warm and fuzzy. Jack was disappointed for sure because he really didn't want to get involved with Danny Watts on this case. He didn't trust him, and he didn't like him. He thanked Harry and they both hung up the phone.

He started the car again and put it in gear and drove to the parking lot exit. There, about 30 yards up the street was the black SUV. He pulled out of the lot and drove down 5th avenue past the SUV. He watched in his rear-view mirror as the SUV pulled out. Jack thought to himself, it's about time to see if the SUV can keep up with this mustang. He stepped on the gas pedal and the engine roared as he shifted into 3rd gear. He passed 2 cars and a bus. The SUV was trying to keep up, but Jack could see that he was falling behind. As Jack got to Broadway, he downshifted, then accelerated down to East 20th Street. He could see the SUV still trying to keep up. He stayed on East 20th Street all the way back down to 3rd Ave. and took a sharp left and accelerated once again up to 50 miles per hour. He passed another car, then a taxi, which doesn't happen often in the city. He stayed on 3rd Ave all the way to East 26th Street, then made a hard right. The SUV was no longer in sight. He had lost them. He didn't know if it was because of his incredible driving skills or because they wanted to be lost. Either way, the ride was exhilarating, and he had worked up an appetite. Fortunately, *Patrizia's Pizza* was right in front of him. It looked like he was going to remember to bring some food into the office after all. He parked his car and went into the pizza place. There was garlic and tomato sauce in the air. He walked up to the counter and ordered a large pizza with everything on it and a bottle of Cola. The young man behind the counter looked like he was barely out of high school. He had several small burns on each arm, probably from reaching into the pizza ovens all day long. He seemed to have a bit of an attitude, probably from sticking his head into 500-degree pizza ovens. The young man said to Jack, "That will be $15.99, and your pizza will be ready in 15 minutes." Jack smiled and dropped $20 on the counter and said, "Hey buddy, keep the change." The young man's demeanor changed. He smiled and said, "Make that 14 minutes."

Jack waited sat and waited for the pizza. He almost expected Blue suit and Leather jacket to walk through the door any minute, but they didn't. About 15 minutes passed and the young man called out to Jack, "Your pizza is up man." Jack picked up the box with the pizza and left the store. He got into his car and put the pizza on the passenger seat. Pizza aroma filled the car. He couldn't wait to get back to the office to score some points with Trudy. He started the car and headed towards the office. He checked in his rearview mirror. The black SUV was nowhere in sight.

CHAPTER 3

Jack parked his car about a block away from the building that his office was in. He grabbed the pizza and locked his car door. He smiled as he walked away from the car. He looked back and admired the car's finish as he could see his reflection in the green car door. He entered the building and went up the stairs to the second floor and entered his office. Trudy was sitting at her desk with her elbow on her desk and her chin resting on her hand. She looked up at Jack and said, "I smell pizza!". Jack smiled and said, "Not just any pizza, this is a *Patrizias* pizza". Trudy was nodding her head up and down, "Oh yeah Jack, that's the best, put it right down here on my desk and I'll forget about you not showing up until noon." He laughed, "I think there is enough here for both of us." He put the pizza box down on Trudy's desk and she opened it up and aroma of the pizza filled the room. It was like pizza incense. You could smell bacon, peppers, mushrooms, onion, spinach, olives, pepperoni, sausage, garlic, mozzarella, and Italian seasoning. It was a feast for the senses and Trudy stood over the box waving her hands towards her nose as if she could consume the pizza through her sense of smell. Trudy said to him, "Jack this pizza is awesome! Can I take the left-overs home?" He laughed, "What makes you think there are going to be any left-overs?" He laughed a sinister laugh.

Jack grabbed a couple of pieces and headed into his office. He took the bottle of Cola into his office with him. Trudy drank only water. He poured some cola into his coffee cup. As he sat in his banker's chair enjoying every bite of the pizza, he got out his cell phone and dialed up the number for the 28th precinct. He figured it was time to touch base with Danny Watts. Danny was one of the biggest putz's on the police force, but he thought that it might be good to work with the police on this case. He was wrong. It rang a couple of times and then someone picked up, "This is the 28th precinct, how can I direct your call?". Jack had a mouthful of pizza, so he mumbled into the phone, "Can I speak with detective Danny Watts?" The voice came back from the other end, "excuse me sir did you say Banny Yats?" Jack managed to swallow what was in his mouth and said, "excuse me, I had a mouthful of pizza. I would like to speak with detective Danny Watts." The voice came back, "hold the line please." Jack was on hold. He finished his first piece of pizza and started on the second piece. The second piece seemed even better than the first. He took a large swallow from the cup of cola and washed down the first piece of pizza. He opened his mouth wide and took a big bite of the second piece of pizza. Then he heard a voice from the other end of the phone, "Danny Watts…." Jack couldn't answer, his mouth was full. The voice from the phone repeated, "This is Danny Watts, is anyone there?" Jack managed to swallow the large bite he had in his mouth and took a swig of cola. He answered the phone, "Hello

Danny this is Jack Trane calling." Danny Watts responded, "Jack who?" Jack laughed a little, "It's Jack Trane, you remember, we met last year on the Alice Lynch case, you suspected me of murder, there was an interrogation, I was innocent, we all laughed, then we solved the case, everything worked out." Danny was squinting and pursing his lips, "Oh yeah, you're that jerk detective that kept getting in my way. What do you want Trane?" Jack laughed a little again so Danny could hear him, "Well, funny thing Danny, I'm working another case and I thought that we might kind of work the case together." Danny scowled, "Why would I work on a case with you. You're nothing but a two-bit second-rate private detective. You probably couldn't even find a hammer in a hardware store." Danny was now laughing on the other end. Jack responded, "That's funny Danny, but I found a dim-wit in a police station." Danny got serious, "Look Trane, I don't know what case you're working on, but I'm just going to warn you once. Stay out of my way. I don't want to see you, I don't want to hear you, I don't want to smell you. Do you understand me Trane?" Jack was smiling and said, "Have a nice day, Danny." And he hung up the phone.

He thought to himself, Danny Watts is still the same cocky, punk detective that he remembered from the last case. He was kind of glad that he wasn't going to be working with him on this case. He put the last bite of his pizza in his mouth and washed it down with a big swallow of cola. He sat back and contemplated his next move.

Trudy was still chowing down in the next office but he needed some information so he yelled into her office, "Trudy can you do me a favor? I need to know what room Billy Bardsley is in at the hospital." The voice came back from the other office, "He's already been released, Jack. Billy Bardsley is at home at his Hoboken address." Trudy always seemed to be one step ahead of Jack and that's one of the reasons he loved having her around. "Thanks, Trudy, you're the best. Why don't you take the rest of the pizza home for leftovers?" She made a face where she raised one eyebrow and opened her mouth wide, "Gee, why didn't I think of that Jack?"

He was already putting on his hat and his coat and he was standing in front of Trudy's desk. 'Look Trudy, I'm heading out to Billy Bardsley's house. I probably won't be back before 5 o'clock so why don't you just lock up when you feel like the time is right." She smiled, "Yeah Jack, that's a good plan, I'll lock up when I think the time is right." He knew that she would probably be out of there by 3 o'clock, but he didn't mind. Trudy was worth her weight in pizza.

He left the office and walked up the street to his car. He got in and put Billy Bardsley's address into his GPS. The trip was only about 6 miles, but because of the Manhattan traffic, it was a 41-minute drive. He put the key in the ignition and started the car and the 500 horses came to life. Before he pulled out into traffic, he noticed in his rear-view mirror a black SUV about 6 parking spaces behind him. He put the car in gear and pulled out into traffic. The black SUV pulled out at the same time. He had been through this game before. He knew that the SUV couldn't keep up with him and he could lose the SUV at any time. But it seemed that whoever was in the SUV just wanted to tail him and not actually impede his activity. Jack decided to play along for now and let the SUV tail him. Maybe this would give him some kind of clue as to who else was interested in the *Henry Graves Supercomplication*". He headed towards the Holland Tunnel. The traffic was heavy on Canal Street, but he made good time and was approaching the tunnel in about 15 minutes. He entered the tunnel and the traffic moved along pretty good. For some reason, the tunnel brought a sense of serenity to the drive. Maybe it was the feeling of being surrounded by water. Once through the tunnel, he snaked his way to Luis Munoz Marin Blvd and eventually ended up on Garden Street. There was a long row of brick apartment houses. There were some trees along the sidewalk, and some apartments had a little patch of grass next to the steps. Even in the city, people like to claim a little land for their own. He found number 132 and parked as close as he could to the building. He was about 2 buildings away from #132. As he pulled into the parking spot, he checked the rear-view mirror, and the SUV was nowhere to be found. Either he had lost them, or they just lost interest. He didn't think either of those was true. He was quite sure that he would be seeing them again.

He locked the car and walked up to 132 Garden Street. He walked up the stairs and knocked on the door. He waited for about 30 seconds and nobody answered. He knocked again, only this time a little harder. The door opened and there was a man who looked to be in his early 40's staring back at Jack. He said, "Yeah, can I help you? Who are you looking for? "Jack answered, "I'm looking for Billy Bardsley." He said, "I'm Billy Bardsley." Jack sized him up. He had a bandage around his head, no doubt from the blow that he had just suffered. He was wearing a pair of grey sweatpants and a red plaid shirt. It looked like he hadn't shaved in a few days, and he was holding a cigarette. Jack hated cigarettes but he couldn't tell him to put it out, it was his house. Jack answered, "My name is Jack Trane, and I'm investigating the robbery that took place yesterday. Do you mind if I come in?" He looked Jack up and down and then slowly waved him into his apartment.

It seemed like a nice place, although it didn't look like Billy Bardsley kept it very nice. Dirty dishes were laying around on the couch, there were several ashtrays full of cigarette buts around the room and the rug looked like it needed a good shampoo. Billy asked Jack, "Would you like to sit down?" Jack looked around to make sure that there was a clean spot on the couch, and he sat down. Billy sat at the other end of the couch. In front of them on a coffee table was a large jar of what looked like aspirins, a bottle of water, and a half-used carton of cigarettes. There was also a prescription bottle of what looked like painkillers. It was obvious that Billy was presently feeling no pain. Jack was hoping that Billy's head was clear enough to remember the details of what happened during the robbery. He started asking Billy questions; "So Billy tell me what you remember about the robbery, and don't worry, no detail is insignificant." Billy took a drag from his cigarette and sat back with his head looking towards the ceiling then he looked at Jack and said, "Me and Donny got hit, and someone stole the piece that we were supposed to pick up." Jack smiled and said, "That's real good Billy, but I was hoping for a few more details. Why don't I ask you some questions?" Billy took another drag of his cigarette and said, "OK, shoot." Jack was coughing from the cigarette smoke coming his way. It always seems that the smoke created by a smoker always ends up traveling over to the non-smoker. He asked Billy, "All right, did you see the person who hit you?" Billy shook his head and took another drag of his cigarette, "No sir, I was just coming around the back of the truck. You see, I was the driver and I got out the driver's door and Donny got out the passenger door and we both went towards the back of the truck. I got there first, so I opened the door to grab the watch, and BOOM, that was it, lights out." Jack stopped him, "Wait a minute did you say that you reached in for the watch? I thought that you were there to pick up the watch?" Billy took another drag of his cigarette and crushed it out in the ashtray on the arm of the couch. "No sir we were hired to deliver the watch. But I guess after I got hit, Donny got hit too, so someone must have taken the watch." Billy opened the prescription bottle and popped a painkiller in his mouth and opened the bottle of water and took a big slug. Then he took a couple of aspirin and popped them into his mouth and took another long swig from the water bottle. Then he took another cigarette out of the pack, put it in his mouth and opened a matchbook, and lit the cigarette. The room was so full of smoke you could literally cut it with a knife.

Jack couldn't tell if the painkillers were affecting Billy or if he just wasn't the brightest bulb in the warehouse. Let me ask you another question Billy, did you notice anyone else in the area before you made the stop?" Billy took another drag from his cigarette, "No sir it was early, about 6:00 AM and it wasn't even that light yet. But I didn't see anybody on the street." Jack was writing all this down on a small pad that he carried in his pocket. "Tell me something else Billy, how long have you worked with Donny?" Billy sat back on the couch and said, "We've been working together now for about 2 months, yeah Donny is a good guy." Jack figured that this was about all he was going to get out of Billy, and he thought that it was probably a good idea to leave before he choked to death on all the cigarette smoke. He said to Billy, "Thank you, Mr. Bardsley, I really appreciate your time and I think you've given me some very good details of this case. Don't bother to get up. I think I can show myself out." Jack got up to leave, Billy took another drag on his cigarette, "No problem detective, what did you say your name was again?" Jack rolled his eyes, "Jack Trane, if I need any more information, we'll be in touch." Billy was smiling an empty smile, probably from the prescription drugs, "Yeah, see you around detective Trane." It appeared that Billy was under the impression that Jack was a police detective. Jack didn't correct him.

Jack left the apartment and breathed in and out about 5 or 6 times to clear his lungs. He smelled like he just came out of an all-night pool room. He started walking up the street towards his car and he noticed a couple of figures coming towards him and one was a familiar face. It was Danny Watts, and he had a partner with him. Jack was going to walk by him without saying anything, but Danny Watts noticed Jack and he reached out and grabbed Jack by the shoulder. Danny squinted at Jack and spoke in a loud voice, "Jack Trane! What are you doing here? You better not be working my case.

I thought that I told you to stay out of my way!" Jack smiled and raised his eyebrows, "Detective Watts, how rude, aren't you even going to introduce me to your partner?" Danny just stared Jack down, his partner was a woman. She looked to be about 5' 7" with an athletic build and she had shoulder-length, reddish-blond hair. She had green eyes and a face that could turn heads. She was wearing a light brown leather jacket and a dark brown turtleneck and a dark brown pair of pants. She held out her hand and said, "Hello I'm detective Debra Thorn. It looks like you already know Detective Watts." Danny chimed in, "Don't be nice to this guy. He's just going to get in our way. He's trouble, with a capital T. And he uses the law like it was his personal plaything." Jack was still smiling, "Come on Danny just because you got demoted from homicide down to the bunko squad, don't blame me." Danny was wearing what looked like a very expensive designer suit and a black trench coat. Jack smiled at him and said, "So Danny you still buying your clothes at Walmart?" Detective Thorn smiled, then laughed.

Danny was breathing heavily, and he looked at Jack in the eyes and said, "I'm telling you for the last time you cockroach, you just stay out of my way." Detective Thorn was just taking all this in. She said, "Hey Danny, lighten up, who do you think this guy is? Public enemy #1?" Danny was still a young punk barely 30 years old and had a lot to learn. Debra was in her mid-40's and a seasoned detective. Danny Watts could have learned a lot from her, but he was too much of a punk. Jack looked at Danny and said, "All right Danny, you work your side of the street and I'll work mine." Danny had his teeth clenched and said, “I’m warning you, if I see you anywhere near my case, I’m going to squash you like a bug.” Jack laughed, “speaking of bugs, you have a huge yellow caterpillar on your shoulder.” The bug had just fallen from the tree that they were standing under. Danny screamed, “Ahhh” and knocked the caterpillar off his shoulder. Debra let out a big laugh. Jack turned to Debra and said, “I think I’m going to like you.”

Danny pushed Jack out of the way and walked up to Billy Bardsley’s door. Jack laughed to himself, “I hope he’s got a gas mask in his pocket.” Jack waved bye to Debra, he kind of hoped that they would run into each other again. She was a redhead.

Jack got back to his car, got in, and sat there for a couple of minutes. He wanted to go over all the information that Billy Bardsley had just given him. It was November and there was a chill in the air, but he had to open the window to air himself out after all that cigarette smoke. One point that had stood out from what Billy had told him, is that they were there to deliver, not to pick up. He was sure the insurance man Harold Chumley told him that they were there to pick up. The only way to clear this up was to visit Don Valley and get his side of the story. He rolled up the window halfway and started the engine. He looked in the rearview mirror and once again there was the black SUV. He pulled into traffic and the SUV followed. It was about 4 o’clock and Jack was headed down to *Big Jim’s Sports* bar for a *Guinness* and some fish and chips, and if whoever was in the SUV wanted to join him, that was OK with Jack. He stepped on the gas and lost the SUV before they even got back to the Holland Tunnel.

Jack pulled into the parking lot across from *Big Jim's*. He parked his car and went in. He loved the atmosphere here. The widescreen TVs, the energy of the crowd, and all the memorabilia that decorated the walls. It was like his own personal man-cave. It was even better in the summer when the Yankees and Red Sox were playing, He loved the purposeful repartee with Yankee fans. And nobody served a better fish and chips than *Big Jim's*. He sat at the bar and yelled down to his old friend behind the bar "Teddy K!" A pint of *Guinness* slid down the bar and stopped right in front of Jack. "You're the best Teddy." Teddy smiled, "Tell me something I don't know Jack." They both laughed. "Hey Teddy, how about an order of those famous fish and chips? Teddy made a high sign with his right index finger, a signal that the fish and chips would be out in a few minutes.

He sipped the *Guinness* and enjoyed the rich flavor of the head on this full-bodied stout ale. Teddy K had walked down in front of Jack and was wiping down the bar in front of where Jack was sitting. Teddy liked to keep track of things, he usually knew a lot of what was going on in the city, at least crime-wise. He asked Jack, "did you hear about the heist outside the MET? I'm not sure what was stolen, but I hear it was worth beaucoup dollars." Jack looked at Teddy with a wry smile, "Actually Teddy, I'm working the case and it's worth over 20 million dollars." Teddy smiled, "Hey Jack you're really coming up in the world, no more 5 dollar-tips, right?" He smiled at Jack and went back to get the fish and chips. Teddy brought back the meal and put it in front of Jack and said, "remember Jack, no $5 dollar tips." He pointed his index and middle finger at his eyes and then towards Jack, then went to wait on another customer.

As Jack began eating, he noticed 3 men enter the bar. A short fat man with a bald head, that kind of looked like "Boss Hogg" from the Dukes of Hazzard. And 2 tall guys with black suits and sunglasses. Jack thought to himself, "sunglasses in a bar? If you're trying to be inconspicuous that's not very effective. They sat in a booth close to the bar and they all seemed to be surveilling Jack. It was obvious that the 2 guys in the black suits were working for Boss Hogg, either that or they were on a secret mission from the government looking for aliens. Jack tried to ignore them, and he ate his meal. When he finished, he put $35 on the bar. $25 for the meal and a $10 tip for Teddy K.

He left the bar and the 3 men in the booth stayed put. In the parking lot, he noticed a black SUV parked directly behind his Mustang. At least now he knew how many jokers were following him. He still didn't know who they were or why. He started his car and let it idle for a minute. He put on the radio and dialed in the classic rock station. The station was playing an old CCR song. Jack sang along with the lyrics "*I see a bad moon a rising*". It was funny how so many of these old songs fit the circumstances of life. He drove off and headed home. He was going to try to get an early start tomorrow, he was sure Don Valley held the keys to this case.

CHAPTER 4

The alarm clock went off and the time on the clock read 8:00 AM. Jack reached over and slapped the top of the clock and the loud buzzing stopped. He sat up in bed and put both hands over his face. It seemed like 8:00 AM was getting earlier every day. He put his feet on the floor and walked to the bathroom in a way that resembled Frankenstein. After about 20 minutes he emerged clean-shaven and showered and ready for the day.

He walked over to the walk-in closet, reached in, and pulled out a pair of navy-blue dockers. The brown dockers, that he had worn yesterday, were still on the floor in front of his bed. He reached into the closet again and pulled out a blue and white stripe tie. He reached in a third time and pulled out a dark blue jacket. The trifecta. He was amazed at how he could randomly pull out a matched outfit day after day. If they gave out prizes for dumb luck he would probably win. He went over to his armoire and pulled out a pristine white shirt with a button-down collar. He put on his ensemble and tied his tie with a classic Windsor knot. Then he left the top button of his shirt open, and his tie was left loose around his neck. One thing you could say about Jack is that he was consistent. He looked around the room and noticed that besides the pants on the floor, there was also yesterday's shirt draped over a chair and a tie on the floor. There was also a pair of brown shoes next to his couch. They were *Nun Bush*, his favorite brand. He felt that they were specially made for a Private Eye. Of course, his shoes had been customized to include 2 ½ inch knife blades in each heel. He put on his shoes but left the rest of the room as it was. He felt that the weekends were meant for cleaning and it wasn't the weekend yet. He put on his favorite hat, and he grabbed his black trench coat. It was a little longer than his tan one, and just a little bit warmer. It was about 30 degrees outside today and according to the weather forecast, it was probably going to stay that way for the whole day. He opened the door, put the matchstick in the bottom of the door jamb, and left his apartment. He headed down the stairs and out to the street. He was going to skip getting the newspaper after the episode that took place yesterday, but he still needed his breakfast. He headed towards the *Coffee Café*.

As soon as he started up the street, he noticed two familiar figures standing about 20 feet in front of him. It was Blue suit and Leather jacket from yesterday. Jack stopped in his tracks. These two gorillas were so big that they were casting shadows like skyscrapers on the sidewalk. You could see the breath coming out of their mouths in the cold air. You could see the breath coming out of Jack's mouth too. They both came at Jack and there was a scuffle. They grabbed at his arms as if they wanted to abduct him and load him into a car. Jack took a swing at one of them. It glanced off Leather jacket's shoulder and didn't do any damage. Leather jacket backed off a little and Jack managed to free himself. He reached down to the heel of his right shoe and pulled out the knife blade and threw it towards Blue suit. It missed and stuck in a tree directly behind the 2 men. They both started towards Jack again but suddenly stopped in their tracks. Jack was facing them ready to defend himself once again, but they both suddenly turned and ran away. They got into a white BMW and sped off. Jack was puzzled. Why did they just stop and run away? Then he looked behind him and saw the 2 men in black suits with sunglasses standing about 30 feet behind him with their arms folded in front of them. They looked quite menacing. They turned around and walked towards the black SUV. They got in and they too sped away. In his mind, he could hear the music from the *Twilight Zone.*

Jack was looking for a pocket watch known as the *Henry Graves Supercomplication*. But it seemed that his life had turned into a super complication of its own. Who were these guys and what did they want with Jack? And where did they want to take him? And who were the guys in the black suits and sunglasses? And why were Blue suit and Leather jacket so afraid of them? All these were questions that he would get the answer to, but not before breakfast. He pulled the knife blade out of the tree and placed it back in the heel of his shoe. He dusted himself off and continued walking towards the *Coffee Café*. This little scuffle had given Jack quite an appetite. He was really looking forward to his Vanilla Latte. Today he was going to take 2 shots.

He walked into the *Coffee Café* and immediately headed for the restroom. He went in and splashed cold water on his face. He looked at his reflection as the water dripped from his chin and he had a conversation with the man in the mirror. "*Are you out of your mind? You're getting too old for this! You could have been killed back there. Is it really worth $200,000?*"

He continued to stare at himself in the mirror and said out loud, "Yes to all the above". He winked at himself and made a smile and walked back into the café.

Betty caught sight of him as he entered from the restroom, "Good Morning Jack, too bad we didn't have a shower, you could live in the restroom." She let out a laugh. He smiled, "Betty if the restroom had a shower, I'd never leave at all." They both laughed. He had sat down at a table near the window and Betty came over. "What'll it be today Jack, another special?" He thought for a moment and said, "Betty, I think this is a blueberry pancake kind of day. And you better bring me a Grande Vanilla Latte with a double shot of espresso." Betty looked shocked, "My goodness Jack, blueberry pancakes and a double shot! I've never heard you order a double shot. Sounds like your day is going to be full of surprises." Jack looked up at her and said, "Betty, I think you might be right." She hit him with her washcloth, and she went to get his order. He reflected on the events of the morning so far. He could deal with Blue suit and Leather jacket, but those 2 guys in the black suits and sunglasses made him nervous. They reminded him of someone that escaped from the *Matrix*. But Blue suit and Leather jacket were just a couple of street punks. He'd deal with them the way he always dealt with street punks. A little muscle, a little brains, and a lot of distance. He looked forward to the next time they made an appearance.

Betty came back with his order. The pancakes were stacked 4 layers high. The maple syrup was 100% pure from Vermont. And the Latte was just what he needed to put things in perspective. "Thanks, Betty, this is just what I needed." She winked at him, "If you say so, Jack." He smiled at her as she walked away. He finished his meal in about 5 minutes, then he savored the Latte for another 5 minutes. He gave Betty a wave and she came over with his check and put it down on the table. She said, "You know Jack, you eat here so much, maybe you should get on a payment plan." She laughed. He smiled, "Then how would you get your tip?" She smiled a big smile, "Maybe you'd have to bring it around to my apartment." She winked at Jack and hit him with her washcloth. He laughed, "That would be one expensive meal, Betty." They both laughed. He put $10 down on the table for Betty's tip and paid the bill at the counter. Then he waved to Betty and left the café.

He walked up the street towards the parking garage. His senses were heightened from his morning scuffle, so he continued to scan the side streets for any white BMWs or black SUVs. He didn't see any. He arrived at the garage and waved to the attendant. He could see from the name tag on the attendant's uniform, that his name was Fernando. He never had actually spoken to Fernando, so this morning he did. "Hey Fernando, how's it going this morning?" Fernando looked up, a little surprised, he responded, "Hey man, good. It's going good man. Thanks for asking. Have a good day man." It was obvious that not many people took the time to speak to Fernando.

He was just a parking attendant, but he appreciated Jack taking the time to make some small talk.

Jack put his card in the machine on the wall and his keys came down a chute. He picked them up and took the elevator up to the second level. He thought that he would avoid the urine and body odor smell of the stairway. He was wrong. The elevator smelled much like the stairs. He got off on the second level and walked over and unlocked his car. He got in and just sat there for a minute exchanging the elevator smell for the nice smell of rich new leather upholstery that he had recently added to his car. He looked down at his watch and it was a little after 9:30 AM. He pulled out his cell phone and called in to his office. Trudy answered, "Trane investigations, Trudy speaking, how can I help you?" Jack answered, "Hey Trudy, that was pretty good, I see that you've added a little something to your repertoire." Trudy was snapping her gum, "Don't get smart Jack, unless you're bringing more pizza for lunch." He answered, "Well I'd like to Trudy, but I'm not going to be around for lunch." She chimed in, "That figures." He continued, "I really have to see Don Valley this morning and he's out in White Plains. So, I'm going to drive out there now and I don't know what time I'm going to be back." Trudy smiled, "So you want me to lock up again when I think the time is right?" Jack rolled his eyes, "No Trudy, stay put, I might need you after I meet with Don Valley. I'll call you when I'm on my way back." Trudy rolled her eyes, "No problem Jack, I'll be here." He thought for a minute and said, "And by the way, be careful of 2 guys in black suits and sunglasses, and for a guy in a blue suit and a guy in a leather jacket". Trudy made a sarcastic face, "what are you wearing today Jack, I'll make a note of that too." Jack told her, "I'm serious Trudy, I've had some run-ins with these guys, and I want to make sure you stay clear of them. They are dangerous." Trudy shook her head, "Oh that makes me feel much better Jack, I'll have them all wait in your office if they show up." He shook his head, "Just be careful, that's all." She smiled and snapped her gum, "No worries Jack, I can handle myself." They both hung up the phone. He thought to himself, "*said the rodeo clown to the bull.*"

He started the car and drove down the ramp and waved to Fernando. Fernando opened the gate and Jack left the garage. He quickly pulled over to the side of the road and entered Don Valley's address into his GPS. It was about a 30-mile drive. With traffic, it looked like it would take an hour to get there. He put the car in gear and pulled out into traffic. He drove towards the Henry Hudson Parkway and made his way up to the Tappan Zee Bridge. The traffic was light, and he made it to White Plains in about 51 minutes. He found Church street. It was a nice clean suburban area with neat well-kept houses. He found number 181 and pulled up in front of the house. It was a white 3 story house with a full porch in front. There was a large tree in front of the house and most of the leaves had fallen off. In the driveway, he noticed that there was a Nissan Sentra, so he figured that someone was home.

He got out of the car and walked towards the house. There were leaves blowing in the street with a cold November wind. He was glad that he had worn his black trench coat with the lining today.

He walked up the porch stairs and knocked on the door. The door opened quickly as if they were expecting him. A woman asked him, "can I help you?" Obviously, this was Paula Valley, Don's wife. She was a fairly attractive woman in her early 30's. She had light brown hair, cut very short, and light blue eyes that seemed to catch the sun. He asked her "can I speak with Don Valley?" She looked at Jack a little suspiciously and said, "Who is asking?" Jack smiled, "Oh I'm sorry, my name is Jack Trane and I'm investigating the armored car robbery that Mr. Valley was involved in." She shot back, "What do you mean involved in?" Jack answered quickly, "Oh, sorry, I didn't mean it like that. The robbery that he was witness to." She looked at him with squinted eyes. "All right wait a minute. I'll see if he can talk to you." A couple of minutes passed, and a large man came to the door. He was about 6' 5" and built like a linebacker. He had cropped black hair and a Fu Manchu mustache. He said, "What can I do for you?" Jack responded, "I'd like to ask you some questions about the robbery that you witnessed the other day." He looked at Jack with steel eyes, "Are you a cop?" Jack answered, "No, I'm a private investigator working for the insurance company. I think you might be able to help me with some of the details that only you would know." He looked at Jack with a suspicious look, "Ok come in, I'll tell you what I know." Don Valley led Jack into the living room, which was the first room as you enter the house. There were several different newspapers laying around. Some on a chair in one corner of the room and a few on the coffee table in the middle of the room. Don's wife sat at a computer on the far side of the room. Don sat down on the couch and Jack sat on another chair opposite from the couch. Don said, "OK what do you want to know?" Jack breathed in deep and let out the breath, "Can you tell me exactly what happened before and during the robbery?" Don now took in a deep breath and exhaled, "Well, it's like this Mr. Trane, Billy and me were picking up this piece, I think it was a watch from the MET…" Jack broke in, "Excuse me, did you say you were picking up the piece?" Don thought for a moment, "Why? Is this important?" Jack smiled, "Well yes, according to Billy, you were there to drop off the piece, not pick it up." Don laughed a little, "Oh did I say pick up? I meant drop-off. You see we were there to drop off this watch. Then when we got to the back of the truck Billy got smacked in the head and before I could see anything I got hit too. I went out for a minute, but when I came to, the watch was gone." Jack was writing all this down in his pad. "So, you didn't get a look at the person who hit Billy when you came to the back of the truck?" Don thought for a second, "Uh, no, I never made it to the back of the truck, I got whacked before I got to the back." Jack had one eyebrow raised, "Ok, this is all very interesting, I think I have all I need for now. Thank you, Mr. Valley, if I need anything else, I'll be in touch." Jack had recently had an app installed on his phone that was capable of tracking the location of any phone that came in contact with his. He noticed Don Valley's phone on the coffee table. He took out his cellphone and let it drop on the table next to Don's. The phones made contact and Jack was now able to track the movement of Don Valley's phone. Don picked up Jack's phone from the table and handed it to Jack. Jack thanked him and smiled a wry smile. Don led Jack to the door. He waved to Paula Valley as he left. He shook Don's hand and thanked him again.

Jack walked back to his car. As he was walking, the old tune from the *Castaways* came to his mind "*Liar, Liar, pants on fire...Liar, Liar, pants on fire.*" There was no doubt Don Valley had more holes in his story than an old colander. He got in his car and headed back towards the city. He put on the radio and the classic rock station was on. The classic Eagles tune was playing, *Lyin Eyes.* Once again popular music lined up with the circumstances of the day. Jack turned up the volume and stepped on the gas. He started to dissect everything that Don Valley had just told him. Don tried to get him to think that they were picking up the watch, but when Jack called him out on it, he changed his story, saying that they were delivering the watch. He said that he didn't see Billy Bardsley get hit and he didn't see who hit him. But that's not likely, as he would have seen someone when he got out of the truck. And why did he have all those newspapers all over the living room? Something was very much looking suspicious here. But he had Don Valley's cellphone coordinates in his cellphone. He would be able to track him if he needed to. And he thought that he would.

It was about 12:30 PM and Jack was back in the city. He drove to E 82nd street and found a place to park. He was right across from the MET. There were a ton of street vendors in front of the MET, so he walked over to a street vendor and picked up a couple of hot dogs and a soda. The dogs had hot mustard and celery salt. An unbeatable combination and he chowed them down in about 2 minutes.

He washed them down with the soda and he was ready for his next move. He looked around and noticed a small shop just towards the end of E 82nd street and saw a small camera on the corner of the building. He was wondering if the camera might have caught the action, the morning of the robbery He walked into the shop. It was a small jewelry shop, *Abe's Fine Jewels*. There was a middle-aged man behind the counter. He had short curly hair and a middle-eastern accent.

Jack introduced himself, "Hello, my name is Jack Trane. I'm investigating the robbery that took place a couple of days ago, right in front of the MET, and I was wondering if your surveillance equipment might have caught any action that went down?" The man stood still and looked at Jack. Everyone was suspicious of everyone in the city. He said, "Robbery? I did not know of any robbery." Jack put $20 down on the counter and said, "Remember anything now?" The man put his hand on his chin like he was thinking. Jack put another $20 bill on the counter. He said, "Is it getting clearer?" The man scratched his head. Jack put another $20 bill on the counter. He said, "How about now?" The man smiled and slipped the $60 into his pants pocket. He looked at Jack and said, "Oh yes, now I remember. I always leave the equipment on overnight, but I haven't checked it because there was no need to. I record a week at a time, then I delete it and start a new week." Jack nodded his head. The man behind the counter said, "If you like, I could download a copy of the last week to a flash-drive and you can look for yourself." He put his hand on the counter and tapped it a few times. Jack put another $20 on the counter and the man slipped it into his pocket. Jack smiled, "Are you Abe?" The man smiled back, "Yes I'm Abe. I'll be right back." Abe went into a back room and was there for about 3 minutes and came back with a flash drive and handed it to Jack. He shook Abe's hand, "Thank you, Abe, I really appreciate this." He handed Abe his card, "If there is ever anything that I can do for you, just call the number on that card." It never hurts to drum up new business. Abe smiled at Jack, "Maybe I will Mr. Trane, Maybe I will."

Jack got back to his car; he still had the flash drive in his hand. He placed it in his shirt pocket, and he started the car. He pulled out his cellphone and dialed up Trudy. He put the car in gear and started to drive back towards his office. Trudy answered, "Trane Investigations, Trudy speaking, how can.." Jack broke in, "Trudy, I'm on my way back to the office and I need you to look at a flash drive on your computer. I'll be there in about 20 minutes, so don't go anywhere." Trudy answered back, "Jack it's 2 o'clock in the afternoon, where am I going to go?" Jack was serious, "See you in a few minutes."

For the next 12 minutes, he exceeded every speed limit, went through 2 red lights, and narrowly avoided hitting a trash truck, but he found a parking spot right outside his office, parked the car, and darted into the building. He ran up the stairs, opened the office door, and bolted in. Trudy looked up as the door opened, she had her mouth open and her hands on her chest. Jack handed her the flash drive and asked her to run it on her computer.

Trudy said, "Slow down Jack, you almost gave me a heart attack the way you just barged in like that!" Jack apologized, "Sorry Trudy,

I think this flash drive is the key to this case." Trudy raised her right eyebrow, "All right Jack, keep your shirt on, let's just see what's on the flash drive." She calmly placed the flash drive in the slot in her computer and hit the play button. Jack stood behind her as the surveillance file popped up on her screen. The day and time appeared in the upper left-hand corner of the screen. He told Trudy to fast forward to the morning of the robbery. She did it with ease. He asked her to slow down the tape at 5:55 in the morning. Then they just watched. They saw the armored car pull up and stop right outside the MET. Then they saw Billy Bardsley and Don Valley exit the truck at the same time. Don Valley stood by the side of the truck. Billy Bardsley came to the back. He opened the door and reached in, but as he did someone came into the picture from the left side of the screen. It appeared to be someone in a black hoodie. He had what appeared to be a pipe and they struck Billy Bardsley in the back of the head and he went down. At this point, Don Valley came to the back of the truck, reached into the truck, and pulled out a box, and gave it to the person in the hoodie. Don Valley then turned around and pointed to his head and the person in the hoodie clocked him in the back of the head. He did not go down. The blow that he received was not nearly as hard as the blow that Billy Bardsley received. The person in the black hoodie then ran off with the box and disappeared from the screen. Don Valley sat down with his back to the truck as if he were hurt.

Jack yelled, "Trudy, stop the tape! It's just what I thought. This was an inside job. Don Valley set this whole thing up. I got him. I can just smell that $200,000 now.

Jack's sense of smell was just a little bit off…

CHAPTER 5

Jack gave Trudy the rest of the day off. He wanted to celebrate a little bit, so he left the office and headed down towards "*Big Jim's Sports* bar. It was still early but he thought that he might shoot the breeze with Teddy K for a while. Teddy knew things. He always listened when people sat in front of him at the bar. In the past, he had proved invaluable to Jack with information that would have gone unknown. For some reason criminals and clients alike, all seem to show up at *Big Jim's* sooner or later, and Jack was hoping that Teddy K had heard something about Don Valley trying to sell the watch that was stolen from the armored truck, The *Henry Graves Supercomplication*. Who would have thought that a little watch could be worth over 24 million dollars? Jack pulled into the parking lot and he was thinking about one of those deluxe burgers that Teddy K serves. But he wasn't thinking about it for long.

Jack got out of the car and started walking towards the entrance to *Big Jim's* and he could sense that something just wasn't right. He had that feeling you get when you know that someone is watching you, that uneasy feeling in the pit of your stomach. Suddenly from behind someone grabbed him and pulled both of his arms behind him. It happened so fast that he couldn't even put up a fight. He could feel the zip-ties going over his wrists and then tightening up so that he could no longer move his arms. He could feel himself being dragged backwards, but he couldn't see who was dragging him. He heard a car door open and then he was thrown in the back seat and the door slammed shut again. As he laid down on the seat, he heard the 2 doors to the front seat open. Then he could hear 2 people getting into the car and then the doors closed again. Jack sat up so he could see who had just zip-tied him and thrown him into the car. He recognized both men. It was Blue suit and Leather Jacket. Blue suit was driving, and Leather jacket turned around and just looked at Jack and smiled. Jack squinted at Leather jacket and said, "What do you 2 jokers want? You've been following me for 2 days. And where are you taking me?" Blue suit turned his head from the driver's seat so he could see Jack. He said, "The boss wants to see you." Then he turned back to looking at the road. Jack was getting angry. His teeth were clenched. He screamed, "What boss? Where are you taking me? You better hope that I don't get out of these zip-ties, because I'll make quick work of you 2 jokers." Leather jacket laughed. He spoke with a Brooklyn tough-guy accent, "Forget about it, Trane. Nobody wants to bust you up, the boss told us not to hurt you. He just wants to talk to you. So, relax, enjoy the ride." Blue suit lit up a stogie and blew the smoke out his window. Jack thought to himself "*these losers can't even afford good cigars.*"

Jack sat up in his seat and looked out the window to try and figure out where they were taking him. They didn't blindfold him, so it was obvious that they didn't care if he knew. So, he asked them again, "Where are you taking me?" Leather jacket spoke up, "Let's just say that we're taking you out for a good meal." Blue suit and Leather jacket laughed.

He could see that they were headed towards lower Manhattan. They had been traveling south on Broadway for about 10 minutes. When they turned left on East Houston Street and right on to Bowery, he knew that they were headed for "Little Italy." They ended up on Mulberry Street and they pulled up in front of what looked to be a closed storefront. Blue suit and Leather jacket both got out of the car. Jack was contemplating making a run for it but figured that they would just catch him again anyway, so he thought that he would play along and see what this meeting with the boss was all about. Blue suit opened the car door. He looked at Jack and said, "Now Mr. Trane, if we cut those zip-ties loose, you're not going to try running, or something are you? Because if you do, we're just going to find you again and bring you back here anyway." Jack nodded his head, "Ok I won't run, let's just meet with your boss and get this over with." Blue suit responded, "Now you're talking sense." They led him into the building. From the front, the building looked like a closed storefront, but once inside, it had the appearance of an old-time Italian restaurant. There were about 7 or 8 tables set up with red-checkered tablecloths and candles were lit on top of the tables. There was a well-stocked bar to the left, and it looked like there was a bartender behind the bar. Towards the back of the building, there were 2 swinging doors. They were black with little round windows about three-quarters of the way up the door. And in the corner was a rather large man sitting at a table and he had what looked like a glass of red wine in front of him. He was wearing what appeared to be an off-white suit, but the lights were low, so it was kind of difficult to tell. And there was a white homburg hat resting on the table. He motioned to Blue suit and Leather jacket like he was waving for them to bring Jack over. Jack walked towards the table. Blue suit and Leather jacket walked about a step behind.

The man sitting at the table spoke, "Mr. Trane, I'm so glad we could get together like this. I've been looking forward to meeting you." The man had a heavy Italian accent, he also had dark hair with a little gray and it was combed straight back. Jack made a sarcastic face and said, "Well, I appreciate the gesture of having your boys here pick me up, but really, all you needed to do was make a call. I'm in the book." The man laughed, "Mr. Trane, I'm glad to see that you have a sense of humor." Jack wasn't laughing. Jack spoke up, "You seem to know who I am; it puts me at a bit of a disadvantage, you never mentioned your name." The man smiled a big smile, "My name is Tony Gumbati. The two men who brought you here are my associates Sylvio Donato and Jimmy Sissi." Jack thought that these guys looked familiar, but he never got a good look at them, and the lights were so low in here he couldn't really make out their faces. The boss was none other than Tony "two shoes" Gumbati. Two shoes because anyone who crossed him ended up in cement shoes at the bottom of the Hudson River. These two guys were Sylvio "Big D" Donato, and Jimmy "the chopper" Sissi. The names spoke for themselves. So now Jack knew who he was dealing with, he just didn't know why.

He started to sweat a little bit under the brim of his hat. He thought back and wondered, "*Did I handle any cases recently that would have stepped on Tony Gumbati's toes*?" He really hoped not.

Tony spoke to Jack, "Mr. Trane, relax, you look a little nervous. Let me get you something to drink," He poured Jack a glass of wine. He was looking at Jack's shoes. He said, "Mr. Trane, I like your shoes. What size are you? About a 9? I'm usually rather good at guessing sizes." He smiled at Jack. It was like he was measuring Jack for some cement overshoes. He said to Jack, "Mr. Trane I'd like to talk some business with you, but I never do business on an empty stomach." He motioned over to Sylvio "Big D" Donato and Sylvio went into the swinging doors and then came right back out. Within about fifteen seconds another man emerged through the swinging doors. He was a short man with thinning hair. He had a thin black mustache and was wearing dark pants and a white shirt. He had an apron around his waist. In his hands were 2 steaming plates of food. He put one plate in front of Jack and one plate in front of Mr. Gumbati. The aroma rose into the air, steam from the food, filled his nostrils. The bartender put on some old Italian music and played it really soft. For a moment Jack thought that he was in Sicily. The food looked wonderful. It was a classic Lasagna with 3 layers of cheese, pasta, and meat. There was also a couple of different vegetables layered in. He couldn't place the sauce for sure, but it smelled like a Bechamel sauce. It was topped with fresh cilantro. In a side dish, there was Arancini. A type of stuffed rice balls filled with Ragu, tomato sauce, mozzarella, and peas.

Mr. Gumbati said to Jack in a kind of a singing voice, "*Mangiare, Mangiare*" Jack lifted his fork and put a full bite of the lasagna in his mouth. It was an incredible treat for his senses. He thought that if he were going to order a last meal, this would probably be it.

Throughout the meal, Tony "two shoes" Gumbati made small talk about the neighborhood, where he grew up, where his family came from. Jack just listened. When they had finished with the lasagna and the Arancini, the short man with the thin mustache came through the swinging doors again and put another plate in front of Jack and Mr. Gumbati. It was Tiramisu. It was kind of like a ladyfinger, but it had a coffee taste to it, and it was covered with cocoa. When Jack finished, he just sat back in his chair, put his hands on his stomach, and took a deep breath. He said, "Mr. Gumbati, do eat like this every day?" Mr. Gumbati looked at Jack and said, "Jack, you got to enjoy the good things in life while you can," Jack took that to mean yes. He pulled a cigar out of his pocket and offered one to Jack. Jack refused because he didn't smoke. Mr. Gumbati looked at Jack and said, "They are Cubans." Jack held his hand up and shook his head. Mr. Gumbati lit up a cigar for himself and then he said to Jack, "Now let's get down to business." He sat back in his chair and blew some smoke into the air.

Jack was wiping his mouth with a napkin; he had just finished the Tiramisu. He threw the napkin down on his plate and said, "OK, Mr. Gumbati let's get down to business, what is it you want from me?" Mr. Gumbati smiled and said, "Mr. Trane it has come to my attention that you are working to retrieve a very expensive watch of which I am extremely interested in finding. I'm going to make this very easy for you. I'd like you to find this watch and then bring the watch to me." Jack opened his eyes wide, "Mr. Gumbati, I really don't want to get involved in any half-baked scheme to steal a 24-million-dollar watch." Jack was shaking his head back and forth. Mr. Gumbati extended his hand towards Jack and said, "Mr. Trane, I don't want you to steal a 24-million-dollar watch. I'm a businessman." Jack thought to himself, "*Yeah, and I'm the starting shortstop for the Boston Red Sox*." Mr. Gumbati continued, "I just want you to return the watch to the rightful owner." Jack smirked and said, "So you are the rightful owner?" Mr. Gumbati responded, "Mr. Trane, I wouldn't ask you to do anything illegal, that watch is mine." Jack tried to measure his words. He looked at Mr. Gumbati with one eyebrow raised and said, "Look Mr. Gumbati, the insurance company hired me to find this watch and return it to them so that they could return it to an unnamed third party." Mr. Gumbati smiled, "There you go!" Jack shot back, "What do you mean, there I go? Are you telling me that you are the unnamed third party?" Mr. Gumbati sat back and took a big puff on his cigar. He blew the smoke up towards the ceiling, and then he put one elbow on the table and let his chin rest on his hand. He said, "Mr. Trane, I own many nice things. I guess I'm just a good businessman." Jack thought to himself "The rightful owner of that watch is probably at the bottom of the Hudson River." Mr. Gumbati continued, "Mr. Trane, all I want you to do is return the watch to me, we can just cut out the middle-man. You won't have to deal with the insurance company, you can just deal with me." Now

Mr. Gumbati was looking down at Jack's shoes. Jack responded, "Mr. Gumbati, with all due respect, the insurance company has offered me a finder's fee of $200,000 upon the return of the watch." Mr. Gumbati laughed, "Mr. Trane, I'm a businessman, I understand these things. Let me make you an offer you can't refuse. I want you to return the watch to me. And I'm going to give you a $400,000 finder's fee." Jack thought for a minute. He imagined his *Nunn Bush* shoes covered in cement. He half-squinted at Mr. Gumbati and said, "But if I give you the watch, wouldn't you collect the 20-million-dollar insurance payment in addition to the watch?" Mr. Gumbati puffed on his cigar again and this time blew the smoke towards Jack, "Mr. Trane, I think that you're starting to see the big picture. You bring me the watch, and you get $400,000. Everybody lives happily ever after."

Jack wasn't buying this, there was no way Gumbati was the true owner of the watch, but he was in a pickle. If he refused to take this deal, he would probably end up at the bottom of the Hudson River with some cement shoes. If he did take this deal, he would be involved in grand larceny of epic proportions. After which he would end up at the bottom of the Hudson River with cement shoes. So, he decided to take the deal until he could figure a way out of this. A way that his *Nun Bush* shoes wouldn't end up at the bottom of the Hudson River.

He said, "Ok Mr. Gumbati, I'll take your offer. But I work alone, I don't want "Big D, or chopper over there tailing me or looking over my shoulder. They cramp my style. Give me about a week and I'll let you know where I am with this case." Mr. Gumbati smiled and put down his cigar in a glass ashtray. He said, "Of course Mr. Trane. I'm a businessman. I'm sure you'll get back to me when you have something." He came over and gave Jack a big hug, Jack would have preferred a handshake. Mr. Gumbati said to Jack, "Let me have Sylvio and Jimmy take you back to where they picked you up." Jack held his hand up and put on his hat, "No that's OK Mr. Gumbati, I think I can find my way back." Mr. Gumbati smiled as he watched Jack head for the door and Jack could hear him say, "Nice shoes." Sylvio and Jimmy let out a laugh. Jack looked at them as he passed them on the way to the door and made snake eyes at them. He opened the door and went outside.

Jack immediately hailed a taxi and one pulled up next to the curb. He got in and closed the door. He let out a deep breath and just sat back in the seat. He had just received an offer he couldn't refuse from an extremely dangerous mob boss. He knew that he had to figure a way out of this, but it was complicated. He sat there in silence. The driver was a young girl in her early 20's. She had dirty blond hair pulled back into a ponytail which came out of the opening in the back of her baseball hat. It was a Red Sox hat. She was patient. Finally, she turned around and looked at Jack. She stared at him for a full minute. It seemed like he was in a trance. Then he shook his head and said to her, "Aren't you in the wrong neighborhood?" She smiled and laughed, "No, I think you are in the wrong neighborhood." Jack laughed and said, "I think you might be right." He gave her the address for *Big Jim's*. That's where he had left his car. He looked up at the driver's tag in the front windshield and saw that the driver's name was Jenny. He asked her, "So Jenny, you been driving long?" She said, "seems like forever." Jack laughed. She was young, but she knew the New York streets and she could drive like a *NASCAR* driver. Zero to fifty in five seconds and she could gesture with the best of them.

As she was darting in and out of lanes and running yellow lights, Jack was trying to figure out how he was going to get out of his deal with Mr. Gumbati. This had certainly complicated things. He didn't even know if Mr. Gumbati was the real third party. Mr. Gumbati could just be using Jack to get the watch. One thing was for sure. Mr. Gumbati was no businessman. But he was the kind of man you didn't want to fool around with. Unfortunately, Jack couldn't think of a way out. Maybe a couple of beers down at *Big Jim's* would help to clear his head. The taxi pulled into the parking lot at *Big Jim's* and Jenny turned around and said to Jack, "That will be $17.50, sir." Jack looked at her Red Sox hat and handed her $40. He said, "I like your hat." She smiled a big smile and said, "Thanks, I come from Boston and this hat reminds me of home." Jack smiled and said, "It reminds me of my home too." She tucked the bills in her jacket pocket, and he got out of the taxi. He watched as the yellow taxi disappeared back into the dark city. Like a tiger heading back into the jungle.

His mind flashed back to Tony "two shoes" Gumbati. Should he get the police involved? Should he let the insurance company know that they are about to be scammed? The wheels were turning, but he was getting nowhere.

He walked into *Big Jim's* and sat down at the bar. There was a Rangers game on the TV. Jack wasn't interested. He noticed Teddy

K at the far end of the bar. He called out, "Teddy K" and a nice cold *Guinness* slid down the bar and stopped right in front of him. Teddy gave Jack a wink and Jack held up the glass towards Teddy. He was hoping that a couple of *Guinness* would clear his head and he would come up with some elaborate scheme to get out the deal that he just made with Tony Gumbati. He looked down at his shoes and imagined what they would look like in cement.

CHAPTER 6

The alarm clock was buzzing, the cellphone was ringing, and Jack was lying in bed with the pillow over his head. He had gotten in quite late last night from *Big Jim's* and he wasn't in the mood for alarm clocks or cellphones. He took the pillow off from his head and sat up in the bed and looked at the alarm clock. It was 8:15 AM and the alarm had been buzzing for the past 15 minutes. He reached over and shut it off. The cellphone was still ringing. He rubbed his eyes, yawned, and took a deep breath. He reached over to the end table and picked up the phone and answered the call.

"Hello, Jack Trane." The voice from the other end had an English accent. It was Harold Chumley. "Hello, Mr. Trane. I hope I didn't wake you. I just called to see how the case was going. Have you made any progress?" Jack rolled his eyes. He didn't like it when clients checked up on him. But he bit his tongue, "Hello Mr. Chumley. Nice to hear from you. Yes, I'm making great progress on the case and I think I will have it wrapped up in a very short time." He left out the part about Gumbati and the cement overshoes. Mr. Chumley sounded giddy on the other end, "Oh, Mr. Trane, you don't know how happy that makes me feel. Please do stay in touch, and if there is anything you need from me, please call directly." Jack thought for a moment and said, "Well there is one thing. Maybe you can tell me who the unnamed third party is. Who actually owns the watch?" Mr. Chumley hesitated for about 10 seconds, "Mr. Trane, you know that I'm not privy to that information. The owner of the watch wishes to remain anonymous. We must respect his wishes." Jack rolled his eyes and made a disgusted face. He thought that Mr. Chumley might be holding out on him. But he really wanted to know if the watch belonged to Mr. Gumbati. Because if it didn't, it would make his next play a lot easier. He spoke into the phone, "Ok Chumley. I guess I'll find out for myself. We'll be in touch." He hung up the phone and fell back into bed.

He laid there with his eyes open, just looking at the ceiling. He noticed that there was a fly in the room. It kept circling the bed. He didn't like flies. He felt that they were competing for any piece of food that they could get their little sticky feet on. The fly had to go, but he didn't have the time or energy to chase him around the apartment this morning. He got out of bed and the fly buzzed away.

He went into the bathroom and completed the morning ritual. Shower and shave in about 20 minutes. He came out and headed directly for the walk-in closet. He stood at the door and reached in and pulled out a pair of olive green dockers. He reached in again and pulled out a paisley green tie. He reached in once more and pulled out a tan jacket. He thought to himself, "close enough". After walking over to his armoire and taking out a perfectly pressed, clean white shirt with a button-down collar, he got dressed. He left the top button of his shirt open, and his tie was tied in a Windsor knot and left loose around his neck. He looked around the apartment and noticed that there were now 3 days of clothes draped over chairs, laying on the floor, and left on the couch. He shook his head and picked up all the dirty laundry and threw it into the walk-in closet. He made a promise to himself to do a thorough cleaning after this case was over. He had made this promise before. That's probably one of the reasons he couldn't walk into the walk-in closet.

He had a plan today to go back to visit Don Valley and see if he could get him to incriminate himself about stealing the *Henry Graves Supercomplication.* Or at least get him to admit that he was somehow in on the job. He grabbed his favorite fedora and put on a black *London Fog* trench coat and headed out the door. He placed the match in the door jamb and closed the door behind him. He walked down the stairs and out the door onto the street. He needed his Latte and a good breakfast, so he headed towards the *Coffee Café.*

It was a sunny day, about 40 degrees with no wind at all. He hadn't taken more than 3 steps when he noticed that black SUV parked about 20 feet from the apartment. Then he felt both arms being grabbed from behind. It was like they were in vice grips. He was being pushed aggressively towards the SUV. He quickly looked left and saw that one of the men in the black suits was holding his left arm. He looked right and there was the other man in the black suit holding his right arm. They still had on their sunglasses.

They put him in the back seat of the SUV and the doors locked automatically as they closed. The 2 men in black suits both entered the front seat of the SUV and didn't say anything to Jack.

They both just sat facing forward like a couple of zombies. Large zombies with very little expression. Once again, it looked like Jack was being abducted and he had no clue as to why or by whom. He started to make some small talk with the 2 black suits. "So, you guys from around here?" They didn't answer. They just continued to look straight ahead. Jack said, "What are the odds on my getting a cup of coffee before you take me wherever you are taking me?" One of the black suits turned around and handed Jack a cup of coffee. It was a vanilla Latte with one shot. This was getting very strange. Why did they have a cup of coffee for him and how did they know he liked vanilla Lattes? Obviously, they had been following him for a while and they were taking notes on his daily routine. But who were they and where were they taking him? He asked them, "Would you guys mind telling me who you are and where you're taking me?" Neither one answered. They just continued to stare straight ahead. The one in the driver's seat started the SUV, put it in gear, and drove off into the traffic.

The windows were blackened so that he couldn't really see where they were going. But he did have his morning Latte, so he figured that he would just sit back and enjoy the ride. He took a long sip of his Latte then just sat back and let this play out.

Jack couldn't tell in what direction they had been driving, but it had been about 20 minutes and they were pulling into a parking garage. The black suit in the front passenger seat turned around and handed Jack a black blindfold and said, "Put it on." Jack was very uneasy. He didn't know where he was, or who these guys were, or where they were taking him. At least in his last abduction, he knew that he was going to see the boss. This time, after he put on the blindfold, he was totally in the dark, literally.

One of the black suits led Jack by the arm to an elevator inside the parking garage. They got in. He could tell that the other black suit was with them too. The elevator traveled up for about 15 seconds and the doors opened. They walked out of the elevator and went left for 12 steps. Then they went right for another 15 steps. Jack counted all the steps in case he needed to come back. He made a mental note. The door opened and they all went in. After they were all inside, Jack's blindfold was removed.

Jack looked around. The room was exquisite. It was a large room with exceptionally large paintings on each wall. He didn't know who the paintings were of, but they looked important. Like Napoleon or Queen Victoria. The floor appeared to be natural dark wood and there were several what looked like oriental rugs in different areas of the room. There were also 6 or 8 dark maroon padded chairs that were placed in pairs on both sides of the room. On the far side of the room, there was a dark maroon couch. And on the couch was the man who looked like "Boss Hogg." The man stood up from the couch and said in a loud voice across the room, "Mr. Trane, please come in, I've been expecting you." The men in the black suits stood at the door. Jack walked over to "Boss Hogg" and smiled. He said, "I hope that you've been expecting me for breakfast because these 2 jokers only got me a coffee." Jack thought that it would be good to break the ice with a little levity, and besides, he really did want some breakfast.

The man laughed. He said, "Mr. Trane, let me introduce myself. My name is George Flax. I work for the Amalgamated Insurance Company. And I believe that you are presently working on a case that concerns my employer."

Jack still had on his trench coat and hat. George Flax continued, "Please take off your coat and hat and let me explain." Things were getting more complicated by the minute. Jack had a lot of questions, and he needed some answers. He took his hat and coat off and draped it over one end of the couch. He sat down on the couch next to his coat and George Flax sat next to him. Jack looked at the small fat man on the couch and said, "What is this, some kind of joke? I'm already working with a guy from Amalgamated Insurance, Harold Chumley." George Flax smiled and said, "Mr. Trane, that man does not work for Amalgamated Insurance and I seriously doubt that his name is Harold Chumley." Jack put his hand on his head as if he had a headache. He said, "Mr. Flax." Mr. Flax interrupted and said, "please call me George," Jack continued, "OK George, what are you saying? This case that I'm on is bogus?" George Flax shook his head from side to side. His jowls jiggled up and down. "Mr. Trane, I assure you that the case that you are working on for the *Henry Graves Supercomplication* is a very real case."

There was a knock on the door. Jack was reaching down to the heel of his shoes just in case there was some action. One of the black suits opened the door and a middle-aged woman wheeled in a small cart with 2 plates of food. The cart ended up in front of George Flax. He smiled from one ear to the other and handed the woman $100 and she left the room. George turned to Jack and said, "breakfast is served." The cart was like a traveling buffet table. There was a little bit of everything. Bacon, scrambled eggs, sausage, home fries, fruit, and more. George said to Jack, "why don't we talk while we eat?" Jack had already munched a piece of bacon and a couple of home fries. "He said, "OK George, you talk, and I'll eat." George buttered a piece of toast and continued to paste it with strawberry jam as he continued to talk, "Mr. Trane, I'm afraid that you've been scammed by an individual who wants the *Henry Graves Supercomplication* for himself. The Amalgamated Insurance Company did not send him to you, but we have been following him, as you are not the first investigator that he has approached with his scheme. We do not know his real name. He has several aliases and may even be part of the robbery plot as well. You would be wise to distance yourself from Harold Chumley." Jack squirted some ketchup on his home fries. He was taking all this in with a grain of salt. He said, "Well this is a good story George, but how do I know that you are who you say you are? Maybe you're the one involved in the robbery plot." Jack smiled and put a fork full of home fries in his mouth. George responded calmly, "Mr. Trane if I was involved in the robbery, I would have the watch." Jack put a sausage in his mouth, he said, "Ok, you got me there. So, this means that the $200,000 finder's fee was a sham too?" George nodded his head and bit down on his toast. He said, "Yes Mr. Trane, I'm afraid that was part of his scam." Jack had finished-off everything on his plate. He dropped his fork on the table and picked up his napkin and wiped his mouth. Then he said, "So George, I appreciate you filling me in on all the details of how I just got scammed, but what do you really want?"

George Flax sat back on the couch and smiled at Jack. He said, "Mr. Trane, we want you to continue with this case. And when you find the watch, and I would like you to return it to me so I can return it to the third party which is indeed anonymous." Jack sat back on the couch as well. He said, "George, what are you offering? Harold Chumley, or whoever he was, offered me $200,000 plus my regular fee if I found the watch. What are you offering?" George Flax rubbed his chin, he said, "Mr. Trane, it appears that much of what Harold Chumley told you was true. We are on the hook for 20 million dollars. The watch was stolen upon delivery to the MET. And there is a finder's fee. But it is not $200,000. The finder's fee is $100,000 and we will pay your normal fee and expenses. George Flax pulled a contract out of his jacket pocket and laid it down on the couch next to Jack. He said, "the case is yours if you still want it."

Jack thought in silence for about 10 seconds. He had just been scammed by Harold Chumley. Tony Gumbati claims he owns the watch and wants it back. Now George Flax claims he's the real insurance man and wants to hire him to solve this case. Well so far, at the very least, he'd gotten 2 good meals out of the deal. Jack picked up the contract from where George Flax had laid it. He looked at it for about 5 seconds. Then he pulled his cross pen out of his pocket and signed the contract and then he handed the contract back to George Flax. George separated the copies and gave Jack a copy. Jack reached out to shake George Flax's hand and George shook his hand. Jack said, "I'll take the case, but I will need my fee in advance. I make $1,000 a day plus expenses. I'll take 2 days now and bill you as I go." So far no one had paid Jack a cent for this case, and he still wasn't sure of who was who. At least if he were making $1,000 a day, it would take some of the edge off.

Jack put on his hat and picked up his coat and put that on. He said, "Ok, I guess that I'll be leaving. How can I get in touch with you?" George smiled, "Mr. Trane, you understand that because this case has such a large amount of money associated with it, there is a great need for confidentiality. My location is not known to anyone except myself and my associates over by the door. I will give you a card with my number on it. You can call me whenever it is necessary." He handed Jack a business card. Jack nodded his head, "I can live with that." George Flax continued, "Mr. Trane, you will need to put the blindfold back on and my associates will take you back down the elevator to the car. And they will drive you back to the location where they picked you up." Jack agreed, "OK George, he pointed towards the breakfast cart, but if I were you, I'd go easy on the bacon, I heard that we are what we eat." Jack smiled, George did not.

Jack put on his blindfold and the 2 men in the black suits escorted him down the elevator and into the SUV. He took off the blindfold and the SUV entered the street and made its way back towards Jack's apartment. Jack looked at his watch. It was now almost 11:00 AM. On the drive back, the men in the black suits did not say anything to Jack or to each other. They just continued to stare straight ahead until they reached Jack's apartment about 20 minutes later. The SUV came to a stop and the doors unlocked. Jack looked at the men in the black suits and said, "We really have to do this again soon, you guys really know how to have a good time." They continued to stare straight ahead. Jack got out of the SUV, and it immediately pulled away.

As Jack stood on the street, his head was spinning. How much more complicated could this case get? He made his way to the parking garage. He waved to Fernando the parking attendant and put his card in the machine on the wall. His keys came down a chute. He put them in his pocket and walked up the urine-stained stairs to the second level and made it to his car. He opened the door and got in and just sat there for a few minutes reflecting. Was George Flax on the level? Or was he trying to scam Jack? Was Harold Chumley on the level? Or who was he really? How was he going to get out of his deal with Tony Gumbati? Jack didn't know who to believe. He started the car and made his way down the ramp. He waved to Fernando and the gate was opened and he drove out onto the street.

He drove to his office and parked about 3 spaces from the building. Not bad for this time of day. It was just about noon. He walked up the stairs and opened the door and went into the office. Trudy was sitting at her desk. She looked at Jack with one eye squinted and said with a sarcastic tone, "Gee, glad you could make it today Jack. What's the matter? A late night at *Big Jim's* last night?" Jack shook his head, "Yeah, well, something like that. But things are getting complicated. Trudy, I want you to check something out for me. I want you to call the Amalgamated Insurance Company and see if there is a George

Flax that is employed there." Through the process of elimination, he was going to find out who was real and who wasn't. Trudy had a pencil in her mouth, she said, "Sure Jack, who should I say I am? The IRS?" Jack looked at her with one eye raised, "Come on Trudy, you're good at this. If you want to be the IRS, be the IRS. Whatever it takes Trudy. But I really need to know this like yesterday."

Trudy was shaking her head up and down. Her blond hair was bouncing on her shoulders, "Ok Jack, I'll tell you what. Why don't you run up to the Taco wagon just up the street and bring back some tacos with everything, and by the time you get back, I'll have your answer. What you say?"

Jack said, "*Volvere enseguida*" which translated means "*I'll be right back.*" He was still kind of full from breakfast, but he thought that a taco or two wouldn't hurt. He left the office and walked up the street to the taco wagon. He ordered 3 tacos. Two for Trudy and one for himself. He paid for the tacos and left a $5.00 tip. The taco guy said "*Gracias.*"

He headed back to the office as fast as he could. The cool air on his face felt good. As he was walking, he noticed a couple of guys standing across the street from his office. It looked like Sylvio "Big D" Donato and Jimmy "the chopper" Sissi. They seemed to notice Jack and they disappeared into an alleyway. Jack brushed it off. Chances are that Tony Gumbati is not going to let Jack out of his sight. Jack went back into the office and up the stairs. He opened the door with one hand and in the other, he was carrying the tacos. He placed two tacos on Trudy's desk and said, "What's the deal, Trudy? What did you find out?" Trudy smiled, she said, "How bad do you want to know Jack?" Jack said, "Come on Trudy, I got you the tacos!" She was twirling her hair with her finger. She said, "George Flax does work for Amalgamated Insurance. He's some kind of executive and he's listed in the national register of who's who in executives and professionals." She looked at Jack with a smile, "Anything else Jack? Or can I just eat my tacos now?" He patted her on the shoulder, "Great work Trudy. You see, that's why I keep you around. You make me look good." She laughed, "Maybe I need to do a better job." He laughed too. He said, "Enjoy the tacos." He walked into his office and sat down at his desk and put his tacos in front of him. At least now he was sure the George Flax was telling him the truth. Harold Chumley was a fraud, and no doubt was looking to make Jack a fall guy in a scheme to steal the watch. Things were starting to come into focus just a little more than before breakfast. He opened his tacos, and a fly came down and landed right on top of the taco. The fly's sticky little feet were stuck in the cheese on top of the taco. He was still kind of full from breakfast anyway. Jack hated flies.

CHAPTER 7

Jack sat back in his chair looking at the fly stuck in his taco. He let the fly have it. He didn't know where the fly had been or what was on his feet. He made a disgusted face and pushed the taco aside. He tried to piece this case together. A line that he had read from Sir Arthur Conan Doyle kept coming back to him, "*there is nothing more deceptive than an obvious fact.*" It seemed like Jack had a bunch of facts, but they really did not lead anywhere concrete. Instead of racking his brain, he decided to read the morning paper since he didn't have a chance to read it this morning. In reality, he wanted to do the jumble puzzle, he felt that it kept his mind sharp. He opened the paper to the last page and pulled out his cross pen from his shirt pocket. He looked at the first jumbled word and let his mind wander. The jumbled letters read; **"YNPIOCCARS"**

He just stared at the jumbled letters for about 10 seconds and then suddenly a word came to him **"CONSPIRACY"**. He dropped his pen. He said to himself out loud, "Of Course!" Trudy yelled from the next office, "Of course what Jack? Did you find a prize in your taco?" He was still deep in thought. It came to him. Maybe I've been focusing on the wrong people. It didn't seem probable that either of the 2 armored car guards was smart enough to devise a successful scheme to steal the watch and get away with it. But it did seem possible that someone with the connections that Tony Gumbati has, could easily put in place a plan not only to steal the watch but then to fence it after he had it in his possession. One thing was for sure. Tony "two shoes" Gumbati did not have the watch. If he did, he wouldn't have pressured Jack into finding it for him. Another thing for sure was that if Jack did bring the watch to Tony Gumbati, he would then become a loose end. No doubt he would be rewarded with a pair of cement overshoes. Jack had to figure a way to return the watch to George Flax but at the same time give Tony Gumbati what he was looking for. He had an idea, but it meant that he would have to put off his visit to Don Valley until he took care of a couple of things.

Jack called out to the next office, "Hey Trudy, would you come in here for a minute?" Trudy came waltzing in. Her blond hair was bouncing off her shoulders. She was wearing a white turtleneck and a very tight red skirt. She had on a rather large gold chain around her neck and her nails were polished red to match her skirt. It was Friday and it looked like Trudy was thinking weekend.

She said, "What do you need Jack? Those tacos a little too spicy for you?" Jack smiled, "No Trudy, I didn't eat the taco. A fly got to it before I did. What I need is for you to get in touch with your friend who does 3d printing." Trudy smiled, "Why? You want to print some tacos, Jack?" She laughed, Jack didn't. He said, "No I need to know if he can print a watch." He pulled the picture of the *Henry Graves Supercomplication* watch from his top drawer and handed it to Trudy. He said, "ask him if he can print this and how long would it take and how much would he charge?" Trudy looked at the picture and said in her New York accent, "It looks like real gold Jack, that could be very expensive." He shook his head back and forth, "No Trudy, it just has to look expensive. As long as it can fool someone temporarily, that's all I need." Trudy said, "No problem Jack, I'll call him and see what he can do." The plan was still forming in Jack's mind. He said, "Thanks, Trudy. I'm going play a hunch and head out to Hoboken and pay a visit to Billy Bardsley. If you need to get in touch with me, just call me on my cell." Trudy made a sarcastic face, "Well duh…I know Jack, that's how I always get in touch with you." Jack raised one eyebrow, "Unless I get in touch with you first." Then he said, "Trudy after you finish with the guy who does 3d printing, why don't you just take the rest of the day off. It's almost the weekend anyway." Trudy picked up her phone and started dialing. She said, "That sounds like a plan."

Jack grabbed his trench coat and his hat and headed towards the door. He knocked on Trudy's desk with his knuckles as he went by and gave her a wave. He knew that she would come through for him. He left the office and walked down the stairs and out onto the street. He could see Sylvio "Big D" Donato and Jimmy "the chopper" Sissi standing in an alleyway watching him. He was sure that they didn't know he was watching them. He didn't want them following him to Billy Bardsley's house out in Hoboken, so he was going to have to lose them somewhere in the city. He had been looking forward to this all day. Sylvio was big, but he was as dumb as they come. And Jimmy was even dumber than Sylvio. He got into his car and started it up. He put Billy Bardsley's address into his GPS and gave Sylvio and Jimmy time to get to their car. He could see them in his rear-view mirror get into a white BMW about 5 car lengths behind his. He thought that he would let them follow him back towards little Italy and then lose them there.

He put the car in gear and pulled out into traffic. He could see the white BMW pull out at the same time. Jack kept the speed at about 35 to 40 miles per hour. Just enough to let them think that they were keeping up. When he got down past Delancey Street, he stepped on the gas and pulled a hard right onto Broome Street. He accelerated quickly and looked back to see if the BMW was keeping pace. The BMW just turned onto Broome Street and Jack went left onto Mott Street. It was crowded with cars parked on both sides of the street. Jack weaved through the traffic. His wheels screeched as he took a hard right onto Grand Street. The BMW had not yet made Mott Street. Grand Street had a lot less traffic, so Jack accelerated again and hit 4th gear. His speedometer read 70 miles per hour. He quickly stepped on the brakes and took a left back onto Bowery. The BMW was nowhere in sight. Jack had lost them. Something they would have to explain to Tony Gumbati.

Jack activated his GPS and headed off to Hoboken. He turned on the radio to the classic rock station. An old Christopher Cross song came on "*I got to ride, ride like the Wind*" He stepped on the gas and sang along.

About 40 minutes later he was pulling up right outside Billy Bardsley's house at 132 Garden Street. He got out of the car and walked towards the house. The shades on the windows were pulled down. But there was a car in the driveway, so he figured that Billy was home. He walked up the steps to the door and he knocked three times. No one answered. He knocked again, this time he knocked five times like a hammer. Still, there was no answer. Jack figured that either Billy Bardsley didn't want to answer the door, or he couldn't. He turned the doorknob, and the door was open. He walked in and called out, "Hello, is anyone here? Billy, it's Jack Trane, I was here the other day. I just had a few more questions for you." It was dead silence. Just the sound of Jack's shoes scuffing the floor.

Jack had been thinking that it was Billy Bardsley that had conspired with Tony Gumbati to steal the watch, and something must have gone wrong. He was sure that there must at least be some clues here that would back up his theory. The first place Jack always looks is the trash can. People always seem to throw away things that become evidence later. As he made his way to the kitchen. He could see that some kind of scuffle had taken place here recently. A chair was turned over. The cabinet drawer under the sink was left open. And there seemed to be some bloodstains on the top of the table. He found the trash can and emptied it onto the floor. He was on his hands and knees looking for anything that would give him some clues. He found some old racing forms. They were all checked off, crumpled up, and thrown into the trash. It was obvious that Billy was a gambler and not a particularly good one. Jack found another piece of paper that had some writing, ***"5,000 dollars, Gumbati"***. So, it appeared that Billy Bardsley was into Tony Gumbati for at least

$5,000 for gambling debts. He continued to sift through the trash. He found a bunch of *Ring Ding* wrappers and a half-eaten *twinkie*. It appeared that Billy Bardsley was not into health-food. Jack couldn't find anything else of value in the trash. He walked into Billy's bedroom and noticed an end table next to the bed. He opened the drawer and found a pad. On the pad was what looked like a diagram of the MET and a truck outside the MET. There was a watch drawn on top of the truck. No doubt this was Billy's diagram of the watch robbery. The only problem was that Billy didn't have the watch. It now became clear. Billy was supposed to steal the watch for Tony Gumbati to pay off his gambling debt. But it looks like Don Valley had a plan of his own. Don Valley had made it look like the watch was stolen from the truck by an unknown thief and now he was going to try to sell the watch without anyone knowing that it was him who stole it. But Jack had already seen the videotape. He knew that Don Valley was in on the robbery, but up to this point, nobody else suspected him. It was only a matter of time before Danny Watts would figure this out. He had to stay one step ahead of him. He still wanted the $100,000 finder's fee. Tony Gumbati just wanted the watch and now Jack was the easiest way for him to get it. At least that's what Tony thought.

Jack didn't want to hang around in Hoboken any longer than he had to. He had what he wanted so he decided to head back to the city. He made sure that he wiped down anything that he had touched as not to leave any fingerprints behind. As he made his way out of the house, he noticed 2 white lines on the floor from the kitchen all the way to the front door as if someone had dragged something across the floor. It was kind of gritty, a little sandy. Jack reached down and ran some of the dirt through his fingers. It had a familiar feel. He just couldn't place it. He walked out the door and down that steps and looked over and saw Billy Bardsley's trash can. On the top of the trash was an empty bag of cement. He thought to himself, "*Billy Bardsley became a loose end and now he's swimming with the fish.*" That was the one thing Jack didn't want to become. A loose end.

He got into his car and headed back towards the city. It was almost 5:00 PM and he thought it might be a good idea to stop in at *Big Jim's* for one of those deluxe burgers and a *Guinness* or two. About halfway back to the city, he pulled out his cellphone and dialed up Trudy's number. She answered, "Hello". "Hi Trudy, it's Jack. I wanted to see how you made out with the 3d printer. Can he do it?" Trudy answered, "Yes Jack, he can do it, but it's going to cost you." Jack nodded his head, "Yeah, I figured it was going to cost me. How much?" Trudy smiled, "He said that he'd do it for $600 as long as you pay for him to take me to a nice dinner at the Rooftop Restaurant." Jack's eyes bulged wide, "What? That meal with probably cost more than the watch!" There were 5 seconds of silence. Then Jack said, "OK Trudy, you got me this time. It's a deal." Trudy giggled, "Thanks Jack, you're the best!" Jack said, "When can he have the watch?" Trudy said, "It only takes about half an hour. You can have it tomorrow." Jack smiled; Trudy really did make him look better. He said, "Thanks Trudy, I'll see you on Monday. Have a great weekend." He didn't like the idea of paying for a meal for the 3d printer, but business is business, and he needed that watch to work out a deal with Tony Gumbati.

Jack pulled into the parking lot at *Big Jim's.* He parked the car and got out and started walking towards the building. He noticed on the far side of the parking lot a white BMW. It looked like Sylvio "Big D" Donato and Jimmy "the chopper" Sissi were waiting for him. Jack figured that he might have a little fun with the situation. He entered *Big Jim's* and walked right past the table that Sylvio and Jimmy were sitting at and made like he didn't even notice them. Sylvio was wearing his blue suit and Jimmy had on his leather jacket. He sat at the bar and yelled down at Teddy, "Hey Teddy K!" A nice cold *Guinness* came sliding down the bar and stopped right in front of him. Teddy gave Jack a wink. Jack raised his glass to Teddy. Jack sipped the head off his beer and Teddy came walking towards Jack with his bar rag over his shoulder. He stopped in front of Jack and said, "What's it going to be tonight Jack?" Jack smiled. He said "How about one of the deluxe burgers and a large order of fries? Oh, and hold the onions on that burger." Teddy looked at Jack close and said, "Jack, I don't think onions are your biggest problem right now. You see those two thugs over there? I'm pretty sure they've been waiting for you. Those are mob guys." Jack laughed, "I know who they are. They are working for Tony "two shoes" Gumbati. And as it turns out so am I." Jack just smiled and took another sip of his beer. Teddy looked startled, "What are you talking about? You're working for the mob?" Jack breathed in deep, "Well it's kind of a long story, but for now, they think I'm working for Gumbati. Those two guys over there are dumber than a rock. Do you want to have a little fun?" Teddy looked puzzled, "What do you mean?" Jack was talking in a low tone. "I'm going to get up quickly and run out the door. These 2 jokers are going to get up to follow me. I'm going to run around the back of the building. Then you let me in through the kitchen. I'll come back in and sit at the bar. When they can't find me outside, and they see that my car is still in the parking lot, they'll come back in and see me sitting at the bar." Teddy said to Jack, "You really need to get a hobby."

Jack got up quickly and ran out the door. Sylvio and Jimmy got up and followed. By the time they got to the door, Jack had already run around the back of the building. Sylvio and Jimmy ran to their car, thinking that Jack was going to make a run for it in his mustang. Sylvio started the BMW and sat there waiting for Jack to make a move. In the meantime, Teddy K had let Jack back in through the kitchen entrance. Sylvio and Jimmy sat there for about 3 minutes until they realized that the mustang was not going anywhere. They got out of the car and walked up to the mustang and saw that Jack wasn't even in the car. Jimmy looked around the parking lot and said, "I guess he's not in the car". Sylvio responded, "No kidding genius." They decided to go back into *Big Jim's*. When they walked back in, they noticed that Jack was still sitting at the bar. Jack gave them both a big wave as they walked in. He turned to Teddy K and let out a big laugh. Sylvio and Jimmy were not laughing. They went and sat down at the table they had just left. They continued to watch Jack.

Teddy K came back with the deluxe burger and fries. He placed them in front of Jack and put a new bottle of ketchup on the bar too. There was no better burger in the city and the fries were done just right. Not too crispy and not too soft. He smothered the fries in ketchup. Jack enjoyed his *Guinness* along with the fries and the burger. As he took a bite, he laughed a little thinking about what he just did to Sylvio and Jimmy. He wasn't through yet. When he had finished the meal, Teddy K came over and put the bill down in front of Jack. Jack didn't even look at the bill, he just put $40 down on the bar. He said, "Teddy K, that was a great meal. Please give my compliments to the chef." Teddy made a face at Jack and made a gesture. Jack laughed and got up and started to leave the bar. On his way out he stopped in front of Sylvio and Jimmy's table. He looked at Sylvio and then at Jimmy and said, "I thought that I saw a couple of guys that look like you two this morning, but that couldn't be true. But they were driving a white BMW just like the one you drive. Oh well, I guess the city is full of coincidences." Sylvio chimed in, "The boss just wants us to keep an eye on you, for your own good." Jack got in Sylvio's face, "Look Sylvio, I work alone. I don't need you and Jimmy cramping my style. And if you guys keep following me, there's going to be trouble. Capisci?" Sylvio smiled and said, "Mr. Trane you don't know what trouble is." Jimmy laughed. Jack backed off and said to both of them, "Look, I'm going home. You don't have to follow me. I'm just going to my apartment to get some sleep. Why don't you guys go home too?" Sylvio smiled, "Maybe we will Mr. Trane. Maybe we will."

Jack left the bar. Sylvio and Jimmy didn't follow. They probably had someone else to harass tonight anyway. Jack got into his mustang and started the engine. He listened to the engine idle for a few minutes as the car warmed up. He loved to hear the sound of his Shelby GT500. He put the car in gear and drove back towards his apartment. There were the normal sounds and scenes of the city. A couple of men standing on the side of a building calling across the street to a couple of other men. At the next corner, some working girls were standing around. And there was a certain quiet in the air. At this time of day, it seemed like there were more taxis on the road than there were cars. He made it back to his parking garage. He drove in and parked his car on the second level and dropped his keys off in the kiosk on the bottom floor. Then he walked the 2 blocks to his apartment.

Jack entered the apartment building and made his way up the stairs to the second floor. It had been a long day and he was just looking forward to a nice hot shower and a good night of sleep. As he approached the door, he noticed that the matchstick that he had placed in the doorjamb this morning was now on the floor. Someone had either been in his apartment or was still there. He opened the door slowly. It was dark. He couldn't see anything inside. He stepped in and saw lights. Not the overhead lights. The kind of lights you see when someone has just hit you in the face. He reacted quickly and spun around and swung his right fist wildly and he connected. He heard a man groan. He had hit the intruder in the ribs, not the face. Somehow Jack was pushed to the floor and the intruder opened the door and fled down the hallway. Jack got up off the floor and ran to the door. Jack got there in time to see a man leaving the building. Jack caught a glimpse of the side of his face. It was a familiar face. It was Harold Chumley. Jack closed the door and put on the light. He was no worse for the wear. His face was a little sore, but it didn't even leave a mark.

He walked over towards his couch and just fell back into a sitting position and sat there for about 3 minutes. A little fly landed on his knee. He thought to himself, "*I really hate flies*". He grabbed the fly with his right hand and squashed it. He thought to himself, "*I'll deal with Chumley tomorrow. Tonight, I just need to get some sleep.*" He flicked on the TV and indeed did fall asleep.

CHAPTER 8

Jack had a few things on his plate today. One, get in touch with Harold Chumley and settle the score with him. And two, drive out to White Plains and see if he can get Don Valley to tip his hand. And three, pick up the 3d printed *Henry Graves Supercomplication*. He rolled out of bed and rubbed his eyes. He didn't remember getting from the couch to the bed last night, but that wasn't unusual. There were times when he didn't even remember how he got home. He stumbled into the bathroom and showered, shaved, and took care of a couple of other necessary things, and came out ready for the day.

He walked over to the walk-in closet, reached in, and pulled out a nice pair of black dockers. Jack had not done any ironing in quite some time, if ever, but there was still a hint of a crease running down the front of the pants. He put them on and reached into the closet again and pulled out a black and white striped tie. He reached in once more and pulled out a dark gray sportscoat. His streak was still alive. A perfect match. He made his way over to the armoire and pulled out a pristine white shirt with a button-down collar. As he was tying his tie into a Windsor knot, he was thinking about what he was going to say to Chumley. He knew what he would like to do to him, but he didn't think he'd get the chance for that. He finished dressing and looked around the room. Dust particles were floating across the room in the sunlight. He shook his head and said to himself, "*I really got to get a maid.*" He put on his black *London Fog* trench coat and put on his favorite hat, the *Flechet Fedora*, and walked out of his apartment. He remembered to place the matchstick in the doorjamb, and he locked the door. As he left the apartment, he whistled the tune "*Zipadeedooda, zipadeeay, my oh my what a wonderful day.*" He was expecting this to be a good day. And he was going to start it right by heading down to the *Coffee Café* for a nice hot Latte and a stack of blueberry pancakes.

He left his apartment and walked briskly down the street. There was no black SUV in sight. There was no white BMW. For a change, it looked like he was all by himself this morning. But looks can be deceiving. He entered the newsstand and picked up the morning paper. He gave Nicky a wave and put $2.00 down on the counter. Nicky gave Jack a New York gesture and mumbled something under his breath. Jack laughed to himself and left the newsstand and continued down the street.

It was a bright sunny day, and the air was as clean as it gets on a November morning in the city. He looked across the street in the store windows and he could see the reflection of what looked like a tall man, probably over 6 feet, dressed in dark clothes, following him about 10 steps behind. Jack didn't like being followed, especially before breakfast. He turned around quickly and spotted the man dressed in dark clothes. As soon as the man realized that Jack had seen him, he ducked into the first alley. He didn't get a good look at the man, but something about him was familiar. Jack turned and gave chase and entered the alley. There were dumpsters on both sides of the alley and garbage was seemingly pasted to the ground the whole length of the alley. The man had a head start, but Jack continued to give chase. The man bumped into one of the posts on the side of a dumpster and ripped the shoulder of his coat. Jack yelled out, "Hey you punk! Stop! Why are you following me?" The man in the dark clothes spun around and he had a gun in his hand, and he shot in Jack's direction. A trace of smoke rose from the weapon. Jack ducked and the bullet grazed the wall on the side of the alley and ricocheted off the wall and clipped the bottom of Jack's left ear. He felt the quick burn, he dropped his newspaper and he immediately ducked behind one of the dumpsters. The man in the dark clothes ran out of the other end of the alley and disappeared into the sea of people on their way to their daily lot in life.

Jack composed himself. He put his hand on his ear and when he took it off, there was a little puddle of blood in his hand. He took a tissue out of his coat and dabbed his ear a couple of times. It didn't appear that the wound was too bad, as the bleeding had slowed. He wondered what this was all about. He knew that Sylvio and Jimmy weren't chasing him, so he wondered who just tried to shoot him in the alley? He had his suspicions, but right now he really needed his morning Latte. He came out from behind the dumpster and picked up his newspaper, tucked it under his arm, and continued on his way towards the *Coffee Café*. He was no longer whistling "*Zipadeedoodah*".

When he got to the *Café,* he headed directly for the restroom so he could clean the wound on his ear and assess the damage. He walked into the restroom and stepped in front of the mirror and looked at his face. He saw a tired man. His left ear was beet red, and the bottom of the ear looked like it had been squeezed in a pair of plyers. He took some paper towels out of the dispenser on the wall and ran them under the water. He dabbed his ear with them to reveal the real damage. After the blood was washed away, there was no more than a little scratch on the bottom of his ear lobe. He laughed and thought to himself, "*Trudy's pierced ears probably hurt more than this.*" He dabbed his ear a couple of more times and threw the paper towels into the trash and went into the *Café.* Betty saw Jack coming out of the restroom and said," Jack I really wasn't serious about you living in our restroom." She laughed out loud, and the other waitresses joined in. Jack said, "It might not smell too good in there, but the view is spectacular." They all laughed, and Jack sat down at a table. Betty came over and said, "Jack, did you know that your ear is all red?" She noticed that there was a little cut on the bottom of his ear. She said, "I'll be right back honey, don't go anywhere." Jack opened his newspaper and started to read the headlines. On the bottom of the first page, it read: "**RARE POCKETWATCH STOLEN IN FRONT OF THE MET"** Jack thought to himself, "*Well, so much for keeping this case under wraps. Every Tom, Dick, and Harry will be looking for the watch now.*" He shook his head. Betty returned and told Jack, "Now sit still." She reached down and put a tiny band-aid on Jack's left ear. Then she said, "Now doesn't that feel better?" Jack smiled and said,

"This really is a full-service restaurant." Betty hit him with her washcloth and said, "Ok Jack, besides your Vanilla Latte, what can I get for you this morning?" Jack smiled, "Come on Betty, you know what I want." Betty smiled, "You can't always get what you want Jack, but sometimes you can get what you need. How about some blueberry pancakes?" Jack laughed, "you're amazing Betty. You read my mind." She smiled and hit him with her washcloth again, "You're an open book, Jack." She walked back to the counter and placed his order.

Jack turned to the back of the newspaper. The front page didn't seem to have any good news. He opened to the sports section and checked out the scores. Although he hadn't been back to Boston in many years, he still followed all the Boston sports teams religiously. In the middle of the page, he could see the hockey scores. **Bruins 6—Flyers 2.** Now his day was starting to look up. Funny how the score of a game, hundreds of miles away can change the outlook of any given day.

Betty came back with his pancakes and a nice full container of Vermont maple syrup. She placed his Latte next to his left hand and said, "Enjoy Jack." The day was indeed looking up. He finished off the pancakes in about 5 minutes and sipped his Latte until it was gone. The first sip was the best, but the last sip wasn't bad either. Betty came over and said, "So how is everything, Jack?" He smiled, "the best Betty, the best." She smiled and said, "I know Jack, but I meant the meal." He loved this banter first thing in the morning. And it didn't hurt that Betty was an attractive woman who kept herself in good shape. He often wondered why she wasn't married. Maybe she liked the banter too.

He put $10 down on the table for Betty, then he paid the bill. He gave her a wave then exited the *Coffee Café*." He walked up the street to the parking garage. It was early Saturday morning, so the traffic was light and there were not many people on the street. Steam rose into the cool November air from the grates in the street. As he was walking, he pulled the business card out of his pocket that Harold Chumley had given him. The address on the card was 112 East 94th Street. That was going to be Jack's first stop. He entered the parking garage and gave Fernando a quick wave. He put his card in the vending machine on the wall and his keys came down a chute. He took the keys and walked up the ramp to the second level. The smell on the ramp was much better than the stairway or the elevator. All he could smell was a faint burning rubber scent. He found his car and got in. He sat for a few minutes contemplating what he was going to say to Chumley when he found him. The smell of the new leather seats helped him to think. He started the car and drove down the ramp. He waved again to Fernando. The yellow bars at the bottom of the ramp raised and Jack exited the parking garage. He made his way to First Avenue and drove straight to East 94th Street. He was there in about 15 minutes. The street had several brick-faced buildings on both sides but when he reached #112, it was just a boarded-up building. No offices, no tenants, no sign of life. Jack's face turned red. He gritted his teeth and pulled his cellphone out of his pocket and dialed the number on the business card. The phone rang and almost immediately there was an answer. "Hello, Harold Chumley." Jack's eyes squinted and he was spitting as he spoke into the phone, "Look Chumley, or whatever your name is, this little charade is over." On the other end of the phone, the man with an English accent spoke, "My dear man, who is this, and what are you talking about?" Jack was fuming, "All right, drop that phony English accent you turkey. This is Jack Trane. I don't know who you really are, or what your involvement is in this robbery, but I'm going to find out. And I'm fairly sure that it was you who took a shot at me this morning in the alley. I don't take too kindly to punks like you taking pot-shots at me. And when I find you, I'm going to put you in a dumpster, English accent, and all. In other words, you're the bug and I'm the shoe. Are you listening Chumley?" The phone hung up. Chumley was no longer on the line. Jack felt sure that he was going to run into him again before this was over.

The next thing on Jack's list was to drive out to White Plains to see Don Valley. He put the address in his GPS and headed out to White Plains. Once he crossed over the Tappan Zee Bridge he started to daydream. He thought about what the *Henry Graves Supercomplication* pocket watch would look like on his nightstand. He smiled because he knew that would never happen. Then he thought about what it would be like to be living in the suburbs. He shook his head and thought to himself, "*No, I already tried that.*" Finally, he thought about detective Debra Thorn and wondered about the possibilities. He smiled to himself.

By the time he had finished all his daydreaming, he was pulling up in front of Don Valleys house in White Plains. He looked at the mailbox and it said 181 Church Street. There was a car in the driveway. It was a late model Nissan Maxima. It was red, but it looked like it hadn't been washed in about 6 months. This was the place. He parked the car and sat for a minute to gather his thoughts. He knew that Don Valley was involved in the robbery and that the stolen pocket watch may even be in the house. But he needed Don Valley to tip his hand so he could catch him in a lie and force him to turn over the watch. Jack wasn't armed, except for the knife blades in his shoes, so he would need to use the delicate art of persuasion. In the past, this had served him well.

He got out of the car and walked up to the steps to the door, and he rang the bell. He heard the chimes. It rang like Beethoven's 5th. The door opened and it was Paula Valley. She answered, "Hello can I help you?" Jack responded, "Hello Mrs. Valley, remember me? I was out here a couple of days ago and I spoke with your husband about the robbery. My name is Jack Trane and was wondering if I could just ask him a few more questions?" Paula made a sour face and squinted one eye. She said, "Oh yeah, Mr. Trane. Yes, I remember you. Come in. I'll tell Donny that you're here." Jack sensed the hesitation in her voice. He entered and stood by the door. She closed the door and walked left towards the kitchen area. As he stood there waiting, he began observing everything in the room. The newspapers were still littered all over the living room. It looked like there were actually more than before, if that was possible. No doubt the

Valleys were monitoring the news for any articles on the robbery. There was a pad of paper on an end table, and something was written on it. There was a lot of handwriting, but he could only make out the last word on the bottom of the page. It said **BOSTON.**

Don Valley appeared from the kitchen area and held out his hand to shake Jack's. They shook hands and Don invited him into the living room to sit down. Jack moved a couple of newspapers over and sat on the couch. Don sat in a chair that was opposite where Jack was sitting. He seemed comfortable and confident. Don leaned back in his chair and said, "So how can I help you, Mr. Trane? I thought that we cleared up everything that last time you were out here." Jack thought to himself, "*funny he should use the words clear up everything…as if something needed to be cleared up.*" Jack responded, "Well Mr. Valley, there were a couple of things that I just wanted to make sure of before I continue on this case. The last time that I was here, it seemed that you were a bit confused as to when the watch was stolen. First, you said it was stolen on pickup, but then you changed your mind and said that it was stolen on delivery. Can you just tell me again, at what point the watch was stolen?" Don looked very uneasy. He rubbed his chin, then he ran his fingers through his hair, then he looked at Jack in the eyes and said, "Well Mr. Trane, for sure it was stolen on delivery. I must have been a little mixed up from the bump on the head." Jack chuckled, "Oh yes, I see how that could happen." Jack paused for a moment and then said, "By the way, I just wanted to let you know, it appears that a videotape of the robbery has been recovered. It seemed that a business across the street had a surveillance camera, and it captured the whole thing. I'm sure that will clear up any inconsistencies." Don Valley looked shocked. He stood up and began pacing back and forth in front of Jack. He said, "A surveillance camera? Well, how about that?" You could see the sweat forming on his forehead as he continued to pace. Jack felt that he had him just where he wanted him. Don Valley now knew that his involvement in the robbery would be uncovered soon, so he would be forced to make his next move. What he didn't know, was that Jack was the only one with a copy of the videotape.

Don called his wife Paula into the room and said to her, "Honey good news. There is a videotape of the robbery, and it will probably answer a lot of questions about who did it." Paula looked perplexed, "A videotape? That could certainly give you some clues into the robbery. Couldn't it, Mr. Trane?" Jack smiled, "Well, I wouldn't at all be surprised." There was a moment of silence, then Jack continued, "Oh and one more thing. It turns out that for some reason this mobster Tony Gumbati is also looking for that watch. Have you ever heard of him, Don?" Don looked terrified. "You mean Tony "two shoes" Gumbati the crime boss?" Jack looked serious with one eyebrow raised. "Yes, that's the one. I really wouldn't want to have that watch in my possession if he was looking for it. I heard he has a rather nasty way of eliminating his enemies." Don put his hand over his mouth.

Jack got up and said, "Well I really have to be getting back to the city now and follow up on a few more leads. You both have been more than helpful." As Jack started walking towards the door, both Paula and Don followed closely. As he got close to the door, he noticed a little nook where the Valleys hung their coats. On the first peg, he noticed a sweatshirt hoodie. It was black. Jack turned back and shook both Paula and Don's hands, and he left the house. As he stood outside the door he smiled. He thought about the look on Don Valley's face when he mentioned Tony Gumbati. It was priceless. Donny was probably picturing his feet covered in cement. Jack knew that he had them just where he wanted them. He knew that they needed to get rid of the watch quickly and get out of town before the real cops showed up at their door. He was sure that he had just forced them into their next move.

As he came down the steps, he noticed a couple of figures coming in his direction. He recognized them immediately. It was Danny Watts and Debra Thorn. Danny was wearing one of his designer suits and a black trench coat with a gray collar. Debra was wearing a dark pair of slacks and a maroon leather jacket. It complimented her reddish-blond hair and green eyes. Jack was glad to see Debra, not so much Danny. Obviously, they were starting to put the pieces of this case together. Danny grabbed Jack's shoulder and said, "Trane, what are you doing out here?" Jack smiled, "What, no hello?" Danny clenched his teeth and gave Jack the snake eye. Jack turned to Debra, "Well, detective Thorn, so nice to see you again. You seem to be holding up well despite the obvious challenges." Debra laughed. Danny angrily said, "What's that supposed to mean?" Jack smiled at Danny, "Relax big guy, nothing personal." Danny asked Jack again, "What are you doing out here?" Jack looked dumbfounded, "Well I guess I just took a little ride to get out of the city and I ended up right here. What a coincidence that I ran into you." Jack smiled, and Debra laughed. Danny got in Jack's face, "Look Trane, I told you before, stay out of my way. I don't want to see you anywhere near this case! Do you understand me?" Jack smiled, "That's funny Danny, I feel the same way." Debra looked at Danny and said, "Hey Danny, lighten up. Let's just focus on the case. Jack's just doing his job." Jack turned to walk away. As he passed Debra Thorn he said, "Maybe we should get together sometime, you know, to compare notes." Debra smiled, "Maybe after this case is over. Why don't you give me a call?" Jack had a wry smile. He said, "Maybe I will Debra, Maybe I will." Danny made a disgusted face and Jack turned and walked to his car.

Jack got into his car and closed the door and just sat back in the seat. He was imagining what he might say to Debra the next time they spoke. He started the car and put it into gear and headed back towards the city. He started to reflect on everything he knew about this case.

Billy Bardsley was into Tony Gumbati for a large gambling debt, which he couldn't pay. Because of that fact, Bardsley was forced to conspire with Tony Gumbati to steal the *Henry Graves Supercomplication* pocket watch in order to pay off Gumbati. Somehow, Bardsley's armored car partner Don Valley found out about the robbery plan and decided to put his own scheme together to steal the watch before Billy Bardsley had the chance. Don Valley's wife Paula was the person in the black hoodie who knocked out Billy Bardsley and made it look like Don Valley was also clubbed. Once the watch had been stolen by the Valley's, Billy Bardsley became a loose end and Tony Gumbati took care of him with cement over-shoes. Obviously, Gumbati doesn't yet realize that the Valleys have the watch, otherwise, they too would be swimming with the fish. It would be way too dangerous to try to fence the watch in the city, so it looks like the Valleys are going to try to run to Boston, either to sell the watch or take off with it on a plane. Fortunately for Jack, because of the app on his phone, he can track the Valley's wherever they go. So, he is now ready to track their every move. But his next step was to pick up the 3d printed watch and put it in his office safe. He had a plan which involved the fake watch that would hopefully take care of Tony Gumbati and help him to keep his *Nunn Bush* shoes out of cement.

CHAPTER 9

Jack crossed over the Tapan zee Bridge and he was back in the city. He was glad to be back, the suburbs made him a little nervous. It was just about noontime, so he decided to get a bite to eat from one of the street vendors. He traveled into the city and found a vendor under the bridge where 119th street intersects with Park Avenue. He was pretty sure the vendor was operating illegally, but he had heard that the Indian food they served was the best and he was willing to take a chance. He parked his car under the bridge and walked up to the vending cart. It appeared that the owners of the cart were of Indian descent, so the food was legit. They appeared to be a husband-and-wife team. They both had a dark complexion and dark hair, and the man was very friendly. He had a little badge on his shirt that said "Raja." Jack assumed that was his name. Raja said, "Good morning sir, how can I help you?" His words were very well pronounced in a sing-song kind of way. Jack studied the menu on the side of the cart. Most of the items on the list he couldn't pronounce so he just ordered the shortest word he could find on the menu. "I think I'll have a bowl of the Dal." Raja responded, "Oh that's a very good choice. My wife has made this Dal special this morning." His wife smiled and prepared the bowl of Dal. She was wearing a mustard-colored shirt, actually a kurta and a light brown salwar, a traditional pants for women. She had a name tag on her kurta, it read "Siya." She handed the bowl of Dal to her husband and then Raja handed it to Jack. "That will be seven dollars and ninety-five cents." Jack gave him a big smile and gave him a twenty-dollar bill and said, "keep the change, my friend." The vendor looked at Jack with big eyes, "Oh, you are too kind. Thank you, Thank you very much." Jack made it a point to support the street vendors, he knew that they all worked hard for their money.

He went back to his car with the bowl of Dal. He had never eaten Dal before. When he opened the lid, the aroma filled the mustang and the windows steamed up. The Dal appeared to some kind of a reddish-orange-colored stew. He couldn't place all the spices, but he was thinking of turmeric, garlic, and ginger. He could also see tomatoes and onions and some kind of red lentils and if he weren't mistaken, there was some finely chopped jalapeno on top of the stew, and on the bottom, there was some brown rice. He took a bite and his eyes opened wide. He was not used to Indian cooking and he was somewhat overwhelmed by the combination of spices and flavors. It was definitely not what he expected. It was much better. He took another bite and closed his eyes and savored the meal. He was done in about 5 minutes and was ready to roll. Although he had finished the meal, his taste buds were still tingling. He made a mental note of the location because he knew that he would be back. He started his car and pulled back into traffic.

It was still before 1:00 PM and Jack's next stop would be to pick up the 3d printed watch and put it in his office safe. This was important to his plan for taking care of Tony Gumbati. The only problem was that Trudy didn't tell him where the printer was located. He took out his phone and dialed Trudy's number. It rang twice and she answered, "Hello Jack, you realize that I have a life. This is Saturday, Jack. I don't work on Saturdays. So, this must be some big emergency, like you can't find the cups to the watercooler." Jack let her finish her complaining with rolled eyes, then said, "Ok Trudy, I don't want to cramp your style, but I need the address for the 3d printer. I really need to pick up that watch today." Trudy snapped her gum, "Jack, no problem, I already picked up the watch last night when I went on my date to the rooftop restaurant. I was going to bring it in on Monday." Jack breathed a sigh of relief, "Trudy, you're amazing. What would I do without you?" Trudy laughed, "You'd probably be broke, homeless, and have a really bad wardrobe." Jack laughed, "I wouldn't be surprised Trudy, I wouldn't be surprised." He laughed, and said, "I'm on my way to your apartment right now, I need to pick up the watch. I want to get it into my safe at the office today." Trudy yawned, "Ok Jack, if you say so. I'll be here." Jack smiled, "I'll be there in about 10 minutes." They both pushed the end button on their phones.

Jack came up to a traffic light and put on his sunglasses, then pulled the brim of his hat low. The light changed, he let up on the clutch and hit the gas pedal hard. He could see blue smoke in the rear-view mirror from the rubber he just burned from his tires. He still enjoyed the sound of an 8-cylinder engine and the feeling of acceleration as he hit all the gears. He drove through the streets at breakneck speed. He even passed 2 taxis, which on any given day is almost impossible. He narrowly avoided a trash truck, and the trash men gave him some pointed New York gestures. Finally, he pulled up outside Trudy's apartment. He jumped out of the car and ran up the steps to the apartment and rang the bell on the side of the door. He heard a buzzer go off and the door unlocked. He opened the door and ran up the stairs to Trudy's apartment. Sweat was dripping down the sides of his face and he was huffing and puffing from running up the stairs. Trudy was waiting for him, standing in the doorway to her apartment. She was holding the watch in front of her. She reached out to hand him the watch, and said, "Jack, you look like you just ran a marathon. Maybe you should start working out." He made a disgusted face, "Yeah, right after I cut out hamburgers, fried foods, and draft beer, I'll start working out." Trudy made a disgusted face, "Speaking of foods, what have you been eating? Your breath is enough to stop an elephant!" Jack laughed, "What? You have something against fine Indian cuisine?" She smirked, "Well, if that's what it is Jack, warn me the next time you eat it and I'll wear a gas mask." He shook his head, "Very funny Trudy." He took the watch. It was enclosed inside a small wooden box. He didn't bother to open the box. He just put it under his arm. He said, "Thanks Trudy, you're one in a million. I owe you one." She smiled, "You owe me more than one Jack, maybe another dinner at the rooftop would make up for it." She smiled. Jack turned around as he was leaving and said, "Would you settle for lunch at the basement café?" He laughed as he made his way back down the stairs. Trudy closed the door and went back into her apartment.

He didn't open the box to look at the watch, he was in too much of a hurry. He felt that it would be better to open the box in the calm setting of his office. He placed the box on the car seat beside him and drove back to his office. He drove much more carefully than he had just a few minutes ago. He treated the watch as precious cargo and wanted to make sure that nothing happened to it. He arrived at his office in about 15 minutes, and he found a parking spot about 3 spaces from the office entrance. He parked the car and went up to his office. He went in and sat down at his desk. He placed the box with the watch in it in front of him on the desk. The box was made of a dark wood, polished to a high gloss. It had a small brass latch on the front of the box that kept it closed. He carefully raised the latch and opened the box slowly. As he opened the box, he could see the gold finish on the watch reflecting the light around him. It looked perfect. The glass crystal looked perfect. The face of the watch with the numbers and hands looked perfect. It looked exactly like the *Henry Graves Supercomplication* pocket watch in his picture. He picked it up and held it in his right hand. The weight too seemed perfect. For a minute he thought about how this watch would look hanging inside a glass container on his desk. He had a love for pocket watches and even though this one was not real, it looked better than any of the 20 gold pocket watches he had in his collection. The short daydream ended. He knew that he was going to need this watch to carry out his plan to take care of Tony Gumbati. He carefully put the watch back in the case, closed the latch, and walked over to his wall safe behind the picture of Fenway Park. He moved the picture aside, opened the safe with the combination 10 right, 10 left, 10 right, and placed the box with the watch inside. He closed the safe, put the picture of Fenway Park back in place, and walked back over and sat at his desk. It had been a full day and it was still early about 2:00 PM. As he sat there, he could see a little sun still coming in through the window. Dust particles were dancing across the room in the beams of light.

He pulled out his cellphone and placed it on his desk. He thought that it would be a good time to start tracking Don Valley's movements to see if he was going to make a run for it with the real watch. He opened the app on his phone and saw that Don Valley hadn't moved. He was still at his home in White Plains. Jack wasn't surprised. He figured that it would take a little time for the Valley's to plan their escape. The Valley's had no idea that Jack was tracking them. This was something that he was going to use to his advantage. It was what he was counting on to retrieve the watch and wrap up this case. But things don't always go as planned.

As Jack was sitting at his desk, looking at his phone, the door to his office opened and he heard someone come in. There were a bunch of footsteps. It sounded like more than one person. Suddenly Sylvio "Big D" Donato and Jimmy "the chopper" Sissi were standing in his doorway. Jack looked up and remained calm. He gritted his teeth and said, "What are you two goons doing here? I thought that I told you that I work alone?" Sylvio smiled and said, "Well, here's the thing, Trane. The boss wants us to keep a real close eye on you and for some reason, you keep losing us and the boss don't like that." Jimmy chimed in, "Yeah the boss don't like that. He told us to keep a close eye on you." Jack thought to himself, "*these two guys are dumber than a box of country dirt.*" Jack squinted at the 2 of them and said, "Well you go back and tell the boss, that if he wants the watch back, I don't want you 2 jokers hanging around me, or following me or even thinking about me. You got it?" Jack was spitting as he spoke. Sylvio smiled, "Why don't you tell him yourself, he's right here." Tony Gumbati came walking in from Trudy's office and sat in the chair right in front of Jack's desk.

Mr. Gumbati said to Jack, "Mr. Trane, so nice to see you again. You have such a nice office. It's a good place to talk." Now Jack was getting a little nervous. He could feel the sweat starting to form on his forehead. He said, "Mr. Gumbati, I thought that we had a deal. I was going to find your watch and bring it back to you, and Sylvio and Jimmy over here would stay out of my way." Mr. Gumbati smiled, "Mr. Trane, I'm a businessman, I need to keep track of my assets. You are one of my assets. And for some reason, Sylvio and Jimmy are having a hard time keeping track of you. I can't have that. It's bad for business. I like you Mr. Trane, so, I tell you what I'm going to do. I'm going to solve the problem." He waved Jimmy over, and Jimmy came and stood in front of Jack. He had something in his hands. It was a round plastic band, gray in color, about an inch in height, and about 8 inches around. Jimmy waved his hand at Jack and said, "Put your foot up on the desk." Jack didn't have many options since he was outnumbered and outgunned. He didn't want to, but he hesitantly put his foot up on his desk. Jimmy put the band around Jack's ankle and locked it with a key. He gave the key to Mr. Gumbati and he walked back towards the door and stood there with Sylvio. Jack knew that they had just placed a tracking bracelet on his ankle and that was really going to put a damper on his plan, but he was immediately thinking about ways to get it off.

Mr. Gumbati smiled a wide smile and said, "Now Mr. Trane, whatever you do, please don't try to get the ankle bracelet off. You see, if you try to open it without this key, the bracelet will explode and probably take off your foot. And we wouldn't want that." Mr. Gumbati was smiling, holding up the key in front of Jack, almost taunting him with it. Jack thought quickly and stepped down on the button under his desk and took several pictures of Mr. Gumbati holding the key. He also reached down to his cellphone and subtly took another picture. Mr. Gumbati put the key in his pocket and sat back in the chair and lit up a cigar. He said to Jack, "Would you like one Mr. Trane? Oh, that's right you don't smoke. Too bad. They are Cubans." He took a big puff of the cigar and blew the smoke in Jack's direction. Jack sat back in his chair and made a disgusted face. He said, "How am I supposed to get around dragging this thing all over the place? I can't even take it off to get in the shower." Mr. Gumbati smiled and said, "Well Mr. Trane, the faster you find the watch, the faster we can get the bracelet off." Sylvio and Jimmy laughed in the background. They were probably thinking that they were going to replace it with some cement shoes. Mr. Gumbati stood up and said, "Well Mr. Trane, this has been very nice. I enjoyed our little visit, but

I really must be leaving now, I have some business to attend to." Tony Gumbati walked out of Jack's office towards the door. Sylvio looked at Jack and pointed at Jack with his index and middle fingers and then pointed at his eyes, sending the message, we are watching you. All three of them left the office.

Jack sat there for a moment in the silence. This was something that he really had not expected. He had to get this bracelet off, otherwise, his plan to return the watch to the insurance company wouldn't work. Sylvio and Jimmy would be able to track him, as he tracked the Valleys. No doubt, if Sylvio and Jimmy found out that the Valleys had the watch, they would get it back and get rid of all the loose ends, which Jack would be one of. But a plan was coming to him. He didn't know if it would work or if it was even possible. It involved the 3d printer. When Tony Gumbati held up the key, Jack had snapped several pictures of Tony holding the key. He was hoping that there would be enough definition in the pictures, that the 3d printer could duplicate the key. Hopefully, he could use that key to open the bracelet without losing his foot. He looked at his cellphone and pulled up the pictures. The pictures that he took with the telephoto lens were quite crisp since there was still some sunlight in the room. He enlarged them on his phone, and he could clearly see the shape and grooves of the key. Now all he had to do was to get them to the printer and hopefully get a 3d printed key. He was hoping that Trudy was still at her apartment.

He dialed up Trudy's phone. It rang once and Trudy answered, "Hello Jack, have you no shame? This is my weekend." Jack broke in,

"Look, Trudy, I'm in a bit of a jam here, and I was hoping that you could help me out." Trudy was concerned, "What's going on Jack?" He continued, "I have an ankle bracelet on my foot that will explode unless I open it with a key." Trudy said, "Well Jack, just open it with the key." Jack as shaking his head, "Trudy, I don't have a key, that's why I called you." Trudy was confused, "Jack, I don't have a key." Jack was getting a little frustrated, "No, listen, Trudy, I was thinking that the guy who printed the 3d watch for you could print up a key. I have some pictures on my phone of the key that I'm sending to your phone right now. I'm hoping that there is enough definition for the printer to print a key. Did you get them?" Trudy looked at her phone, "Yeah Jack, it looks like I got them." Jack continued, "Ok, I know it's late. It's about 4 o'clock, but I want you to run over to the 3d printer and see if he can print up this key for me. It's very important that I get this bracelet off before I start tracking the Valleys. Can you do it?" Trudy smiled, "Of course I can do it, Jack. Is it worth another dinner at the rooftop restaurant?" Jack rubbed his forehead, "Well Trudy, if this works, I was thinking about a field trip to Boston for a couple of days. How about that?" Trudy was smiling, "Boston, oh yeah Jack that sounds great. Do I have time to do a little shopping while we're there? I've never been to Boston, Jack. Do they really make baked beans there?" Jack was rolling his eyes. "Trudy, just get the key and everything will fall into place. When you get it, you can't bring it here, I'm being watched. So just take it home with you and call me to let me know that you have it. I'm going to drive my car to my apartment and leave it in the garage just up the street. In the morning, there will be 2 gorillas watching me, so I'll go up to the Coffee Café and take them with me. I'll call you in the morning before I leave so you will know the coast is clear. Now, what I need you to do, is while I'm at the Coffee Café, you go to the garage and place the key on top of the front tire on the driver's side. You can call me when the key is in place." Trudy smiled, "No problem Jack, I got this." He could hear Trudy in the background singing "*Please come to Boston in the springtime.*" Jack was feeling good about his plan. They both hung up the phone. If the key worked, he had a plan that would send Sylvio and Jimmy all the way to Washington DC. If the key didn't work, he was either going to end up in cement overshoes or missing one foot.

He got up from his desk and put on his hat and coat and left the office. He got in his car and drove home. He was sure Sylvio and Jimmy were close behind. He parked his car in the garage and walked to his apartment. He went inside and waited for Trudy to call. He laid down on his bed and closed his eyes, he was just going to take a quick nap. As it turns out, some naps are quicker than others.

CHAPTER 10

The alarm clock next to Jack's bed was ringing and ringing. He reached over and turned it off. The clock read 8:00 AM. He rubbed his eyes and then picked up his cellphone from the night table. He noticed that Trudy had sent him a text message last night at about 11:30 PM. It read, "I have the key Jack, I'm going to drive over to your garage tomorrow morning at about 8:00 AM I will place the key on your tire. Then, I'll call you when everything is in place, Trudy." He smiled to himself and laid back down on the pillow and thought about what a great assistant Trudy is for him. Even though she acted a little ditzy on occasion, and she liked to give him a hard time, he knew that she was really smart with a good sense of humor and personality that complimented his in more ways than he could say. He laughed, if it weren't for her, he probably would be broke, homeless, and have a really bad wardrobe.

He sat on the bed for a minute and looked around. It looked like laundry day had come and gone. There were pants and shirts from every day of the week hanging on the backs of chairs, on the floor, and on the couch. He gathered up all the clothes and put them in a big pile just inside the walk-in closet. He figured that he would get to it sooner or later, but for now, it was a really quick way to make the apartment look clean. At least he thought so. He made his way into the bathroom and showered, shaved, and took care of a few other necessary things. By the time he finished and came out he was alert and ready for his day. He had to get the key to the ankle bracelet and then lose Sylvio and Jimmy. He had a plan. He walked over to the walk-in closet and could barely get in far enough to reach any clothes. He struggled but eventually pulled out a pair of light brown dockers. He reached in again and pulled out a paisley yellow tie. He couldn't reach in any further, so he fished out a brown jacket from the pile on the floor just in front of him. He had the trifecta. The jacket was a little wrinkled, but under his trench coat, no one would know anyway. He went over to his armoire and pulled out a perfectly pressed, immaculate white button-down shirt. He put on the pants and shirt, then tied the tie with a strong Windsor knot. Today, he pulled it tightly around his neck. He put on his jacket and grabbed his hat and light brown trench coat, and he was ready to leave the apartment. His cellphone rang and he picked it up, it was Trudy. "Hello, Jack, everything is all set. The key is right on top of the tire on the front driver's side." Jack smiled, "Great job Trudy, I owe you one." Trudy was smirking, "Yeah right Jack, one hundred maybe." Jack continued, "OK Trudy, now you just go back to your apartment and stay out of the way. I'll call you if I need you for anything." Trudy was still smirking, "Right Jack like I have nothing else to do with my Sundays. But I'm sure you're going to make up for all this when we get to Boston right?" He was shaking his head up and down, "Yeah right Trudy, when we get to Boston, I'll make it up to you." Trudy smiled, "Sounds like somebody's going shopping. Bring your check-book, Jack." He closed his eyes, "Right Trudy, we'll do some shopping in Boston." They both hung up the phone. He was dreading going shopping in Boston, but he knew that he owed her, so to make Trudy happy he was going to let her spend some money and get something nice. Getting the watch back to the insurance company was something that he needed to do as quickly as possible. His expenses were building up quickly and that finder's fee was going to give him what he needed and a little more.

He walked out the door and put the matchstick in the door jamb. His plan was to go down to the Coffee Café for breakfast. He knew that Sylvio and Jimmy would be outside and follow him down to the Café. After he had eaten breakfast, he would walk down to the garage to get his car, lift the key from the front tire, open his ankle bracelet, and then take Sylvio and Jimmy on a ride that they wouldn't forget for a while.

He left the apartment and started walking towards the Coffee Café. He noticed Sylvio and Jimmy get out of their white BMW and start following him. He walked into the newsstand, picked up the paper, and put $2.00 down on the counter. He waved at Nicky and Nicky grunted something and made a half-wave in Jack's direction. The normal morning banter he had with Nicky. He walked down the street with the paper under his arm and entered the Coffee Café. Sylvio and Jimmy were about 5 steps behind. Jack yelled out to his favorite waitress, "Betty, how's it going this morning my friend?" Betty smiled, "Nice to see you're on time today Jack." He smiled and walked over to a table near the window. Sylvio and Jimmy followed and sat down at the same table as Jack. Betty came over and said, "Jack, aren't you going to introduce me to your 2 friends?" She had a big smile. Her short blond hair had a particularly nice shine this morning. Jack said, "Oh these 2 gorillas? They're not really my friends." He pointed at Sylvio, "This is King Kong and this other one is Godzilla. They are on loan from the zoo." Sylvio and Jimmy gave Jack the snake eyes. Betty laughed, "Come on Jack, they look like a couple of nice young men." Jack smiled, "Well looks can be deceiving." She hit Jack with her washcloth. Betty worked on tips and she always tried to work the crowd. Finally, Sylvio spoke up, "I'm Sylvio, and this is my associate Jimmy over there, and we're just keeping Mr. Trane company for a while." Betty smiled, "Well isn't that nice. It sounds like you have a couple of good friends here Jack." Jack smiled, "Yeah, kind of like being friends with batman. You don't know if he's there to help you or hurt you." Betty laughed, "Come on Jack, you're such a kidder."

Jack looked up at Betty with a half-smile. Sylvio and Jimmy just sat there looking dumb. Their normal look. Sylvio was dressed in a blue suit. Jimmy had on a leather jacket.

Betty said, "Well what can I get for all you boys?" Jack spoke up first, "Betty, how about a stack of those blueberry pancakes?" She smiled, "Of course Jack, and a vanilla Late." Sylvio chimed in, "I'll just have a coffee, black. And the same for Jimmy over there." Jimmy protested, "Hey, those pancakes sound pretty good, I'm going to have some of those too." Betty smiled, "OK, that's 2 pancakes, a vanilla

Late, and 2 black coffees." Jack smiled, "You got it Betty, and by the way, Sylvio over here is going to pick up the check." He smiled at Sylvio. Sylvio just stared back at Jack with cold brown eyes. Betty said, "I'll be right back with your coffee, boys." She went back to the counter to put in their order.

Sylvio said to Jack, "So you're a funny guy, Mr. Trane? I know a lot of funny guys at the bottom of the Hudson River." Jack smiled, "Come on Sylvio, I was just joking around." He looked at Jimmy, "Right Jimmy?" Sylvio looked at Jack with a serious face, "You know Mr. Trane, I think by the end of this, you're not going to cracking so many jokes." Jack looked back at Sylvio with a serious face, "You know something Sylvio, it depends on who ends up on the bottom of the Hudson River." Betty came back with the coffee, "Here you go boys, I'll be back with the pancakes in a minute." She gave Jack a wink. Jimmy was drumming his fingers on the table, "I can't wait for those pancakes, man. I haven't had pancakes in a long time." Jack looked at Jimmy, "Well Jimmy, just remember, everything can have drama if it's done right. Even a pancake. Julia Child said that." Jimmy smiled, "Hey, that's real deep man." Sylvio rolled his eyes. Betty came back with the pancakes and Syrup and put them down in front of Jack and Jimmy. She said, "Enjoy boys" and she went back to the counter.

Sylvio spoke to Jack, "So what have you got planned today, Mr. Trane? Me and Jimmy have to follow you all day, so we want to know the plan. Jack put a large fork full of pancakes in his mouth and started speaking with his mouth full, on purpose, "Ok Sylvio, here's the deal. After I finish these pancakes, I'm going down to my garage and get my car. Then I have a good lead. I'm supposed to meet a guy right outside of Grand Central Station. I think he's going to give me what I need to find the watch. If you guys are going to follow me don't get too close. I don't want to spook this guy. If he runs, I won't get anything. Do you think you can do that? Give me a little space?" Sylvio squinted at Jack, "Well you better not try any funny stuff. Remember you have on that ankle bracelet, and we can track you wherever you go." He took out his cellphone and pointed to the app on the phone. Jack put another full fork of pancakes in his mouth and turned to Sylvio and said, "No funny stuff Sylvio. I know when I'm beaten. Let's just finish this job, get the watch to your boss and we'll all call it a day." Sylvio smiled, "Yeah, we'll all call it a day." Jimmy was too busy eating his pancakes to hear any of the conversations they just had. He just continued stuffing his mouth with pancakes.

About 10 minutes later Betty came back to the table. "How was everything boys? Can I get you anything else?" Sylvio chimed in, "Your address would be good." Jack spoke up, "I told you Betty, King Kong, and Godzilla." Betty put the check down on the table and went back to the counter. Jack said to Sylvio, "Thanks for the breakfast Syl, we'll have to do this again sometime." Jimmy chimed in, "Yeah, we'll definitely have to do this again sometime." Jack rolled his eyes. Sylvio looked at Jimmy with a disgusted face. Jack put $10 dollars on the table for Betty's tip and Sylvio went up to the counter to pay the bill. Jack said, "Wait for me outside the garage, then we'll head over to Grand Central." Sylvio pointed his index and middle finger at Jack and then at his own eyes, to say, "I'm watching you." Jack winked at Betty and left the Café. Sylvio and Jimmy were about 10 steps behind.

Jack walked up the street and took a large breath of the cool morning air. Then he let out a couple of coughs. He kept turning back to make sure Sylvio and Jimmy were following him. He entered the garage and gave Fernando a wave. Sylvio and Jimmy got into their BMW and drove close to the entrance of the garage. Jack put his card in the vending machine and his keys came down the chute. He put them in his pocket and walked up the ramp to the second level. His car was just inside the second level against a retaining wall. He reached under the front fender and felt around on the top of his tire and he found the key. It was a gold color and it appeared to be made of a hard metal, but it was smooth like plastic. There was sweat forming on his brow under his hat. He wanted to get the ankle bracelet off, but he also wanted to keep his foot. He was hoping the key was going to work. He thought that it would be best to open the bracelet outside rather than inside his car, just in case something went wrong. There was no need to damage the car too. He walked over to an open space in the garage and put his foot up on a cinderblock that was being used as a divider. He put the key in the bracelet, closed his eyes, and turned it slowly. He heard a click and stopped. Nothing happened. He turned it just a little more and the bracelet popped open. He let out a huge breath and wiped his forehead. It looked like he was going to keep his foot. He took the ankle bracelet off and closed it shut again and put it under his jacket in a large side pocket. He put the key in his shirt pocket, then he got into his car and started the engine. He sat and listened for just about a minute. The low idle of the motor helped him to get his thoughts together.

Jack drove down the ramp and gave Fernando another wave. Fernando smiled, waved back, and opened the gate. He drove out into the street. Sylvio and Jimmy were waiting for him in their white BMW. Jack headed towards Park Avenue; his destination was Grand Central Station. He allowed Sylvio and Jimmy to keep up with him. It was all part of his plan. About three blocks from Grand Central, Jack ran a red light and left Sylvio and Jimmy behind. Sylvio slammed his fist down on the steering wheel. Jimmy was just chewing gum, looking out the window. Jack was not trying to lose them; he knew that they could track him. He just needed a little time to set them up. Jack pulled his car up to the curb near the Hyatt Hotel. He waited until he could see the white BMW, then he got out of the car. He let Sylvio and Jimmy see him go into the station. Jack entered the station and made his way to the terminals. The train from New York to Washington was scheduled for 10:00 AM. It was now 9:55 AM. Jack could see Sylvio and Jimmy entering the terminal from across the open hall. Jack stood, leaning against a marble support column, and acted like he was waiting for someone. He looked up and down, back, and forth, and finally, at 9:59 AM Jack entered the train. Quickly, Sylvio and Jimmy ran to the train and got into the next car. Jack walked to the front of the car that he was in and exited the front of the car back onto the terminal deck. The train started to move, and Jack watched as Sylvio and Jimmy headed for Washington DC. He laughed out loud and said under his breath, "Those two are as dumb as a couple of cane toads." He laughed all the way back to his car. The next part of his plan was to get rid of the ankle bracelet in a way that would throw them off the trail.

He got into his car and headed north on Park Avenue towards East 60th street. He cracked the window open and listened to some of the sounds common to the city. He could hear the beeping of a truck backing up to make a delivery. There was the sound of voices. He couldn't make out what they were saying. It was just white noise common in this sea of people. When he got to East 60th street he took a right and made his way up to the Queensboro bridge. About a quarter way across the bridge, he slowed down to about 30 miles per hour and opened his window. He took the ankle bracelet out of his pocket and with his left hand, he flung it over the car to his right and it cleared the guard rail and floated down into the East River. Now if Sylvio and Jimmy tried to track the ankle bracelet, the only signal they could possibly get was from the bottom of the East River. He laughed again. He could picture Sylvio and Jimmy with scuba gear searching the bottom of the East River. Now that he was free of those two goons, he could track Don Valley on his cellphone and hopefully get the *Henry Graves Supercomplication* pocket watch back without any further problems. That was wishful thinking for sure…

CHAPTER 11

Jack turned the car around and headed back towards his office. He thought that his office would be the best place to track the movements of Don Valley and his wife. He was expecting them to make a run for Boston, but it was still possible that they would try to sell the watch in New York before they left the city. For some reason, the sky looked a little brighter as he drove back into the city. He turned on the radio and the old Beatles song was playing "*Good day Sunshine.*" Jack stepped on the gas and whistled along with the song.

He pulled up outside his office. He got a parking place right in front of the building. Before he got out of the car, he pulled out his cellphone and opened up the app to track the Valleys. He could see that they hadn't moved. They were still in White Plains. Jack figured that they were probably still working out the details of selling the watch to a buyer in Boston, otherwise they would have already come into the city. He got out of his car and walked into the building. He had recently purchased a stun gun that had the appearance of a small handgun. It was capable of delivering enough volts to stop a horse. It could also be used as a taser upon contact. He kept it in his office safe. He never carried a gun, but he thought that it might be a good idea to at least have a stun gun in case Sylvio and Jimmy managed to track him down. He walked up the stairs to his office. He noticed the matchstick in the door was still there, but it was just above the first door jamb. He could have sworn that he had put it below the first door jamb. He had a bad feeling in the pit of his stomach. It was like there was a dark cloud hanging over his head. He knew that Sylvio and Jimmy were still on the train, so they couldn't possibly be in his office. Still, someone had been in his office, or may still be in there. He bit down on his lower lip and opened the door slowly. The hinges creaked. He looked inside without going in, and everything appeared to be in its place. The office was still and silent. He walked a couple of steps into the office and suddenly he saw a shadow out of the corner of his eye, then there was a bright light, and then everything went dark.

When he came to, he was tied to one of the old chairs that he had in his office. The cords from the window blinds were wrapped around his body several times and around the back of the chair. It was tight enough to keep him in place for now. He couldn't move his arms or hands. Standing in front of him was a dark figure, about 6 feet tall. Jack's vision was still a little fuzzy and he had a nasty bump on the back of his head. He could feel pain radiating from his head down the back of his neck. He shook his head and blinked his eyes a few times and his vision became clear. The man standing in front of him was Harold Chumley. Harold pulled up the other old chair that was in the room and sat directly in front of Jack. He sat there and just stared Jack in the eyes. Jack could smell alcohol on Chumley's breath. That was probably not a good sign. Many times, people under the influence of alcohol do stupid things. Chumley smiled and said, "Mr. Trane, so nice to see you're awake, I was afraid that I might have hit you a little too hard." Chumley laughed and said, "I wouldn't want anything to happen to you, at least not until we have completed our little business arrangement." He was no longer speaking in an English accent. His true Brooklyn accent now rang true. Jack squinted at Chumley and said, "I'm glad you dropped that phony accent Chumley, or whatever your name is. Let's get one thing straight, we have no business arrangement. And if I wasn't tied up in the chair, I'd kick your sorry butt down those stairs so fast you'd come out of your shoes. Then I'd throw you out into the street like the trash that you are." Chumley laughed out loud, "Oh, I forgot, you're a tough guy. But Mr. Trane, you are tied up, and we do have some business. Remember, when we first met, I hired you to find the watch? But of course, I realize that things have changed, we seem to be on conflicting sides now. But understand this, I still want the watch." Jack laughed out loud, "I'll bet you do Chumley, but what makes you think I'm going to help you?" Chumley smiled, "Because Mr. Trane if you don't, I'll kill you." Chumley pulled out a small-caliber pistol and placed it on Jack's desk so he could see it. Jack's cellphone was also on the desk. Jack had been in tight situations before, usually, he was able to outsmart the other guy, but it was awfully hard to outsmart a handgun. There were beads of sweat starting to form on Jack's forehead. He looked at Chumley with squinted eyes and said, "Why should I believe that after I help you, you won't kill me anyway?" Chumley smiled, "Well Mr. Trane, I guess you'll just have to trust me." Jack smiled at Chumley and said, “Chumley, I trust you like I trust the weatherman. If you think I’m going to trust you, you’re a bigger idiot than I thought you were.” Chumley gritted his teeth, squinted his eyes, and swung his right fist at Jack, and caught him squarely on the jaw. Jack’s head twisted to his right and a slight flow of blood trickled from his upper lip. Jack looked up at Chumley and smiled, then he spit a little blood on the floor and said, “Chumley, I hope that wasn’t your best shot, my secretary hits harder than that.” Chumley’s eyes opened wide, he stood up and raised his fist again, then stopped. He knew that he couldn’t beat it out of Jack. He said, “Look Trane, I don’t have time for this. Now you tell me everything you know about the watch right now or that’s it.” He picked up the gun from Jack’s desk and pointed it at Jack. At this point, Jack believed that Chumley would indeed kill him if he didn’t tell him what he wanted to know. But he thought that maybe he could stall him until he could think of a way out of this. Jack took a deep breath, “Ok Chumley, what do you want to know?” Chumley gritted his teeth, “OK, Trane, that’s better. Who’s got the watch? And where can I find them?” Jack shook his head, “I don’t know Chumley, I need more time to track down some leads.” Chumley made a disgusted face, “Trane, I think you know a lot more than you’re telling me. But that’s OK, I think I can get what I need out of your cellphone.” Chumley picked up Jack’s cellphone from the desk and slipped it into his jacket pocket. Jack blurted out, “Chumley, without my password, you’ll never get into that phone!” Chumley laughed and started walking towards the door. As he approached the door he turned towards Jack and said, “I know a guy who can help me with that." He raised his gun and pointed it at Jack and said, "Nice doing business with you Trane." Chumley had a cold look on his face, and he gently squeezed the trigger. A white flash and a puff of smoke came out of the barrel of the gun along with a bullet shot in Jack's direction. Jack felt a strong force on his chest and the chair went over backward and he hit the floor. His life was flashing before his eyes, his mind was racing, and he was breathing heavily. As he looked up at the ceiling, he was hoping that he was still alive. He wasn't feeling any pain. He wondered if this was what it felt like just before you died. When the chair hit the floor, the cords around the chair and Jack's body were loosened. He put his hand on his chest expecting to feel where the bullet went in, and then he looked down at his shirt. But there was no blood. His shirt was dry. But there was a tiny hole where the pocket was. He reached into the pocket and pulled out the 3d printed key. And there, in the little hole on the top part of the key was embedded the 22-caliber bullet from Chumley's gun. The bullet never reached Jack's chest. He breathed a deep sigh of relief. No doubt the key had now saved his life twice. He thought to himself, "I'm going to have to give that 3d printer a huge tip the next time I see him"

Jack got his thoughts together and got up from the floor and ran down the stairs after Chumley, but he was too late. By the time he reached the outside door, he could see Chumley in the street, get in his car and drive away. This was not good. Chumley had Jack's phone, and he needed that phone to track the Valleys. He needed to get that phone back before the Valleys left for Boston or he'd never be able to get the watch back. He ran back up the stairs to the office and picked up the phone on Trudy's desk and dialed Trudy's number. The phone rang a couple of times and Trudy answered, "Hello Jack, I see that you're calling from the office now, let me guess, you forgot what day it was." Jack was frazzled, "No, listen, Trudy, my cellphone has been stolen. I need to borrow your cellphone to track mine. I'll be at your apartment in 10 minutes. Be outside with the phone." Trudy was trying to take all this in. She hesitated then said, "Wait, what? Jack, slow down, what are you talking about?" He continued speaking at a rapid pace, "I can't go into it now. I got knocked out, my phone was stolen, and I got to get it back!" She could hear Jack breathing fast and heavy on the other end of the phone. She tried to calm him down, "OK Jack, but where my cellphone goes, I go." Jack nodded, "OK Trudy, be outside your apartment in 10 minutes. I'll pick you up." Jack hung up the phone and hurried over to his safe. He opened the safe and took out the stun-gun. It came with a holster which he placed under his left arm. He closed the safe, put on his jacket, and hat and ran out the door. He didn't have time to place the matchstick in the door jamb, he just ran down the stairs and out the door. He jumped into his car and started the engine all in one continuous motion. He put the car into first gear, let up on the clutch and the rear wheels screamed on the pavement. Blue smoke rose into the air and his mustang fishtailed out into traffic.

Within 10 minutes he was pulling up in front of Trudy's apartment. She was outside waiting. She got into the car and before the car door was closed, Jack had stepped on the gas and he was back in traffic. Trudy looked at him with bulging eyes, "Jack if your car had wings, we'd be flying!" He stared straight ahead at the road with no expression, "Sorry, Trudy, I really need to get my phone back before Chumley figures out my password and tracks down Don Valley before I do." Trudy said in a calm voice, "Don't worry Jack, I'm tracking your phone and it looks like it's only about 10 minutes away. According to this map, it's at 260 west 52nd street." Jack had a serious look on his face. There was sweat dripping down from around his hat and on his face. He said, "I know that area. That's a low-rent district. Sounds like where the old Elsworth Hotel used to be. I'll be there in 5 minutes."

The rain started to fall in the city and the roads became slick. The buildings and cars reflected off the pavement like an old French painting. He drove down 2nd avenue until he took a right onto East 53rd Street. He drove all the way to 7th Avenue and took a left onto 7th Avenue. The rain was falling hard now, and the windshield wipers were barely keeping up with the rain. Trudy was staring down at her cell phone and not paying much attention to the weather. She shouted out, "take a right at West 52nd." Jack turned right and the car fishtailed until he compensated for the shift in momentum. Directly in front of them was a 12-story apartment building. He pulled the car into a parking space about a half a block from the building. He turned off the car and turned to Trudy and said, "Trudy, I want you to stay in the car. I'll need your cellphone to track my cellphone's signal. It should lead me to the room that my phone is in. I'm going to leave you, my keys. If I'm not out in 10 minutes, just drive back to your apartment. Don't worry about me, I'll be OK." Trudy looked at him with her mouth open like he was crazy. She said, "Jack, what are you nuts? You can't go in there with no protection. And I'm not just leaving and going back to my apartment like I just got out of a movie." Jack put his hand on her shoulder, "Relax Trudy, I got this. I have a stun gun under my jacket and the heels of my shoes are loaded with knife blades. I'll be fine, let's just stick to the plan." Trudy was hesitant, but she agreed, "OK Jack, but I don't like this." The rain poured down heavily and sounded like someone was playing a snare drum on the roof of the car.

He opened the door and got out. He had on his trench coat and his hat, so the rain didn't bother him. By the time he reached the door, water drops were falling from the brim of his hat. The building was locked and secure, He needed a badge to get in. Since he didn't have one, he stood near the entrance, under the overhang, hoping that someone would come out. Within about 3 minutes an older woman came out the door. Jack held the door open for her and she politely thanked him. As she passed, Jack went through the open door into the apartment building. He looked down at the phone and could see that the signal from his phone was coming from the third floor. He walked up the stairs to the third floor. He started walking down the hallway on the 3rd floor and as he was walking, he was also looking down at Trudy's cellphone. He could see that signal from his phone was coming from the left. He walked down the hallway and stopped at apartment 311. The signal from his phone was definitely coming from apartment 311. Now that he had found the apartment, he had to figure out how to get in without a key and somehow get his phone from Chumley without getting shot at again. He didn't have a solid plan, but he reached down and grabbed the doorknob. He couldn't believe it; the door was unlocked. He turned the knob slowly and the door opened. He stood there for a minute in the hallway looking into the apartment. He was trying to get a feel for how the apartment was laid out. He could see a room straight ahead in the apartment that appeared to be an office, and there was a desk, and on the desk, there was what appeared to be his phone. He did not see Chumley in sight, but he also couldn't see any other room either. He had to take a chance. He slowly made his way into the apartment. The floor was a natural wood finish, and he could hear his wet shoes squeaking on the floor. "*squeak...squeak...squeak*" He made his way straight ahead into the room that looked like an office. He picked up the phone from the table. It was his. He breathed a sigh of relief and put it into his pocket. He still didn't know where Chumley was, but the apartment was still and quiet. It appeared to Jack like he was the only one there. He decided that he better get out of there quickly before things changed. As he approached the door, he could hear footsteps coming towards the door from the other side. He figured that it must be Chumley. He must have left the apartment for something and now he was coming back. Jack thought fast. He hid behind the door and pulled his stun gun from under his jacket and held it by his side. Now he waited for the door to open.

As he stood there, he reflected for a moment on the bullet that lodged in the key in his shirt pocket, the one that was meant for his chest. He thought to himself, "Yeah, I'm going to enjoy this." The door opened and Chumley came through. Chumley swung the door closed and didn't notice that Jack was standing behind the door. He headed directly for the room that looked like an office. Jack came up behind him and placed the stun gun against Chumley's neck and pulled hard on the trigger. Eighty thousand volts rushed through Chumley's neck and then down through his body. He became rigid and his muscles contracted. He started to shake as his whole body convulsed and he hit the floor face down. Jack stood over him for a few seconds and then he put the stun gun on the other side of Chumley's neck and pulled the trigger again. Chumley let out a low moan and his body convulsed again. It appeared that Chumley had passed out. He was very still on the floor, still face down. Jack put the stun gun back in its holster. He turned and ran out the door and back down the stairs. He had his cellphone back and Chumley didn't even know who had just tased him. Things were once again starting to look up. He left the apartment building and walked through the rain back to his car. He opened the door and got in. Rainwater was dripping from the brim of his hat. Trudy was just staring at him. She said, "So Jack, what happened? Did you get it?" Jack smiled, "Mission accomplished." He held up his cellphone and gave Trudy back hers. He started the car and put it in gear and headed back towards Trudy's apartment. He looked at her and said, "Now Trudy, I'm going to drop you off at your apartment and I want you to make sure that you have everything packed for Boston. I'm expecting the Valleys to make a move at any time. We have to be ready to roll." Trudy smiled, "Jack,

I'm ready to roll right now. I'm going to be able to do some shopping there right?" He rolled his eyes, "Trudy, let's remember, we're going there to get the watch. The *Henry Graves Supercomplication.* There's a $100,000 finder's fee that's waiting for us." Trudy smiled a big smile, "Like I said Jack, plenty of time for shopping." He shook his head, "I swear Trudy if you had a choice between being the queen or going shopping, you'd choose shopping." Trudy looked at him with one eye squinted, "Well Jack, queens shop too."

They pulled up outside Trudy's apartment and she got out, put her hands over her head, and ran through the rain into her building. He watched to make sure that she got in OK. Then he drove his car back to his apartment and parked his car on the street. He knew that he would probably be back in the car again before the evening news aired on TV. It was about 4:00 PM and he hadn't eaten anything all day. He had some frozen pizza in his fridge so he thought that might hit the spot. The rain had all but stopped. There was just a little drizzle coming down. He got out of his car and went into his apartment building. He went up the stairs and unlocked his apartment and went in. He took off his hat and jacket and threw them on the couch. He opened the freezer door and there, in the back of the freezer, was a box of frozen pizza. Ice crystals were forming all over the outside of the box. Jack thought to himself, "a little freezer burn never hurt anyone." He put the pizza in the microwave and let it run for about 4 minutes. The bell went off and he took the pizza out of the oven and dropped it on the table. He ripped off some paper towels and put a couple of pizza slices on the towels and went over and sat on the couch and put his cellphone on his lap. He took a bite of the pizza. It tasted a lot like a piece of frozen cardboard with tomato sauce and a little garlic. Not the best pizza he ever had, but he was hungry, and this would have to do. He turned on his cellphone and opened the app to follow the Valleys. As he was taking his second bite of the pizza, he noticed that the little red dot that represented the Valley's cellphone had started to move. This was it. They were on their way to Boston to sell the watch and get out of the country.

Jack threw the pizza back down on the paper towel and made a disgusted face. The pizza wasn't that good, but it was the only meal he had all day and now that wasn't going to happen either. He picked up the cellphone from his lap and dialed Trudy's number. The phone rang a couple of times and Trudy answered. "Jack, tell me you're not in trouble again." He responded, "No Trudy, listen, the Valleys are making a run for it. It looks like they just left for Boston. I'm going to come over and pick you up in a few minutes. We're going to track them to their hotel in Boston and get the watch back." Trudy smiled, "I'll be ready Jack, and we're going shopping, remember." Jack shook his head, "Yeah, we'll go shopping." They both hung up their phones and Jack took one last bite of his pizza and deposited the rest in the trash can. He put on his trench coat and his hat. He felt the inside of his jacket and made sure he still had the stun gun. He thought that this might come in handy in Boston. He put a matchstick in the door and left the apartment. He ran down the stairs and out the door. The sky had cleared, and the sun had almost set. The sky was a nice pink color. Things were really starting to look brighter. He started the car and sat there for a moment. He listened to the sound of the engine. He breathed in the scent of the leather seats. He enjoyed the simple things in life. And he was also thinking that $100,000 could buy a lot of the simple things. He put the car in gear and drove off in the direction of Trudy's apartment.

CHAPTER 12

He pulled the car up outside of Trudy's apartment. It was about 5:00 PM. Trudy was waiting outside. She threw a small bag in the back seat of the mustang and got in. She looked at Jack and said, "I hope we're going to stop for something to eat, I haven't had anything to eat all day." Jack shook his head, "Ok Trudy, we'll stop for something to eat as soon as we get out of the city." Trudy smiled, "You're not talking about some burger joint, are you, Jack? How about someplace with napkins and a waiter?" He made a disgusted face and looked at her, "Trudy, you're eating up all my profits." She raised her eyebrow and said, "Come on Jack, you look like you could use a good meal too." He smiled and she smiled back. He had intended on taking her to a nice restaurant anyway, but he just liked the back-and-forth banter. It was part of their work relationship.

He handed her his cellphone and said, "Now Trudy, I want you to track the location of Don Valley's cellphone so we can follow them wherever they are going. But I'm pretty sure they're headed to Boston." Trudy took the phone. She was a whiz with computers, phones, or anything else with buttons that were connected to the internet. She opened the "find your friends" app on Jack's phone and located the Valley's cellphone location quite easily. She turned to Jack and said, "It looks like the Valleys are on Route 95 in Port Chester. They are headed north." Jack smiled and made a pleased face, "Just as I figured, they are headed for Boston." He put the car in gear and headed for FDR Drive. The night was setting in and now the sky was layers of pink stretched across the skyline like cotton candy. Even a city dominated by gray skyscrapers and graffiti looked like a work of art when the evening sky provided the canvas. It would soon be dark. He put on the radio to the classic country station and an old Garth Brooks song was playing. The lyrics seemed to fit his mood. "*I Ain't going down til the Sun Comes up.*" Jack cranked up the volume. Trudy made a disgusted face and said, "Are you into country now Jack? I don't think I can take this all the way to Boston." Jack shook his head, "Trudy, this is a classic country song. It was released back in 1993. Can't you feel the vibe?" Trudy squinted and arched her upper lip, "Jack, the only vibe I'm feeling is the seat vibrating from the sound of your speakers." He laughed, "All right Trudy, I'll turn it down." Trudy smirked, "It would be better if you turned it off or changed the station." Trudy didn't care much for country music. Jack laughed, "You really have to get out of the city more Trudy, you know, expand your horizons." She made a face, "Whatever." He continued on FDR Drive all the way to Harlem River Drive and followed that until he crossed over to the Bronx and picked up Route 95. He stepped on the gas and got into the passing lane. The engine in Jack's mustang came to life and they were cruising at about 85 miles per hour. The Valleys had about a 45-minute head start, but Jack wasn't too worried. They had no idea that he was following them, and he also knew that he could catch up with them quite easily if he really wanted to. That little Nissan that they were driving was no match for the 500 horses he had under his hood. He was going to track them right to their hotel. Then he was going to get a room in the same hotel and hopefully get the watch back in the morning before they had a chance to move the merchandise. At least that was the plan.

They traveled for about 40 minutes and Trudy was complaining about being hungry, so Jack took an exit in Greenwich Connecticut and found a plaza with about 15 different restaurants. He turned to Trudy and said, "OK, Trudy, pick one." She picked the first place they passed. It was called the Southern Bay. He pulled into the parking lot and turned off the car. He said to her "Take a look at the phone. How far ahead of us are the Valleys?" She looked at the phone and said, "It looks like they are on route 95 in Darien." Jack smiled, "That's good. They're only about 10 miles ahead of us. We can have a nice meal and still catch up with them before they hit Massachusetts." They both got out of the car. Jack looked around. He didn't think that he was being followed, but you never know. Too many people were after the *Henry Graves Supercomplication* pocket watch, it made him a little paranoid. He had to watch his back. He noticed a few black SUVs parked in the parking lot and he thought to himself, "I hope those guys with the black suits and sunglasses aren't in here." He shook his head and under his breath, he said, "No."

Forty-Five minutes later they came out of the restaurant. Jack had ordered some fish and chips with a bowl of clam chowder. Trudy had some grilled Calamari with a cup of chowder. Trudy said, "That really hit the spot, Jack." He smiled, "I've got to say, Trudy, you sure know how to pick them. For $50 bucks that was a pretty good meal." She smiled, "It's a gift Jack, what can I say?" He laughed and started the car. He put it in gear and made his way back to the highway. He gave Trudy his phone and asked her "Where are the Valleys now? How far did they get?" Trudy opened up the app on the phone. She was humming the theme from *Mission Impossible* to herself. She looked at the phone for a few minutes and said, "It looks like they're just past Bridgeport." Jack smiled. "Fasten your seat belt, Trudy. In an hour and a half, I'll be right behind them." There was a little box on the dashboard. Jack never skimped when it came to electronics. He had a radar detection system that was second to none. He had the Escort Max 360-degree radar detector with built-in wi-fi. He pushed the button to turn it on. The light blue bar on the front of the unit became illuminated. There was no better radar detector on the market. But he felt that the peace of mind knowing that he was not going to be stopped for speeding was worth the price tag of the unit. He stepped on the gas and Trudy's head snapped back and hit the car seat. Soon they were cruising at 90 miles per hour and passing every car in sight. Trudy gave Jack's phone back to him and she closed her eyes and fell asleep to the rhythmic sound of the wheels going over the cracks in the road.

He had been driving for about half an hour and his cellphone rang. He looked down at the phone, but he didn't recognize the number. But he could see from the area code that it was a number from New York City. He thought that it might be George Flax from the

Amalgamated Insurance Company. So, he picked up. "Hello, Jack Trane." The phone was silent for a moment, but he could hear breathing on the other end. Finally, a voice spoke up, "Trane! I thought that I took care of you." Jack laughed, "Harold Chumley, so nice to hear from you. Tell me, has anything shocking happened to you lately?" Jack was laughing out loud. Chumley was fuming, "Look Trane, I don't know how you did it, but I'm going to get you for this. My neck is burned on both sides and I can't even turn my head." Jack smiled, "And oh, I suppose that the bullet that you fired into my chest was just a joke." Chumley was silent for a minute and said, "OK Trane, I guess we're even. But I still want that watch. I'm not going to give up. I don't know where you are but I'm going to find you. And I'm going to get that watch!" Jack responded in a calm voice, "Relax Chumley, relax. There is no need to get all "*Mortal Combat*" about this. I think we can work something out." Chumley agreed, "That's more like it, Trane. What have you got in mind?" Jack smiled a big smile, "Well Chumley, here is how it's going to go down. It seems like you and Tony Gumbati both want this pocket watch really badly. You offered me $200,000 to get the watch and Gumbati offered me $400,000 for the watch. So, to me, this looks like a bidding war and you 2 chumps will have to bid against each other." Chumley thought for a moment. There was the sound of fear in his voice, "Look, Trane, why don't we just do a deal right here, right now. I'll give you $500,000 for the watch. We don't have to get Gumbati involved." Jack knew that Chumley wanted nothing to do with Tony "two shoes" Gumbati. At this point, Chumley was competing with Gumbati for the watch, and he was way out of his league. Chumley had already double-crossed George Flax by hiring Jack. Now his plan was to take the watch and sell it for himself and leave Gumbati and Flax with nothing. Chumley knew if Gumbati found out about him making a deal with Jack, his shoes would be covered with cement at the bottom of the Hudson River, and he would be in them. Jack told Chumley, "Well $500,000 is a good place to start, but I think we can do a lot better than that." Chumley was rubbing his hand across his forehead, wiping off the sweat. Jack continued "Here's the deal Chumley. When I get back to the city, I'll have the watch in hand. I'll call you and I'll call Gumbati. Then we'll have a little auction, and then we'll see who wants the watch more." Chumley said, "No, wait Trane, there must be another way we can handle this. Why don't you..." Jack cut him off, "Nice talking with you Chumley, have a good evening." He hung up the phone and he laughed to himself. He looked over at Trudy, and she was still fast asleep. All those Omega 3 fatty acids from the Calamari must have calmed her nerves and Jack wasn't about to wake her up at least until they hit Massachusetts.

Jack had just put a plan in motion, that if it were successful, would get both Chumley and Gumbati off his back. The next part of the plan was to get Gumbati involved. He dialed up the number for Tony Gumbati. The phone rang twice and a Brooklyn voice with an Italian accent answered, "Yeah?" Jack responded, "Mr. Gumbati, is this you?" Gumbati responded, "Yeah, this is me, who is this?" Jack answered, "This is Jack Trane, I thought that you might be looking for me." Gumbati answered with a calm voice, "Mr. Trane, I hope you are still walking on 2 feet. For a minute I thought that you took a dive into the East River." Jack smirked, "Well, you know Mr. Gumbati, that ankle bracelet just wasn't the right fit. I hope that Sylvio and Jimmy enjoyed their little ride to Washington." Mr. Gumbati spoke slowly, "I'll deal with them." Jack smiled, "Well Mr. Gumbati, good help is hard to find today." Mr. Gumbati laughed, but was not amused, "Mr. Trane, I thought that we had an arrangement? You were going to get me the watch, and I was going to pay you $400,000 for your trouble." Jack smiled, "Well no offense, Mr. Gumbati, but I don't like walking around with a bracelet and a bomb tied to my foot. And I told you I work alone." Mr. Gumbati responded, "Mr. Trane, I'm a businessman, I was trying to protect my assets." Jack smiled, "OK, Mr. Gumbati, since you're a businessman, you'll understand this. Our business arrangement has changed. From here on in, I'm calling the shots. You see, it seems that there at 2 parties that really want this watch. Let me fill you in. There is this guy that hired me before we made our little business arrangement, and he's offered me $500,000 for the watch, just 10 minutes ago, so it looks like we have a little dilemma here." Gumbati broke in, "Mr. Trane, I'll give you $1Million dollars for the watch right now." Jack spoke in a slow calm voice, "Mr. Gumbati, I think the best way to solve this little problem is to have a little auction. You against my friend Harold Chumley. I think you're familiar with Mr. Chumley, at least that's what he is calling himself now. I believe that he's an associate of yours, at least I think he was. I thought that it would only be fair to let the two of you bid against each other and the winner gets the watch. I'm out of town right now.

I should be back in a couple of days with the watch. When I get back, I'll call you and we'll set it up." Gumbati broke in, "Wait, Mr. Trane, I think there is a different way we can handle this. If you...." Jack cut him off, "So nice speaking with Mr. Gumbati, have a really nice evening." Jack hung up the phone and laughed out loud. Trudy woke out of her sound sleep. Her eyes opened wide. She said, "Jack, what's going on? Why are you laughing so loud to yourself?" Jack was still laughing just a little bit, "I think I'm going to keep my shoes from getting stuck in cement. But I can't say the same for Harold Chumley." Trudy went back to sleep.

He was hoping to get Tony Gumbati and Chumley to start fighting with one another for the watch before he got back to New York. For the time being, that would take their focus off of him. He figured that by the time that he got back to the city, only one of them would be left to deal with and was pretty sure that would be Mr. Gumbati. If everything went to plan, he would never have to deal with Harold Chumley again, Mr. Gumbati would end up in prison, and the *Henry Graves Supercomplication* would end up back in the hand of the rightful owner. That was the plan. The only things that were standing in his way were the Valleys, a full tank of gas, and the city of Boston. He pulled off the highway at the first rest stop and filled up his gas tank. Now there were only 2 things standing in his way.

After another hour and a half of driving, Trudy woke up. She said, "Where are we?" Jack handed her the phone. He said, "I was hoping you could tell me." She squinted at the cellphone and opened the app on the phone. The blue light from the phone illuminated her face. She said, "It looks like we're in North Stonington Connecticut." He felt good about that. They were approaching Rhode Island. He said, "Ok, now where are the Valleys?" Trudy moved her finger on the surface of the phone. She said, "It looks like they are just a little past Providence." He smiled. "We'll catch up with them before they hit Route 128." He put his foot on the gas and gave Trudy a nod. He was cruising at just about 90 miles per hour. The radar detector lit up and beeped at about every 10-mile interval. In each instance, Jack slowed down until he was past the speed trap. Then he would accelerate back to 90 miles per hour again. The money that he had saved from speeding tickets had already covered the $650 price tag of his radar detector. They passed through Rhode Island pretty quickly. As they drove through Providence, he could clearly see the state capital and the Superman building that dominates the skyline. This was all familiar to Jack. It truly felt like home. Quickly they entered Massachusetts and in another short 20 minutes, they were approaching Norwood. Jack turned to Trudy, "Ok where are they now?" She squinted at the screen again and said, "It looks like they are right in front of us Jack." He had a smile of satisfaction on his face. "What did I tell you, Trudy? I told you that we would catch them before we hit 128. He had a measured grin on his face. Trudy just rolled her eyes.

Jack was a native of the area, so he was very familiar with the route into Boston. There was a point in the road where Route 95 converges with Routes 128, 93, and route 1. Then it defies all logic. You actually have to go south in order to go north. It was very confusing to anyone who didn't live in Massachusetts. He was wondering if the Valleys would figure this out. He said to Trudy, "OK, continue to track them. I want to make sure that they take the right exit." To Jack's surprise, the Valleys took the right exit. Trudy shouted out, "They are going south on route 93 Jack." He smiled, "That's perfect. We'll just follow them into Boston and check in at the same hotel that they are staying at. And in the morning, I'll pay them a friendly visit and get what we came for." Trudy smirked, "You're pretty sure of yourself aren't you, Jack?" He laughed, "Come on Trudy, this will be like taking candy from a baby." Trudy was still smirking, "More like taking honey, out of a bee's nest."

About 15 minutes later Trudy was still looking at the cell-phone, she said, "It looks like they exited off the highway, Jack. They are on India Street." Jack was familiar with the area, he figured that they were headed for the Marriott. He exited the highway and zig-zagged through the streets until he came upon India Street. It was dark so he couldn't make out much detail of the city. But he could see what looked like young people with hooded sweatshirts hanging around on the corner streets. He thought to himself, "*New York or Boston, sometimes the scene remains the same.*" There was a garage near McKinley square, and he watched as the Valley's car pulled in. He waited on the street for about 5 minutes to make sure that the Valleys had parked the car. Then he entered the garage and drove to the top level and parked his car. Trudy looked at him and said, "Geez Jack, couldn't you get any higher, I can see the stars." He looked at her, "Come on Trudy, I'm trying to stay off the radar. I don't want to let the Valleys know that we're following them. I'm pretty sure they know what my car looks like." Trudy made a face, "Jack, everyone from Boston to New York knows what your car looks like." Jack made a face, "Very funny Trudy. The other reason that I parked up here, is to make sure that my phone has good reception. We need to track where the Valleys are going so, we can stay in the same hotel they check into." She handed the phone back to him. "OK, Jack, your turn. You track them from here. Staring at this little blue screen is giving me a headache." He took the phone and watched as the Valleys exited the garage and walked directly to the Marriott. Jack yelled out "We got them, they're in the Marriott." Trudy was half-listening. She said, "Jack, is Faneuil Hall around here somewhere? I hear that's like a really cool place. Can we go there? I'm really hungry from the ride. How about *Cheers*? Can we go to *Cheers?*" How about some stores? You said we could go shopping." Jack's thoughts were spinning, "Trudy relax. Yes, we can do all those things but not tonight. Let's just get a room at the Marriott and we take care of our little business in the morning, then we get breakfast and look around." Trudy made a face at Jack, "What do you mean a room? We need 2 rooms right, Jack?" He smiled, "Oh, yeah, I meant 2 adjoining rooms." Trudy smiled, "That's better Jack. You're always trying to save a couple of bucks."

They left the garage and walked over to the Marriott. The Valleys had already checked in. Jack held his phone up to his face and noticed that Valleys were staying on one of the upper floors. He wanted to get as close to their room as possible. They walked up to the desk clerk.

The clerk was a young girl, attractive and very pleasant. She had long dark hair and looked to be of Asian descent. She was wearing a light blue blazer, a white shirt, and a blue tie. Her name tag said "June", and she looked like she knew what she was doing. "Can I help you, sir?" Jack smiled at her, "Yes I'd like 2 rooms that have an adjoining door, preferably on one of the higher floors." The girl smiled, "I see. Well, perhaps you and your (she paused) associate would like room on the 10th floor. You'll have a nice view of the city from there. How long will you be staying with us?" He looked at Trudy, he said "Oh, this is actually my assistant. Where here on some business. Why don't we book it for 2 nights? That should be enough." Trudy smiled and laughed a little. The clerk said, "Of course sir, I'm sure 2 nights will be enough for you and your (she paused again) assistant." Jack shook his head. The clerk handed Jack all the paperwork and he signed the register as Mr. Johnson and Miss Jones. The desk clerk smiled and handed Jack the key to the rooms. They walked over to the elevator and pushed the button for the upper floors. June continued to watch them as they got into the elevator. As they got into the elevator, June yelled out, "Have a nice stay (she paused again) Mr. Johnson. Trudy laughed, "Well, that went well." Jack rolled his eyes, "I had to give them different names, I don't want anyone to be able to track us here. I don't know why everyone always gets the wrong idea." Trudy smiled, "Maybe it's because you wear that long trench coat and that hat. You do kind of stand out in a crowd." He smiled, "I'll take that as a compliment." They got off on the 10th floor and walked down the hallway. He looked at his phone. He could see that the Valleys were on the same floor. He walked down the hallway to the right for about 30 feet and the signal for the Valley's phone was coming out of room 1024. Now he knew for sure where the Valleys were.

He walked back down the hallway and went left for about 25 feet and came to his room 1065 A & B. He turned to Trudy, "Here we are Trudy." It was late, about 11:30 PM. He said, "Why don't you just get a good night's sleep. In fact, why don't you sleep in tomorrow? I'm going to get up early and confront the Valleys by myself. I was thinking that it could get a little dicey and I don't want you to get hurt. My insurance premium is already through the roof." Trudy crossed her arms and smirked, "Good thinking Jack, it's not like you ever get hurt." He ignored Trudy's comment. "I should have the watch back by 9:00 AM, then we can go out for some breakfast, you can do your shopping and then I show you some of the sights." She smiled, "OK Jack, it's a deal. I'll be ready at 9:00 AM. Don't be late." He smiled, "Don't worry, what could possibly go wrong?" He would find out soon enough.

CHAPTER 13

Jack laid back on his pillow and he was looking up at the ceiling. If anyone asked him what he was thinking about, he could honestly say nothing. Rays of sunshine were beaming in through the window on the far side of the room. He continued looking up at the ceiling and now he was just trying to get his thoughts together for the day. He was hoping that the Valleys would give up the watch easily, but that was probably not going to happen. He needed a plan, but nothing was coming to him. He threw off the covers and walked over to the window. In the distance, he could see the Prudential building and it looked like steam was coming off the top of the building. And just off to the side of that, he could make out the lights at Fenway Park. At least he thought that he could. He was thinking to himself, "Too bad it's not July, I would love to catch a Red Sox game." He thought back to the days when his dad would take him to a Red Sox/Yankees game. He still savored the memories. He just stood there and smiled as he remembered the hot dogs and ice cream bars. The days when $10 would get you a good seat and the 3rd string players were not making more than the President of the United States. He shook his head and came back to reality. It was still early, about 6:45 AM but as he looked down from the 10th floor, the traffic on the street was already buzzing, the commuters seemed to be prematurely in the city, and there were also people walking along the sidewalks. New York was the city that never sleeps, but Boston wasn't far behind. He looked more closely at the buildings. They all looked familiar. It had been several years since he had visited Boston, but it still felt like home every time he came back.

He picked up his pants from the chair on the side of the bed and put them on. They weren't any more wrinkled than they were when he put them on yesterday. It really needed a good washing, but he put them on anyway. This wasn't the first time he had worn the same clothes 2 days in a row, and it probably wouldn't be the last. He put on his white shirt and buttoned it up to the collar. It was killing him that this shirt wasn't fresh and clean. The only piece of clothing that he always made sure was pristine every day was his white shirt. He made a disgusted face as he looked in the mirror and tied his tie. He tightened the knot of the tie around his neck and then buttoned the collar down around it. He put on his shoes and made sure that the knife blades were still in the heels of the shoes. Then he put on the holster for his stun-gun and placed the gun in the holster just under his left arm. Now he felt that he was now ready for the day. The problem was that he didn't know what today would bring.

He sat down on the side of the bed and tried to come up with a plan. He thought that he should go directly to the Valleys room and knock on the door. When they answered, he would confront them about the pocket watch and demand that they turn it over to him. He figured that they would probably just laugh at him. Then he would threaten them that if they didn't comply, he would turn them in to the authorities. It wasn't much of a plan and seeing that the Valleys probably had a gun, it wasn't going to be very effective either. The Valleys weren't just going to give up a 24 million dollar watch without a fight. But in the past, when Jack didn't have a working plan, he would just wing it. More times than not, he was able to work things out. This was certainly turning out to be one of those times that he was going to have to just wing it. He stood up from the bed and tightened his tie again. He put on his jacket and his hat, left his room, and closed the door. He walked down the hallway and went past the elevator. He came to the end of the hallway and had to take a right to get to room 1024, where Don Valley was staying. He turned the corner, and he noticed some movement down by the Valleys room. He quickly walked across to the other side of the hallway and continued to observe what was going on outside the door to the Valleys room. There appeared to be a man exiting from room 1024 with a box under his arm. He seemed to be putting a handgun into a holster under his jacket. He was backing out of the room, looking into the room as he closed the door. The man started walking in Jack's direction. He was a tall man, about 6 feet 4 inches. He looked like he weighed about 240 pounds. He looked like Hercules, so that's what Jack called him. Hercules was wearing a maroon jacket and dark gray pants. He was wearing a black turtleneck shirt. He was probably about 40 years old, with dark hair and that chiseled look. His features were well defined. Jack figured that the box under his arm was no doubt the box that contained the "*Henry Graves Supercomplication.*" He had to get that box back before Hercules left the hotel with it, along with his $100,000 finder's fee. Jack thought fast. He stood adjacent to the wall on the right side of the hallway that Hercules was coming down. Hercules would have to take a left to get to the elevator. Jack pulled out his stun gun and patiently waited for Hercules to come up the hallway and take the left. It seemed like every step that Hercules would take was in slow motion. Jack could hear Hercules's shoes scrape the carpet with every step he took. Time always slowed down for Jack during his planned power maneuvers. Finally, Hercules got to the end of the hallway, and he went left. He was not aware Jack was standing in the hallway to the right. Jack waited for Hercules to get a distance of about 6 feet from him, then he sprang into action. He aimed the stun gun at Hercules's neck and pulled the trigger. The gun made a zip sound and a crack, and the electrodes traveled like a dart directly into the back of Hercules's neck. Hercules stood motionless for a second, then he started to shake. His body convulsed and he dropped to his knees. He continued shaking for about 5 seconds. Jack reached forward and lifted the box with the watch out from under Hercules's arm. Hercules fell face down into the rug. Jack removed the electrodes from the gun. He knelt down next to Hercules and placed the barrel of the gun against the left side of Hercules's neck. He changed the settings on the gun and tased Hercules with about 80,000 volts to his neck. Hercules moaned deeply and then stopped. He had passed out. Jack removed the electrodes from Hercules's neck and folded them up and put them in his pocket. Jack had barely broken a sweat, but now had the "*Henry Graves Supercomplication*" in his possession, and Hercules didn't even know who had taken it from him.

Jack stood up and smiled to himself, satisfied that he had just taken down 6 foot 4 Hercules with the skill of a ninja. He kind of wished someone had just seen all that, so they could tell him how smooth he looked. He put the box under his arm and started walking towards his room. As he walked past the elevator, he pushed the button for the elevator to come up to the 10th floor. He wasn't sure how long Hercules would be out, but he needed to make it look like the elevator had just gone down to the bottom floor so that Hercules would think that whoever had taken the watch from him had just left the building. The elevator reached the 10th floor. Jack stepped in and pushed the button for the ground floor. He got out of the elevator, the doors closed, and the elevator went down to the ground floor empty. Jack continued walking down the hallway towards his room. Before he took a left to go down the hallway that led to his room 1065, he noticed on the wall, a large mirror. He was hoping that Hercules wasn't looking in the mirror all the time that Jack was tasing him. He was hoping that he got away with the watch scot-free. Time would tell. He walked down the hallway and put his keycard in his door. The door opened and he went in. He walked over and sat on the bed and put the box with the watch on his lap and he just stared at the box for a few minutes.

The box itself wasn't anything special. It was a very dark wood, with dark grain and it was highly polished. There were gold hinges and a gold clasp in front of the box. But sitting on Jack's lap was

24 million dollars. Jack considered himself to be an honest person. A man of integrity. But for just one half a millisecond, he thought about Hawaii, the beach, and holding a strawberry pineapple mojito in his hand. He shook his head back to reality. He would never steal the watch or anything for that matter, but he was still human and like everyone else, from time-to-time crazy thoughts entered his head. He carefully and slowly opened the box. There it was. A three-inch mix of gold, glass, and numbers that seemed to reflect all the light that was in the room. It was uniquely beautiful. Instead of the numbers on the face going from 1 to 12, they went from 1 to 24. There was a blue circle in the middle of the face that seemed to be filled with stars. There were also 3 smaller dials on the face of the watch that had different functions. The gold on the case of the watch was the deepest gold he had ever seen, and it was flawless with no scratches or marks. He picked it up and turned it over. On the other side of the watch was yet another face with yet more dials. Inside the box, it said **"PATEK PHILIPPE GENEVE".** This was the real deal. He thought to himself, "This was some watch!" He started to get a little nervous realizing the value of what he was holding in his hand. One little slip and watch would be worth a lot less than 24 million dollars. He ever so carefully placed the watch back in the spot made for it in the box.

He needed to make a video of the watch to send to Tony Gumbati to make him think that he was bringing the watch to him. He pulled out his cell phone and opened up the camera setting. He recorded a video of the watch as it sat on his bed. Then he turned the camera towards himself. As he looked at the camera, he said,

"Mr. Gumbati, as you can see, I have the pocket watch in my possession. I will be coming back to New York in a couple of days, then we can finish up our business arrangement." He attached the video to a text message and sent it off to Tony Gumbati. He was pretty sure Tony Gumbati would be mixing the cement as soon as he got this message. Jack was going to do everything he could to make sure his Nunn Bush shoes stayed out of the cement. He put his phone away and then stared at the watch for about 5 minutes just admiring all the different facets of the watch. Before he closed the box, he put a very small tracking device inside the box just under the watch. It was clear like a piece of tape so that it couldn't easily be detected, but it would allow Jack just a small measure of security in case something happened to the watch between his room and the hotel lockbox. Then he gently closed the box and hooked the latch and left the box on the bed.

He had to keep the watch safe until he could return it to George Flax at Amalgamated Insurance. He picked up the phone in the room and dialed the main desk. A woman answered "Hello, can I help you?" Jack said, "I'd like to use one safe deposit box here at the hotel. I need someplace to store my valuables while I'm here in Boston?" She answered "Yes, of course, sir. Please come down to the front desk and ask for the manager, and he will be able to get you a box." Jack responded, "Thank you, I'll do that." He hung up the phone and sat back down on the bed. He reflected on his plan to keep the watch safely in the lockbox until they returned to New York. He had promised Trudy a little shopping spree and he felt that she deserved it for all that she had to put up with working for him. He thought that the best idea would be to put the watch in the safe deposit box before he knocked on Trudy's door. It was still early, about 7:30 AM. Trudy wouldn't be up for another hour or so he had plenty of time to bring the watch downstairs before he took Trudy to breakfast.

He wanted to check on the Valleys first to see if they were OK, or if Hercules had done something sinister to them. He couldn't walk down the hallway, because he didn't know if Hercules was still on the floor, or if he had recovered and gone down the elevator to chase whoever he thought just took the watch from him. Jack picked up the phone again and dialed down to the main desk. The desk clerk picked up, "Hello, this is the main desk, how can I help you?" Jack made his voice sound nervous and alarmed, "Hello, this is Mr. Johnson on the 10th floor. I was just getting some ice and I heard some loud noises and screams coming out of room 1024, and then I heard what I think sounded like a gunshot. Then I saw a man running down the hallway and I think that something bad has happened to the people staying in that room." The desk clerk now sounded alarmed, "My goodness, thank you for reporting this. I will send up security right away!" The desk clerk hung up the phone and so did Jack. He knew that security would see Hercules if he were still in the hallway and if not, that would mean that Hercules had already gone down the elevator. Jack came out of his room and waited to hear the beep of the elevator arrive on the 10th floor. At this point, he would just look like an observer as he came out to see what all the commotion was about.

The elevator door opened, and 2 good-sized men came out dressed in dark blue uniforms. They both had nightsticks, and stun guns by their sides. They came out of the elevator and went left. Jack followed. He could see now that Hercules was no longer on the floor. He had obviously recovered and gone downstairs in the elevator. Hercules would have no idea that Jack was the one that took the watch from him. (Unless he had seen Jack in the mirror. Jack was hoping that was not the case.) The security guards reached room 1024 and knocked on the door. There was no answer. One of the guards had a master key. He put the card in the door and the door opened. Jack slid into position so that when the door opened, he could see inside. He caught a glimpse of Don and Paula Valley tied up to chairs, back-to-back with each other and they had gags around their mouths. The door closed as the security guards went in. But at least Jack knew that the Valleys had not been rubbed out by Hercules or whoever he was working for. He wasn't sure, but there was a chance that Don Valley had caught a quick glimpse of Jack too before the door closed. He hoped that he hadn't recognized him. Jack went back to his room and waited for the dust to clear.

Jack had been in his room for about fifteen minutes, and he thought that the time would be right to bring the watch down to the main desk and ask for a safe deposit box to put it in. He didn't want to get into the elevator with the box in plain view, in case he ran into the Valleys along the way, so he took a towel from the bathroom and folded it around the box and tucked in the ends so that all you could see was a white towel. He put on his coat and his hat and placed the wrapped box under his arm and started for the door. About 2 steps before he reached the door, there was a knock from the other side. Jack stopped in his tracks. The door knocked again. Jack looked through the peephole on the door. It was the 2 security guards. He took off his hat and jacket and placed them on the foot of the bed. He kept the towel with the watch under his arm. Jack opened the door. He could see their name tags on their uniforms. One was named Tim and the other was named George. Tim spoke first, "Hello, Mr. Johnson, are you the one that called the desk about the disturbance down the hall?" Jack was sweating just a little bit under his arms and over his forehead. He said, "Oh yes, I was concerned that something might have happened, and I just wanted to make sure everything was all right." Jack smiled and waited for a response. The other security guard, Gorge, said "Well Mr. Johnson, it appears that a man had broken into that room, and he tied up the two people inside and stole a box with some valuable jewelry." Jack looked shocked, "You don't say! Imagine in a nice place like this. What's this world coming to when you can't even stay at a nice hotel without getting robbed?" Tim responded, "Yes, well what we really want to know is, did you see anybody in the hallway when you heard the disturbance outside room 1024?" Jack shifted the box from under one arm to the other. He looked up at the ceiling and said, "No, there was no one in the hallway, just me. I'm kind of glad I didn't run into anyone; I really don't like confrontation." It was getting very hard for Jack to maintain a straight face. George responded, "Well, Mr. Johnson, according to the desk clerk, she said you saw a man running down the hallway."

Jack grimaced, "Hmm, no, she must have misunderstood, I didn't see anyone," George made a skeptical look, "OK, Mr. Johnson, if you remember anything else, please let us know. We'll be downstairs in the main office." Jack looked very serious and raised one eyebrow, "Oh yes, for sure, if I remember anything else, I'll come right down. Whatever I can do to help." The 2 security guards thanked Jack and went back to the elevator. Jack closed the door and went back and sat on the bed. He was glad now that he used the fake name Johnson when he checked in. He didn't want to get mixed up in any investigation that might keep him in Boston any longer than he had to be here. His main focus now was getting the watch back to New York and collecting his $100,000 finder's fee.

After sitting on the bed for about 2 minutes there was another knock on the door. He wondered who this could be. Nobody knew he was there, and nobody knew that his name was not Johnson. He put the towel with the box under the blanket on the bed and placed it up near the pillow so that it looked like part of the pillow. Then he walked over to the door. He looked through the peephole. It was Don Valley on the other side of the door. Jack contemplated whether or not he should open the door. Valley knocked again. Jack opened the door slowly. Don Valley had a surprised look on his face. "Mr. Trane! What are you doing here? The security guard told me that your name was Johnson, and you saw what happened outside my room." Don Valley was speaking fast, he was very agitated. Jack smiled, "Relax Don, come in. I think I can explain some things for you." Don Valley came into the room. Jack had pointed to the chair next to the bed for Don to sit down on, but instead, Don Valley sat on the bed, right next to the pillow where Jack had covered the towel and the box which contained the watch. Jack's blood pressure was rising just a bit. He could feel his face getting red. He looked at Don Valley with a serious face and said, "Look, Don, the reason that I'm here is that I was hired to retrieve the watch that you and Billy Bardsley stole outside the MET in New York. I figured that you were going to sell the watch here in Boston and then hop a plane to somewhere until all this blew over. How am I doing? Am I close?" Don Valley looked down at the floor. His face was empty of expression. He said, "Mr. Trane, we didn't expect anyone to get hurt. We just saw this as a way to start over. We were going to get 10 million dollars for that watch and then live comfortably on some island in the Bahamas. But after we made the deal to sell the watch, we were supposed to meet with the buyer this morning at 10:00 AM in the restaurant downstairs. But we got a call at 6:30 AM and the buyer told us that there was a change in plans. He wanted to come up to our room. We agreed and came up to our room with a gun. He tied us up and he took the box with the pocket watch. He took the *Henry Graves*. I need to get that watch back." Jack sat back in the chair, "Don, consider yourself fortunate. That guy could have killed you. Do you know how many people are looking for that watch? The New York police department is no doubt looking for you right now. If they catch up with you, you're going to the slammer. Tony Gumbati is looking for that watch. If he finds out that it was you who stole it, well, let's just say that you and Paula would be swimming with the fishes at the bottom of the East River.

My advice to you, is to forget about the watch, get on that plane and take a nice long vacation somewhere and hope that this whole thing has blown over by the time you get back." Don Valley shook his head, "No, I can't do that. I'm in too deep. I need that watch back. What if I hire you to find the guy that took the watch? You said that you were hired to find the watch anyway. I don't know what your fee is, but I'll give you a million dollars if you find it for me." Valley rested his hand back about 2 inches from where the box was hidden next to the pillow. Jack rubbed his chin, took a deep breath, and said, "I don't know about you Mr. Valley, but for me, this case is over. I'm going back to New York and I'm going to tell my client that the watch is gone and it's time to move on. I advise you to do the same." Don Valley sat up on the bed and put his hands on his eyes. He was obviously in great mental anguish. He looked at Jack and said, "Just think about my offer, you know where you can find me." Jack was shaking his head up and down, "Yes, I'll think about your offer, I know where to find you. Now, why don't you and Paula just go have a nice breakfast and think about what I said." Jack smiled and pointed to the door. Don Valley rose from the bed. He shook Jack's hand, and he left the room.

It was barely 8:30 AM and Jack already had a full day. He reached down to the bed and turned down the blanket. He looked down at the towel with the watch wrapped in it. It stood out like Carry Grant in a three stooge's film. He couldn't believe that both the security guards and Don Valley were so close to the watch but suspected nothing. He shook his head and laughed to himself and thought about how Gumbati was going to respond when he read his text message. One thing was for sure. He needed to get this watch into a safe deposit box before anyone else knocked on his door. He put his coat and hat back on and he picked up the towel with the box in it from the bed and placed it under his right arm. He left the room and walked towards the elevator. The floor was empty. He could hear faint noises coming from the different rooms. As he passed one room, he could hear the muffled sound of a hairdryer. As he passed another room, he could hear the sounds of what appeared to be a rather loud conversation between a man and a woman. As he passed another room, he thought that he heard the sound of a dog barking. There were no pets allowed in the hotel so he wasn't sure how that could be. He shook his head and thought to himself, "*you can change the city, but you can't change the people.*" He reached the elevator and pushed the button for the elevator to come to the 10th floor. He could hear the cables and gears humming beneath the door as the elevator rose. He hoped that once the watch was in a safe deposit box, it would take some of the pressure off. He also hoped that the Red Sox would win the World Series next year, both probably had the same chance of coming true.

CHAPTER 14

The elevator reached the bottom floor and the doors slowly opened. Jack stepped out and looked around. Based on the events that took place earlier in the morning, he couldn't be too cautious. It was still early but in the hotel lobby, people coming and going. As he walked towards the main desk he looked to his left and saw and man and a woman who appeared to be arriving from a warm-weather climate. The man was wearing a pair of light blue shorts with a white polo shirt and sandals on his feet. The woman was wearing a short yellow dress with open-toed shoes. They obviously had never been in Boston in early Winter before. November in Boston is definitely not sandals weather. That's probably why they were hurrying to get in the door. Jack also noticed a man in a dark suit standing against the wall towards his right. He appeared to be reading a newspaper. There were also several people waiting at the desk to be checked in or checked out. Jack felt very uneasy about standing in line with a 24 million dollar watch under his arm. He still wasn't sure that Hercules hadn't seen him in the mirror while he was being tased. He continued to scan the room just in case Hercules showed up.

After about 5 minutes in line, Jack reached the desk. There were 3 clerks working the crowd. They were all wearing the same dark blue uniforms with their name tags on their shirt pockets. There was a man, Dave, and 2 women. An older woman named Sue and a younger one named Jessie. Jessie smiled at Jack and asked, "Can I help you, sir?" Jack held the towel with the box in it with both hands. He said, "Yes, I'm in need of a safe deposit lock box and I was told that you have rental units here." Jessie kept the same smile that she had from before, "Yes, sir. The lockboxes are free of charge as long as you remain a guest in the hotel. If you decide to leave your possessions here after checking out, the fee will be $10 a day." Jack smiled back, "Well Jessie, that sounds like a good deal to me. I'd like to get access to one of those lockboxes." Jessie had the same smile on her face, "No problem sir. Could you tell me what room that you're staying in?" Jack was still smiling at her, "Yes, that would be room 1065." Jessie was still smiling. Jack wasn't sure if it was a birth defect or Jessie just like to smile. She said, "Oh yes, Mr. Johnson, let me have our security staff help you." She picked up the phone and pushed a few buttons and said something into the phone. Jack couldn't hear what she said, but about 30 seconds later George, the security guard that had just been up to his room, entered from behind the desk. He approached Jack and looked at him carefully. He said, "Oh yes, Mr. Johnson, did you remember anything from the hallway this morning?" Jack was thinking to himself, "*I hope this guy doesn't put 2 & 2 together and figure out that I have the Valley's box under my arm.*" Jack spoke to the guard in a calm voice, "No I didn't remember anything, but I just need to check something into a lockbox, and they told me that you have the keys." There was a moment of silence. Jack was waiting for

George's response. George seemed to be studying Jack up and down. He raised one eyebrow and put his hand to his chin. He said, "No problem. Come around the desk and follow me." Jack was relieved that George didn't exactly seem to be the ace of the staff. Jack came around the desk and followed George into a back room. The lighting was that low industrial fluorescent lighting, and there seemed to be large gray standing files on both sides of the room. George opened a door to yet another room. The lighting was much better. In this room, there were small little workstations enclosed with curtains. There were four of them. At the far end of the room, there was another door that led to the room with the lockboxes. It was protected with a metal door. George looked at the towel that Jack had under his arm. He said, "Is that what you're putting in the lockbox?" Jack was going to say, "Good thinking Einstein," but he didn't. He bit his cheek and said, "Well, not the towel, but what's inside the towel." George laughed a dumb laugh. He said, "Well that's good because that looks like one of our towels and I couldn't let you put one of the hotel's towels in a lockbox." Jack turned away for a minute and rolled his eyes. He turned back and said to George, "No you can have your towel back, I just want to use the lockbox." George turned and opened the metal door. He went in and came back with a small black box and placed it in one of the small workstations. Jack went into the workstation and closed the curtain. George waited outside. He could hear George say, "Let me know when you're done, and I'll put the box back in the safe." Jack took the towel off the wooden box, and he opened the lockbox. It was almost a perfect fit. When Jack placed the wooden box in the lockbox there was about an inch to spare on the top and the bottom. He closed the box and flipped the towel over his shoulder. He pulled the curtain back and came out of the workstation. George was standing there waiting for him. He dangled the key in front of Jack's face like a carrot in front of a rabbit. Jack took the key and flipped the towel onto George's shoulder. He looked at the key and noticed the number 125 and put the key into his pocket. Then he watched as George brought the box into the safe. He heard a drawer open and close, then a click, and George came back out of the safe room. George closed the metal door and locked it. The slam of the metal door reminded Jack of a prison cell. Not that Jack had ever been in prison, but many of his clients over the years had hired him from inside prison cells.

A sense of calm came over Jack. That was one less thing he would have to worry about. George said to Jack, "Just make sure you bring the key when you come back to get your stuff." Jack smiled, "Someone else is going to come to pick up the contents of my box, but thanks for the reminder." Jack turned his head and rolled his eyes. George quickly shot back, "Just make sure whoever you send has the key. That's the only way they can get into the box." Jack thought to himself again, "*Good point Einstein.*" But he said, "Thanks George, you've been very helpful."

Jack exited the room with the workstations and headed towards the elevator. He was going to go back upstairs to get Trudy for breakfast. As he approached the elevator, out of the corner of his eye he could see a rather large man coming through the swinging entrance doors. He turned to get a better look. It was Hercules. He must have seen Jack in the mirror last night when he was being tased. The elevator opened and Jack got in. He pushed the button for the 10th floor about 6 or 7 times, thinking it would work faster the more times he pushed the button. The doors finally closed as Jack could see Hercules coming towards the elevator. The elevator rose, but it seemed like an eternity to reach the 10th floor. The doors opened again, and Jack got out. He ran down the hallway to his room and slid the card in the door and went in. Jack was sure that Hercules didn't know his name or his room number, so he was safe for now. He knocked on the adjoining door to Trudy's room. He could hear the loud humming of the hairdryer, so there was no use in trying to get Trudy's attention. He would just have to wait until the hairdryer went off. Trudy was meticulous about her hair. He knew this was going to be a while. He sat on the edge of his bed and took out the key and looked at it. A small bronze key with a number tag 125. He thought to himself, "*This little key is going to get me $100,000 or killed.*" He really wasn't sure which one it was going to be.

The hairdryer stopped. Jack went over to the door and knocked again. The door opened and Jack heard a familiar voice, "Hello Mr. Trane." Jack's mouth fell open. He was totally shocked by who was on the other side of the door. It was Harold Chumley, and he had a gun pointed directly at Jack's head." Jack said, "How did you find me, Chumley? Nobody knows that I'm here." Chumley smiled a half-smile, and he laughed a sinister laugh, "Come on Mr. Trane, that's elementary detective work. I put a tracker under the rear bumper of your car the last time I was at your office. When you left the city, I didn't know who you were trailing, but I knew that you were following the watch. When I got here, I knew that it was the Valleys. I should have suspected them in the first place. It would have saved a lot of time." Jack gave Chumley the stink eye, "Sound's to me like you're just lazy. You just wanted me to do all the work." Chumley laughed, "That's right Trane. Why should I do all the work when I can get a chump like you to do it for me?" Chumley laughed out loud. Jack just kept looking at him with squinted eyes. Chumley continued, "I've already been to the Valley's room, and I know they don't have the watch. They told me it was taken from them this morning. And based on the shape that they are in right now, I believe them. So that only leaves you. I'm only going to ask you one time. Where is the Watch? And be careful how you answer Mr. Trane, I won't miss this time." He had the gun pointed at the middle of Jack's head. Jack needed to buy some time. He started speaking slowly, "Ok, Chumley, I'm going to level with you. The watch is….." Suddenly there was a loud crack over the back of Chumley's head and pieces of wood were flying in the air. Chumley went down to the floor holding the back of his head. He started to get up and Jack hit him hard with a right hand to the left side of his jaw and then hit him with a left to his right temple. Chumley went down again, but this time he didn't get up. He was out cold. Jack shook his right hand. His knuckles went a little numb after hitting Chumley's jaw. Jack looked up and saw Trudy standing in the next room. She was standing there with pieces of the chair in her hands. She was shaking. Jack stepped over Chumley's crumpled body on the floor. He hugged Trudy and said, "Trudy, are you OK? He didn't' hurt you, did he?" Trudy smiled, "No problem Jack, I'm just taking care of business." She held up her arm and made a fist and a muscle. It was a good act, but he could see that she was still shaken. He said, "Trudy, that was an awesome move with the chair, I think that you just saved both of our lives. At least for now." Trudy raised one eyebrow, "What do you mean, at least for now?"

Jack grabbed Trudy's hand as they both stepped over Chumley's body and led her into his room. He said, "I don't have time to explain everything, but we have to act fast before Chumley wakes up. He took the key out of his pocket, and he put it in Trudy's hand. He looked her in the eyes and said with a very serious tone, "Trudy, I want you to take this key and hold on to it. Keep it safe, it opens a safe deposit box that contains the "*Henry Graves Supercomplication*." There is a guy in the hotel that's looking for me. Actually, he's looking for the watch and he thinks that I have it. So, we need to split up. You can't be seen with me. It's too dangerous." Trudy's eyes were wide open, she said, "OK, Jack, what do you want me to do?" Jack patted her on the shoulder, He said, "First, I want you to help me drag Chumley into my room. Then you go back into your room and stay there for about 30 minutes. Then just go about your day as if nothing happened." Trudy broke in, "As if nothing happened?" Jack continued, "That's right. When you leave the room take your bag and all your stuff with you. We won't be coming back to our rooms." Trudy was just standing there looking at Jack with a dazed look on her face. She said, "Jack, what are you saying? A guy trying to kill you, and you want me to go shopping?" Jack smiled, "Yeah that's pretty much it. I'm going to give you a call when it's safe. So, don't worry about anything, just go out and do some shopping and I'll call you later." Trudy broke into a half-smile, "Can I have your expense card, Jack?" He pulled his credit card out of his wallet and Trudy grabbed it out of his hand. Jack looked at her with a serious look, "I trust that you'll use this in a responsible way." She laughed, "Come on Jack, you know who you're talking to? He smiled, "Yeah, that's what I mean." She smiled, "I'll be so responsible that when you get the bill, you'll think that you made all the purchases yourself." She laughed. Then she said, "Speaking of responsible, if you need me to get you out of any more jams, you just give me a call." Trudy laughed again. Jack said, "Yeah, you'll be the first one that I call." They both dragged Chumley's limp body into Jack's room.

Jack took off his coat and his hat and threw them on the bed. Trudy went back into her room and locked the adjoining door.

Chumley was laying on the floor next to Jack's bed and he was starting to move a little. Jack picked up the phone in the room and dialed down to the main desk. Jessie answered the phone, "Hello, main desk, can I help you?" Jack broke in, "Yes, this is Mr. Johnson in room 1065. Can you send security right up to my room? A man broke into my room and threatened me with a gun. Right now, he's unconscious on the floor but I think he's coming to. Please Hurry." Jessie was startled, "Oh my, yes, security will be up there immediately." She hung up the phone. Jack had his hand on his taser in case he had to use it on Chumley. A plan was developing in his mind. If it worked, he was going to get rid of Chumley, hopefully for a long while. He kicked Chumley's gun into a position so that it was visible. He wanted the security guards to see it and view Chumley as an imminent threat. Jack stood over Chumley for about 4 minutes, then there was a knock at the door. Jack opened the door and the 2 security guards Tim and George stood in the doorway looking like they were ready to brawl at the main event at WrestleMania. They both had their nightsticks in their hands. Tim said, "We got a call, you got some trouble up here." Jack pointed to Chumley on the floor. "This guy broke into my room and held me at gunpoint. That's his gun on the floor. Then he threatened me, that if I didn't give him some kind of watch, he was going to kill me." George spoke up, "Is this the same guy that you saw in the hallway this morning?" Jack let a little silence fill the air. This was part of his plan. He said, "Yes, now that you mention it, I'm quite sure this is the guy in the hallway from this morning. In fact, he even said that he was down at the Valley's room before he came to mine. Fortunately, I got the jump on him and hit him in the face before he had a chance to use his gun." Tim's eyes were bugging out, "Mr. Johnson, that's pretty impressive, how did you do it?" Jack smiled, "It's just reflexes I guess." George said, "Don't worry Mr. Johnson, we'll take it from here." Chumley was coming to, and he started to get up from the floor. George and Tim grabbed him and put zip ties around his wrists and picked up the gun from the floor. Tim spoke to Chumley, "You're coming with us. The police are on the way, and I think you have a lot of explaining to do. I hope that gun hasn't been involved in any crimes or you may be going away for a long time." Jack smiled and waved goodbye to Chumley as they dragged him out of the room.

He thought to himself, "*one problem solved.*" Now his focus was on Hercules. He knew that he was in the building, he just didn't know where. It was possible, that with the security staff running around, Hercules could have left the building until things cooled off. But Jack didn't think that was likely. He had to assume that Hercules was still somewhere in the hotel. It was now after 9:00 AM and Jack was getting hungry. He still wasn't sure that Hercules had recognized him in the mirror, so he thought that he would go down to the restaurant and get some breakfast. If Hercules recognized him as he was having breakfast, then he could make his next move. He put on his coat and his hat and left the room and walked over to the elevator. He pushed the button and the elevator opened immediately. He stepped in and pushed the button for the bottom floor. The cables clanged and the car gently descended towards the 1st floor. The car stopped and the doors opened. Jack looked left and right as he walked out of the elevator. The restaurant was just to the right. He walked into the restaurant and sat down at a small table against the wall. He wanted to make sure that he could observe anyone coming into the room. A young waitress came up to the table. She had on a blue skirt and a white shirt. She looked to be in her early 20's. She had short brown hair and had a look that resembled a young Audrey Hepburn. She said, "Hi, my name is Doris. Can I take your order?" Jack smiled, "Hello Doris." He was thinking to himself, "*I haven't had any blueberry pancakes in a while.*" He asked Doris, "Do you have any blueberry pancakes on the menu?" Doris smiled a big smile, "Oh yes sir, it's one of our most popular items. They are made with fresh Maine blueberries." Jack thought to himself, "*That's funny, blueberry season ended back in late August.*" Jack smiled, "That will be perfect Doris. I'll have an order of blueberry pancakes with fresh Maine blueberries. Would you happen to have Lattes here?" Doris made a sad face, "I'm afraid not sir, but we do have fresh Columbian breakfast blend." Jack looked disappointed, "Ok Doris, I'll have a cup of the Columbian blend and a small orange juice." Doris smiled her big smile, "I'll be right back with your order." She left and went back towards the kitchen. Jack continued to scan the room to make sure Hercules was nowhere in sight. He was drumming on the table with his fingers to a tune that came into his head. An old Jimmy Buffet song, "*Come Monday, it will be all right.*" He was hoping that the song rang true.

Doris came back with the pancakes. There was a stack of 4 half-inch pancakes. They looked to be done just right. She also placed a steaming hot cup of coffee on the table, along with some natural maple syrup from New Hampshire. She said, "Is there anything else I can get for you?" Jack smiled, "Not a thing Doris, not a thing." She smiled and went back towards the kitchen. He took a sip of his coffee, it was strong, but it was good. He poured the syrup on the pancakes and watched as the syrup drizzled around the sides of the pancake and down onto the plate. He put his fork into the stack and swirled a fork full of pancakes into the syrup, then he put a large bite into his mouth. The syrup must have been grade "B" dark. It was rich and flavorful. The pancakes were outstanding, even though the blueberry season had ended in August. While he was eating, he called Trudy. She answered, "Jack, where are you?" He answered, "I'm in the restaurant having breakfast." Her mouth was open, "Jack, you have a lot of nerve. I'm stuck up here in the room and you're having a great breakfast downstairs!" He said in a calm voice, "Now relax, Trudy. You can come down and have breakfast. Just make like you don't know me. We can't let anyone know that we are connected." Trudy's voice was raising, "Why Jack? Are you still in trouble? Is someone after us?" Jack responded, "Not you Trudy, just me. And we're going to keep it that way. The key that you have, we need to deliver to the Amalgamated Insurance company back in New York. They will come and get the watch out of the lockbox. But until then, there is this big guy, I call Hercules, that has already tried to get the watch once and I don't think he is going to give up." She sounded worried, "Shouldn't we just drive back to New York right now then, Jack?" He thought for a moment, "No Trudy, I don't want anyone following us back to New York. I need to think this through. You just come down when you're ready and have a nice breakfast. Take everything with you when you leave the room. Go do your shopping and I will call you when we're ready to go back to New York." She hesitated for a moment, "OK Jack, if you say so. Be careful, I don't want to have to save you again, or go back to New York by myself." Jack smiled, "That's why I keep you around Trudy, you're such a stone-hearted intimidator." She made a face, "Very funny Jack." They both hung up the phones. Jack finished his pancakes and drank down his last drop of coffee. He reached over and picked up the glass of orange juice and drank that too. He thought to himself, "*That was one fine meal, things are finally starting to look up.*" That thought was a little premature. From where he was sitting, he could see into the lobby. Although it was a fairly long distance, he looked into the lobby, and standing at the main desk he could see Hercules. He looked even bigger than he did before. A little sweat was starting to form on the back of Jack's neck. He motioned for Doris to come over with the check. Doris came over to the table and asked, "How was everything, sir?" Jack was in a hurry, but he didn't want to be rude. He pulled out $50 from his wallet. He said, "It was this good" He handed the $50 to Doris. He said, "Thank you, Doris, have a great day." Doris smiled her big smile, "Thank you, sir, you have a good day too!"

Jack got up from the table and tried to remain inconspicuous and calm. He moved slowly and tried to blend in with the environment. He stayed near the wall as he made his way towards the main lobby. When he reached the entrance to the lobby, He stuck his head inside the entrance, and he could see that Hercules was not there. He picked up his pace and made his way across the lobby and into the swinging circular door. As the door was swinging around, he looked back, and he could see that Hercules was standing in the open elevator, and he was looking right at him. Jack went out the door and onto the street. Hercules was close behind. The chase was on.

CHAPTER 15

It was a cool November morning in Boston. The temperature was in the high 40's with a stiff breeze coming off the Atlantic. The sun was low in the sky and Jack was hoping that the bright sun would give him some cover by shining in Hercules's eyes. As he exited the hotel, he ran south down India street. He always prided himself in his physical conditioning. He used to run 10 miles a week. But that was 10 years and about 20 pounds ago, and by the time he was about 50 steps down the road, he was already huffing and puffing. He looked back and he could see Hercules about 30 yards behind. It also looked like Hercules had 3 of his buddies with him. They were all about six feet five inches tall and looked like they all weighed at least 250 pounds. They were all younger than Jack and apparently in better shape. With every step, they were all gaining on him. Jack went left onto Central Street and spotted an old warehouse. He could see that the large receiving doors were open. He headed towards the warehouse as fast as his 49-year-old legs could carry him. By now he was sweating profusely and wished that he had changed his shirt this morning. He approached the warehouse in full stride and ran in through the open doors. None of the warehouse workers had noticed him. They were all involved in their own mundane Monday morning shift. He could see a couple of workers loading some skids on the floor with what looked like large wooden crates. There were also a few guys just hanging around watching them. And there was also a forklift driver, driving back and forth between aisles of the warehouse. Jack quickly ran to the right side of the building and ducked down behind some of the large crates. He sat there on the floor, trying to be as quiet as possible, even though he was breathing so heavily it was hard to catch his breath. He listened carefully to the sounds coming from inside the warehouse. He could hear the high revving of the forklift going back and forth. He could smell the propane fuel being expelled into the air and he could hear the workers arguing over who's babe was better looking. Then he heard several footsteps and the voice of Hercules, "We know you're in here Johnson. Make it easy on yourself and come out now. Because if we have to find you, you're really going to be sorry."

Jack thought to himself, "I already am sorry that I didn't take care of you when I had the chance." Hercules must have gotten the name Johnson from the desk clerk at the hotel. That was good because once Jack got out of this mess, they would never be able to trace him to the name Johnson.

The workers all started walking towards Hercules and his 3 buddies. One of them said, "Hey, what are you guys doing in here? This is a restricted area. You're all going to have to leave." Hercules turned towards them and raised his gun. He said, "Boy's don't you think it's time for a little coffee break? Why don't you all just make yourselves scarce for the next 10 minutes? Why don't you all just go get a cup of coffee?" The workers all stopped and looked at each other. Immediately, Jack picked up a large nail from the floor and threw it towards the other side of the building. Hercules and his 3 buddies heard the cling-clang of the nail and they all started in that direction with their guns drawn. The workers on the floor all scattered. Hercules yelled out, "Come on out Mr. Johnson. We're not going to hurt you. We just want to talk." Jack thought to himself, "*that's the kind of talk where someone ends up face down and not breathing.*" Jack figured that this was as good a time as any to make a move. He stood up slowly and came out from in back of the wooden crates. He walked slowly and as quietly as possible towards the center aisle in the warehouse. As hard as he tried, you could still hear the pebbles crunching under his shoes. Hercules spotted him and turned towards Jack and raised his gun in Jack's direction. Just as Hercules turned, the forklift suddenly moved to the front of the center aisle. The worker jumped out of the forklift and ran. Hercules got off a few shots, but they rang off the metal side of the forklift. Hercules and his 3 buddies all started running towards the center aisle. But by the time they got around the forklift, Jack had already reached the back of the building. He looked up and there was the most beautiful sight that he had seen all day. A bright orange sign that read EXIT. He pushed the bar on the door and the door opened. He ran through and found himself on McKinley Street. He was running out of options. There was a taxi coming down the road and Jack jumped in the middle of the street, hoping that unlike in New York, the taxi would stop. It did and Jack ran around the taxi and got in. He crumpled himself low in the back seat and yelled to the driver, "Drive, just drive!" Hercules and his 3 buddies had made their way out of the warehouse, and they could see that Jack had gotten into the taxi. The taxi driver turned around as asked Jack, "Hey man, where would you want me to drive to?" Jack yelled back, "If you don't want to get shot, you'll step on the gas and ask questions later." Shots rang out and there was a sound like pop, pop in the lid of the trunk. The driver said, "What the?....." and floored the gas pedal. Hercules and his 3 buddies continued to fire off shots at the taxi. The taxi had gotten about 100 yards away and then it started listing to the right side. Then there was a sound of thud…thud…thud. The right rear passenger tire had been hit by a bullet and had gone flat. Jack pulled $20 out of his pocket and threw it in the front seat at the driver. The driver was just staring at Jack with his eyes wide open in disbelief. The chase continued.

Jack exited the cab and started running down State Street. He knew that all he had to do is get back to India street. Then he could run into the garage and get his car, and hopefully get away from these 4 thugs. He was hoping that he had enough of a lead that Hercules and his 3 buddies wouldn't be able to catch him before he reached the garage. He reached back and ran just a little faster than he thought that he could, and he made it to the garage. As he entered, he looked back, and he could see Hercules and his 3 buddies coming around the corner of State Street. They saw Jack as he went into the garage and stopped in their tracks. Jack's car was on the top floor, but Hercules had no way of knowing that. In fact, he didn't even know what kind of car that Jack was driving. Jack didn't want to take the elevator because it would tip off Hercules as to which floor he was on. So, he took the stairs. Jack had a gym membership, but it had been about 6 months since he had shown up for any workouts. It showed. He was dripping sweat from his chin and the sides of his face. His shirt was drenched. He was breathing so hard he sounded like a donkey, but he made it to the top floor in about 60 seconds. Once on the top floor of the garage, he walked over to the rooftop railing and looked over the side to see if Hercules and his boys were anywhere in sight. All he could see were 2 dark-colored Lincoln town cars right outside the exit to the garage. No doubt, Hercules and his boys were in the Lincoln town cars, and it appeared that they were going to wait for Jack to come out of the garage, and then chase him down in the city. Jack smiled a broad smile. He liked his chances with his mustang against the 2 Lincoln's. Now he was actually looking forward to exiting the garage. Since they didn't know what Jack was driving, they would have to try to identify him when he came out of the garage. Jack took off his hat and his coat and put them in the back seat of his car. He wanted to be free to make all the driving maneuvers that he knew he was going to make. He sat in the driver's seat for a moment just gathering his thoughts. He felt that now he had the advantage. He was literally in the driver's seat, and he felt good about that. He planned out his route in his mind, "*take State Street down to Court Street and enter some heavy traffic. Get on to Cambridge Street and hook a right on to New Sudbury and get back on 93 going north.*" It sounded like a good plan. He started the engine and let it idle for a minute. It sounded good. A low roar of the 500 horses.

He let up on the clutch and slowly made his way down the ramps in the center of the garage. Around and around, he went until finally, he was at ground level. He drove up to the yellow gate and put his card in the machine. Then he slipped his credit card back out and the gate slowly opened. Jack could see the 2 Lincoln town cars on each side of the exit. He tightened his seat belt and revved his engine a couple of times. They recognized him. He jammed his foot on the gas pedal and his wheels peeled out of the garage down State Street. The 2 Lincolns followed closely. The cars left a trail of dirt and leaves that kicked up onto the sidewalk. Jack was forced to run a red light. As he approached the intersection, he tried to use his peripheral vision to see both ways. He jammed on the gas pedal and entered Court Street, but instead of continuing straight to Cambridge Street, he took a hard right onto Tremont. Traffic was heavy and Jack was weaving around cars, bicycles, and pedestrians. Where Cambridge Street meets Tremont, a large blue trash truck was merging. Jack served to avoid it, but one of the Lincolns couldn't swerve fast enough and clipped the rear bumper of the truck. The rear end of the truck moved into the road and blocked the path of oncoming traffic. The Lincoln had to stop until the truck was moved out of the line of traffic, but the other Lincoln continued following Jack's mustang's every move. Jack continued racing up Tremont Street. It was a one-way street. He could see Boston Common on his right and the large buildings towards Government Center in front of him. He was going about 70 miles per hour. That was certainly not an exceptional speed on the highway, but in the city, it was like driving in NASCAR. He slowed down to about 40 miles per hour and took a hard right onto Boylston Street. His tires screeched on the pavement. A pedestrian in the crosswalk jumped out of the way to narrowly avoid being hit. Jack shook his head and wiped his forehead. He thought to himself, "*That was a little too close for comfort.*" He was driving on the edge of what he considered out of control. The Lincoln stayed right with him. Jack looked in the rearview mirror and he could see Hercules in the passenger seat. Hercules was sticking his head out the window and he had his gun drawn. He squeezed off a couple of shots at the mustang. Jack could see a flash and smoke coming from the front of Hercules's gun. Jack swerved into the other lane and back again to avoid any bullets. Pedestrians on the sidewalk were running for cover. Jack was able to get his speed up to 80 miles per hour, but he was coming up on some heavy traffic. He downshifted and reduced speed to 40 miles per hour and swerved into Charles Street. There were 4 lanes of open traffic on Charles Street and Jack was going to need all of them. He checked his rearview mirror again and now there were 2 Lincolns behind him again. The other one must have caught up. Jack was in the far-right lane. He accelerated and changed quickly to the far-left lane. The 2 Lincolns followed, and they were closing.

Jack could see up ahead, a flatbed truck unloading port-a-potties for the common. He smiled to himself because he had a plan. He accelerated again until he came right up on the port-a-potties, then he swerved quickly into one of the middle lanes. The first Lincoln could not react fast enough and tried to stop but instead ran head-on into the port-a-potties. Jack looked back in the rearview mirror and started to laugh. That Lincoln was out of the chase. Their next stop would be the car wash. Jack checked his rearview mirror again and the second Lincoln, the one with Hercules, was still on his tail. Jack figured that if he could get back onto Beacon Street and take Storrow Drive, he could get on to the Expressway and lose Hercules once and for all. He took a left onto Beacon Street and there was not much room for maneuvering. The Lincoln was right on his bumper. He took the exit for Storrow Drive and accelerated again quickly up to 85 miles per hour. He put a little distance between himself and the Lincoln. Storrow Drive at rush hour is brutal, so he had to downshift and slow down quickly. New York traffic was bad, but there was never anything personal. In Boston, however, these gestures and screams coming from cars were extremely personal. Sometimes even mothers, sisters, even grandmothers were mentioned in the curses. Jack negotiated his way to the J F. Fitzgerald Expressway South. He entered the expressway and now the race was on.

Jack merged into the traffic and the Lincoln was about 3 car lengths behind. As he entered the Expressway, the traffic was heavy and as he approached the Tip O'Neill Tunnel, he could read the speed limit sign. It read 45 miles per hour. In Jack's mind that was just a suggestion. He stayed in the right-hand lane and quickly accelerated past an 18-wheel freight truck, and he entered the tunnel. Inside the tunnel, the light was an eerie orange color, and the tile on the wall on both sides of the tunnel seemed to close in on you. Jack switched lanes and cut out in front of the 18-wheeler. He was now in front of the 18-wheeler and behind a white pickup truck. This was all part of his strategy. He had slowed down to 45 miles per hour and on his left side, the Lincoln appeared. He could see Hercules roll the window down and lift his gun towards the window. Jack quickly changed back to the far-right lane and slowed down until the truck had passed him. He changed lanes again, this time to the far-left lane. He could now see the Lincoln in front of him, about 4 car lengths ahead. He stepped on the gas and came up on the Lincoln's rear bumper. Hercules turned around and looked at Jack through the rear window of the Lincoln. Jack could see the anger in his eyes. Both the Mustang and Lincoln were traveling in the lane to the left of the 18-wheeler. There was not much room for maneuvering. Hercules turned around in the front seat and hung out the front window. Jack could see him raising his gun. Jack immediately slowed down and again got behind the 18-wheeler. Jack could keep this up all day, but he decided to make a move. He veered into the right lane and accelerated quickly up to 75 miles per hour. He zoomed by the 18-wheeler and the pickup truck. The Lincoln changed lanes and tried to keep up, but Jack had too much of a lead. Most of the new Lincoln's have a 3.0L V6 engine which advertises 400 horsepower, but that was not enough to keep up with the Mustang GT-500's 500 horsepower. Still, the Lincoln accelerated and tried to stay with Jack. When the Lincoln got about 5 car lengths behind, Jack switched to the middle lane. There were cars, SUVs, dump trucks, busses all trying to negotiate the same space of the expressway. Whenever the Lincoln would accelerate and change lanes, Jack would do the same at about 5 car lengths ahead. This went on for the length of the tunnel and finally, the dark orange glow of the tunnel gave way to daylight as they burst out of the tunnel onto Route 93 at about 70 miles per hour. This was the Southeast Expressway and at this time of the morning, there were more cars on the other side of the road coming into the city, than those heading out. There was plenty of room to maneuver now. Jack purposely slowed down and let the Lincoln catch up to him. A plan was developing in his head. Both the far-left and far-right lanes were protected by Jersey barriers. Unless there was an exit ramp, there was really nowhere to go on either side of the road. Up ahead, he could see a small orange cone in the left lane. Someone had left the grate off one of the storm drains in the high-speed lane. This would work right into Jack's plan. He got into the left lane and the Lincoln followed almost on Jack's bumper. Jack accelerated up to 85 miles per hour and the Lincoln followed. Just before they got to the storm drain, Jack veered right to avoid the storm drain. The Lincoln never saw the drain. The Lincoln ran over the orange cone and hit the open hole in the road and blew out the front tire on the driver's side. The Lincoln swerved violently to the right, then flipped over onto the roof of the car. The Lincoln's slid down the expressway for about 120 feet and came to a stop. Jack looked back in the rearview mirror with a pleased smile on his face. He could see Hercules and the driver crawling out of the Lincoln. They didn't appear to be badly hurt, but he wouldn't have to deal with Hercules again, at least not for a while. Jack's mustang had gotten him out of many jams over the years. He had spent a lot of money keeping the car in top condition, but it was experiences like this that convinced him that it was all worth it. He turned on the radio. An old Bob Dylan song was playing "*How does it feel…Like a Rolling Stone*" He put on his sunglasses, took the next exit, and headed back into Boston. It was time to check on Trudy.

CHAPTER 16

By the time Jack got off the expressway, he was in Quincy. He was on Adams Street heading back towards Boston. It had been years since he had traveled these old streets, but they all had that familiar feel. Suburban neighborhoods with white picket fences and trees lining the sidewalks. It was mid-November, but there was still a little color on the trees. He loved the big city but there was still something about a small town that made him feel at home. He made his way to Dorchester Ave. and drove through the center of the city. There was a mix of old and new. Old tenements on one side of the road, 3 stories high, and on the other side, a brand-new office building surrounded by a black wrought iron fence. There was a nice mix of beauty parlors, dry cleaners, pizza shops, liquor stores, and the occasional auto repair shop lining the street. The nice thing about New England is that many of the towns and cities all somewhat resemble each other. If you feel comfortable in one town, you will probably feel comfortable in most.

As he was making his way back into Boston, he took out his cellphone. He pulled over to the side of the road turned off the car and dialed up Trudy. It was now about 11:30 AM, so he was hoping that Trudy had finished up most of her shopping. He knew that was a long shot. He could see Boston in the distance. It was a clear blue day with just a few puffy white clouds straddling the city, and the buildings stood out against the deep blue sky. Trudy answered the phone. "Hello Jack, you're not calling me because you're in trouble again, are you? I hope not because I'm just getting started on my shopping. There is so much to see. You know Jack, I found this place called Newbury Street and there are so many places that I have to stop in to….." Jack broke in, "Trudy, slow down. How many cups of Columbian blend did you have this morning? The reason I called, is that I wanted to see if you were done with all you're shopping. I'd like to get back to New York as quickly as possible." Trudy laughed, "You're kidding, right Jack?" You know, I've only been to like 3 stores. There is this place called "*Lord and Taylors*" and I just have to get over there. I heard that they are having a sale." Jack was rolling his eyes, "Trudy, how did you hear that there was a sale? You're not even from around here and you just got to Boston last night!" Trudy was laughing, "You know me, Jack, I can smell a sale." He was shaking his head up and down. "OK Trudy, I'm just outside the city. I don't think we'll be having any trouble with Hercules and his buddies for a while and Chumley will probably be tied up at the police station for a few days. So, just continue with your shopping. *Lord and Taylor* is on Boylston Street. I'll pick you up there in 1 hour and then we'll head over to the North End for some real Italian pizza." Trudy hesitated for a minute, "OK Jack, that sounds good, but an hour is not that long, how about 2 hours?" Jack smiled, "Trudy, I forgot to tell you. There is only a $2,000 daily limit on the expense card, I think you'll have that covered in less than an hour." Then he laughed. Trudy smiled, "I think I'm almost there now." They both hung up the phone and Jack started his car and got back onto Dorchester Ave. He looked in the rearview mirror and it appeared that there were a few more lines on his face than the last time he looked. He figured that they were character lines, and he was good with that. He took a left onto Columbia Road and made his way onto Massachusetts Ave. He was headed towards Fenway Park. He thought that this was probably as good a place as any to spend an hour, and besides, he was hoping that the Team Store on Jersey street would be open for business. He could always use a new Red Sox hat. About 15 minutes later Jack was on Jersey Street. Because it was November, he was easily able to find a place to park right on the street. He remembered when the street was named "*Yawkey Way*" after the former owner, but times and politics change. Now it was named Jersey Street.

He went into the Team Store and walked up to the counter and looked over the wall of Major League caps. There was only one that he was interested in. A lone clerk was working behind the counter. He was a man who looked to be about Jack's age, mid to late '40s. He looked like he hadn't shaved in a few days, and he had a high-pitched husky voice. He asked Jack with a Boston accent "What a ya like?" Jack smiled because he kind of missed that accent. He felt that his accent wasn't far off from the clerks. Jack said, "Give me a Red Sox cap, size 7." The clerk pulled a cap from the bottom of the stack and handed it to Jack. He put it on, and it fit like a glove. Ever since he was a kid, the experience of putting on a real major league cap was something special. Jack said, "How much?" The clerk pointed to the sign that read, $39.99. Jack said, "Hey this is off-season, can't we make a deal?" The clerk smiled, "Hey buddy if it was up to me, I'd give ya the cap for free. But if I give you a deal, everybody's gonna want a deal" Jack laughed, "Yeah, whatever." He took the cash out of his wallet and paid the clerk. The clerk took the money and put the cap in a bag and handed it back to Jack. Then Jack asked the clerk, "Would you mind putting a New York cap size 7 ¼ in a bag too? I got a secretary who's a native New Yorker, I think she would like it." "New York!" The clerk grumbled, "New York! If I knew you were taking it to New York, I would have charged you double!" Jack laughed. He knew that would get the clerk going. He paid the clerk another $39.99, and he put the New York cap in the bag. As Jack was leaving the clerk continued grumbling at Jack. He couldn't make out what the clerk was saying, but he was pretty sure it should be banned in Boston.

Jack got back into his car and put the bags with the caps in the back seat. He started the car and drove around Back Bay a couple of times just to take some time off the clock. He looked at his watch and was 12:25. The hour was almost up. He headed back on Boylston Street and pulled up in front of *Lord and Taylor*. He could see Trudy standing in front of the store, with about 4 bags on the ground in addition to the overnight bag from last night. Jack got out of the car and popped the trunk open. Trudy piled all the bags into the trunk. Jack said, "It's a good thing that I only gave you an hour, we couldn't fit one more bag in the trunk." She looked at him with squinted eyes, "Maybe you need a bigger car." Jack shook his head and smiled. He closed the trunk and they both got into the car. Trudy sat there looking pleased with herself. He said, "So did you have a good time spending all my money?" She looked at him with one eyebrow raised, "Come on Jack, you said that I could do some shopping. And besides, you're making $100,000 on this job. You can afford a couple of bucks." Jack smiled, "I was just kidding Trudy. I hope you maxed out the card. You're worth it." She smiled, "I'm glad you feel that way Jack because I don't think we can use the card again today. Two thousand dollars adds up pretty fast." Jack smiled, "Don't worry Trudy, I kept the good card in my wallet." She laughed, "I know that, Jack. Who do you think pays all the expense accounts?" They both laughed and Jack drove towards the North End.

He drove for about 15 minutes and arrived in the North End. Trudy said to Jack, "So you know this area pretty well, don't you?" Jack smiled, "It's been a while but it's all coming back to me. There is this restaurant I remember Mamma Mia, or Mamma Marie or something like that. It had the best Italian food you can ever imagine. The pizza is out of this world." Trudy yelled out, "Jack is that it?" He looked over to his right and there it was, an old historic circa 1830 brick townhouse overlooking the Public Square, "*Mamma Marias.*" The streets were cramped but there was a parking place less than a block away. Jack parked the car and he and Trudy walked into the restaurant. The maître de greeted them as they entered the restaurant. He was a young man in his late 20's, he had on black pants and a white shirt. His hair was jet black and slicked back. He said,

"Two for lunch?" Trudy spoke up, "Yes and we'd like a table with a view." The maître de smiled at Trudy and she smiled back. He said, "You mean a table near a window?" Trudy was still smiling. She said, "Yeah, something like that." He led them into the main dining room and showed them a table next to a window with a view of the Public Square. He said, "How is this?" Trudy was still smiling at the maître de, just staring at him. Jack broke in, "Yes, this will be perfect, thank you." The maître de responded, "Your waitress will be with you in just a moment." He put the menus on the table in front of Trudy and Jack. Trudy was still looking at the maître de and smiling. Jack said, "Thank you." The maître de left and Trudy watched him walk away. Jack was waving his hand in front of Trudy's face. "Hello, earth to Trudy." She turned to Jack and said, "Wasn't that an interesting after-shave the maître de was wearing?" Jack rolled his eyes, "Yeah, I think it was called "Boston predator." Trudy hit Jack on the arm. "Come on Jack, I think you're jealous." Jack laughed, "Jealous of that little punk? Are you kidding? Don't make me laugh. Five years from now, he'll probably still be waiting tables and his aftershave won't be smelling so good anymore." Trudy looked at him with one eyebrow raised and a smirk on her face. She said, "I was right, you're jealous."

The waitress came to the table. She was wearing a blue skirt and a tight white top. She had short black hair and gold stud earrings. She had striking features, dark eyes, and olive skin, quite attractive. She looked to be in her early 30's. She said, "What can I get for you both to drink?" Jack was silent. He was just looking at her and smiling. Trudy answered, "I'd like a glass of the Cabernet Sauvignon Red."

Jack was still silently smiling at the waitress. Trudy kicked him under the table. He said, "Oh, yes, I'll have a *Sam Adams* draught." The waitress smiled, "I'll be right back to take your order." She walked away and Jack watched her walk to the bar." Trudy said to Jack, "Why don't you just take a picture Jack, it will last longer." Jack laughed, he said, "Come on Trudy, she's not even my type." Trudy looked at him a little puzzled, "Yeah, I'm still trying to figure out, what your type is." The waitress returned with the drinks and said, "Can I give you both a little more time to look at the menu?" Jack responded quickly, "No we know exactly what we want. We'll have a large deep-dish pizza with everything on it." The waitress smiled, "Everything?" Jack smiled back, "Well, everything you got." The waitress laughed. She said, "I'll be back in about 20 minutes with your order." She walked back towards the kitchen.

Trudy sipped her wine and Jack had a large swallow of his *Sam Adams*. He said to her, "Well Trudy, it looks like this case turned out pretty good so far. You got to do some serious shopping. I avoided getting rubbed out, and the *Henry Graves Supercomplication* is locked away safely in a secured lockbox back at the hotel. Jack was feeling very satisfied with himself. He took another sip of his beer. He said, "By the way, you can give me back the key now for the lockbox. I'm going to have to deliver that to George Flax at the Amalgamated Insurance Company as soon as we get back to New York. Trudy said, "No problem, I have it right here in my purse. You can have it back." She fished around in her purse for about 30 seconds, then she looked at Jack with both eyes wide open. She said, "It's not here. The key is not in my purse." Jack looked at her with an eyebrow raised. "Come on Trudy, quit fooling around." Trudy was panicking, "No Jack, it's not here. I know that I put it in here this morning and it's not here." Now Jack was starting to panic. Without the key, the hotel would never release the contents of the lockbox. "Ok, Trudy, let's retrace your steps. Where have you been since you left the hotel?" She looked up at the ceiling and started counting on her fingers, she said, "Well, I got into a taxi, then I went to Newbury Street, there was a nail salon, then there was this Second Time store, and a sunglass store, a dress store, I think it was Marlene's or something, then I stopped for a drink at Starbucks. And then you called, and I went over to *Lord and Taylor*. But I think that's it. That shouldn't be too hard to trace right?" Jack was rolling his eyes. "Trudy that's like 7 different places. It could be on the floor someplace, or in the street, in the cab." Jack was starting to sweat. "Trudy, there is a 24-Million-dollar watch sitting in a lockbox and whoever has that key can walk right in, open the box, and walk away with the watch. We have to find that key!" Trudy smirked at him, "Come on Jack, you've been in tighter jams than this, and you always find a way." He looked at her with one eyebrow raised, he said, "Let me see your purse." She picked up her purse and said, "Jack, it's not here." She emptied the contents of the purse onto the table. There were 3 different tubes of lipstick, a small makeup compact, a mirror, some tissues, a keychain in the shape of New York with about 5 keys on it, some loose change, chapstick, two pens, and about 6 other items all rolling around on the table. She handed Jack the purse. He held it upside down and shook it violently for about 5 seconds. Then you could hear the bright tinkle of a key bouncing off the table. He picked it up and showed it to Trudy with a deadpan face. She looked at Jack with a half-smile and said, "Well, how about that. It must have been caught in the seam or something." Jack looked into the purse. There was a little pocket on the inside of the purse specifically meant to hold a key. He asked Trudy, "What do you think this little pocket is for?" She smiled, "Gee, Jack, I didn't even know that was there. What will they think of next? I guess all's well that ends well." Jack dropped the purse back on the table and put the key in his shirt pocket. Then he sat back and took another long swallow of his *Sam Adams*. Trudy picked up the contents of her purse from the table and started putting it back into her purse.

The waitress came over and placed the piping hot pizza on a little stand on the side of the table. She looked at the table which was strewn with all the contents of Trudy's purse, and said, "Why don't we just leave the pizza here, and that way you will have more room on the table for whatever is going on here." She made wide eyes and looked at Jack. Trudy looked embarrassed. Jack was laughing a little bit under his breath. He said, "She's just trying to get organized. Some people just have a hard time keeping things in their place." Jack and the waitress looked at each other and laughed. Trudy looked at Jack with squinted eyes. "Yeah, some people have a hard time knowing what their place is." Jack looked at Trudy with a half-smile and the waitress drifted back towards the kitchen. For some people, this might be uncomfortable, but this was the normal banter between Trudy and Jack. They both understood the rules and almost never crossed the line. But he was getting very close. Trudy said to Jack, "You're quite a comedian, aren't you, Jack?" Jack looked at her with one eye and the other eye on the pizza. He said, "Come on Trudy, I was just kidding. Let's enjoy the pizza. It looks fabulous." Trudy smiled, "You're right Jack it does look good." They could smell the aroma of the tomato sauce, the pepperoni, the garlic, and a mix of the "everything" that was on top of the pizza. Jack took a piece and put it on Trudy's plate. Then he put a slice on his plate. They both started to eat. Jack took a bite and closed his eyes. He swallowed, opened his eyes, and took a sip of his beer. He said, "Oh my, that is just about the best pizza I have ever had." Trudy was still chewing her first bite. She swallowed and said, "Jack, you're right. This pizza is amazing." She took another bite and savored the flavor. She said, "That is one awesome pie, Jack." Jack's mouth was full, he couldn't answer. He just nodded and gave her a thumbs up.

They continued eating for about the next 15 minutes along with some small talk and finally, the entire pizza was gone. Jack sat back and put his hands on his stomach and said, "Whew...I don't think I can get up." Trudy laughed. "Jack, I only had 3 pieces. That means that you ate 5 pieces. You're going to be a real porker by the time we get back to New York." She blew her cheeks real full of air and mimicked Jack holding her stomach." He smirked, "Very funny Trudy. But speaking of New York, we should be getting back." He looked at his watch and it was just about 2:00 PM. He said, "If we leave now, I think I can get us back to New York by 6:00 PM." Trudy looked at Jack with a serious face, "Knowing you Jack, I think you could." The waitress came back over and said, "I hope everything was OK." Trudy spoke up, "It was awesome, even if I only got to eat 3 of the 8 pieces." Jack was sitting there with his elbow on the table and his hand on his chin. He said, "I guess some of us just need to watch our weight." Both the waitress and Trudy looked at Jack with the expression of "I can't believe you just said that" and there was an uncomfortable silence at the table. Jack realized that he just crossed the line. You never ask a woman if you can kiss her, you never ask if you can have her number, and you never talk about her weight. Jack had learned all these the hard way, but he still put his foot into his mouth from time to time. He cleared his throat and said, "Well, I guess we'll just take the check. The pizza was outstanding."

The waitress ripped the check off her pad and put it in front of Jack. The total for the entire meal was only $25. He took $50 out of his wallet and gave it to the waitress. He said, "Keep the change." She looked at the $50 dollars and said, "Thank you very much, please come back again." She smiled a big smile at Jack. It looked like the $25 tip had washed away his smart-aleck remark about watching your weight. They got up from the table and headed towards the exit. They passed the maître de on the way out and Trudy gave him a big smile and he smiled back. He said, "Have a great day." Trudy waved at him, and they left the restaurant.

They both got into the car. Jack turned the key in the ignition and started the engine. He put the car in gear and started on the drive back to New York. He asked Trudy, "So how did you like Boston?" She said sarcastically, "Well Jack, from what I saw in the day and a half that we've been here, this is a really cool city. I'm thinking of coming back with some of my friends so I can really have some fun." Jack smiled, "So almost getting killed by Harold Chumley, and bashing him over the head with a chair wasn't enough fun for you?" She looked at him with one eyebrow raised, "No Jack, that's your kind of fun. But thanks for sharing." They both laughed and he headed towards the Massachusetts Turnpike. His plan was to take the Mass Pike to Route 84 in Sturbridge and follow that all the way down to Route 95. He thought to himself, "*this should be a piece of cake. I'll be back in the city by 6:00.*" The only problem is the cake was going to be Devil's food.

CHAPTER 17

Jack got back to the city just a little after 6:00 PM. By this time of the day, darkness owned the city. All that was visible were the rows of lights that dotted the buildings as far as the eye could see. There were no shadows, just a dark mood that filled the air. Trudy was sleeping in the passenger seat. From the glare of the lights on the dashboard, he could see that her head was back, and her mouth was open and from time to time she let out a quick snore. He was tempted to take a picture with his cell phone, but he resisted because he was sure that Trudy would get him back with something twice as bad. He made his way to Trudy's apartment and pulled up in front of the building and turned off the car. Trudy woke up. She snapped her head upright and yawned. She said, "I must have dozed off for a few minutes." Jack laughed and said, "Yeah, you dozed off for the last three hours." She looked at Jack with eyes of apology, "Gee, sorry Jack, I must not have been very good company." He smiled, "Sometimes, Trudy, a sleeping passenger is the best company." He got out of the car and opened the trunk and took out her 4 shopping bags plus her overnight bag and brought them over to the front door. She got out of the car and walked towards the front door. Jack passed her on the way back to the car. He said, "Thanks for everything Trudy,

I couldn't have gotten the watch back without you. Why don't you take tomorrow off?" Trudy smiled, "You're right Jack, but I think the 2,000-dollar shopping spree about covers it. But if you insist, yeah, I'll take tomorrow off." She turned to put her key into the door and Jack said, "Hey Trudy!" She looked over and Jack scaled her Yankees hat towards her like a frisbee. She reached out with one hand and caught it and put it on her head. Jack said, "All that and she can catch too! Trudy, you're amazing." She smiled, "I know Jack, that's what I keep telling everybody." They both laughed and Trudy went into her apartment. Jack closed the door to his car and drove off in the direction of his parking garage.

He pulled into the garage and gave Fernando, the parking attendant a wave. Fernando waved back. Jack drove up the ramp and parked his car on the second level where he could easily access it if he needed to. He kept his keys in his pocket. There was always an extra set in the vending machine on the wall in case he needed them. He walked a couple of blocks to his apartment and entered the building. He hadn't been there for a couple of days, so he didn't know what to expect. Sylvio and Jimmy were no doubt still looking for him, so he was very cautious. He walked up the stairs and stood outside the door to his apartment. He looked down and to his surprise, the matchstick was still in the doorjamb. He opened the door and went in. There was a distinct stale odor to his apartment. It smelled like dirty socks and stale pizza. It could be because he hadn't done laundry in over a week and there was a load of dirty clothes on the floor in the walk-in closet. Jack was about to add to the odor. He took off his coat and placed his cell phone and the lockbox key on the coffee table. He peeled off his 2-day old sweaty shirt and pants and dropped them on the floor in the middle of the living room in front of his couch. Then he jumped into the shower. Nothing feels as good as a nice hot shower after 2 days on the road. After about 20 minutes he came out of the bathroom. He didn't want to take the time to shave, so he gave himself a once-over with his Remington electric shaver. It wasn't the best shave, but it would do for now. He was starving and he was planning a trip down to Big Jim's sports bar for some of their fabulous fish and chips. He thought about picking up the pants from the floor and putting them on again but then he took a good whiff of the air and decided not to. He walked over and reached into his walk-in closet and pulled out a pair of plain black pants. Then he walked over to the armoire and instead of picking out a pristine white shirt, he pulled out a dark green turtleneck shirt and put it on. It felt like he was out of uniform, but it felt good. He imagined this must be how Steve McQueen felt when he was off-screen.

The November air was cool in the evening, so Jack put on his black trench coat and put on a black pork pie hat. He felt that it gave him more of a casual look. He put his cell phone and the key to the lockbox back into his jacket pocket and he left the apartment. He made sure to replace the matchstick in the doorjamb. He wanted to get to Big Jim's because the Bruins were playing the Islanders tonight and he wanted to catch it on the big screen, but he also wanted to make sure that he delivered the key to George Flax as soon as possible. On the way down the stairway, he pulled out his cell phone and dialed the number for George Flax. The phone rang twice, and George Flax picked up. "Mr. Trane, so nice to hear from you. I trust you have good news for me." Jack had a big smile on his face, "Yes George, I have the watch in a lockbox in Boston and want to give you the key." There was a slight pause, then George Flax spoke, "Very good Mr. Trane, well done. I'm not at my office right now but you can come over to my apartment and deliver the key. I will be here all evening." Again, there was a slight pause and Jack spoke, "Well, George, I'm going to be at *Big Jim's* sports bar for the next couple of hours. Can you send one of those guys in the black suits down and I'll hand it off to them?" This time there was a little longer pause and George Flax spoke, "OK, Mr. Trane, My associates will be down at *Big Jim's* within the hour. But Mr. Trane, I will not be able to deliver your finder's fee until the watch is fully in my possession, you understand." This time there was no pause, "Of course George, that's not a problem. All your associates will have to do is present the key at the Mariotte hotel just off India street in Boston, open the lockbox, and walk away with the watch." George Flax responded, "You make it sound so easy Mr. Trane. Let's hope you're right." Jack was shaking his head, "Don't worry George, your guys should have it by the morning." George responded, "Let's both hope that they do." They both hung up their phones and Jack entered the street and immediately waved down a taxi.

A taxi pulled over and Jack got in. Jack said, "*Big Jim's* sports bar." The driver was an older man, probably older than Jack and very short. He could barely see over the steering wheel, and he was wearing a vintage brown leather flat cap which was about even with the top of the steering wheel. He had a very distinct Brooklyn accent. The name tag on the visor read "Mike Jordan". Jack read the name tag and he laughed to himself and thought, *"there's probably nothing I can say that the poor guy hasn't heard before."* The driver drove off in the direction of *Big Jim's*. He may have been short but that didn't stop him from going from 0 to 40 in three seconds and changing lanes twice in the process. He turned back and looked at Jack and said, "Big Jim's ehh? You looking for a little action? If you was to place a bet on a particular team, I might be able to see that your bet gets covered if you knows what I mean?" Jack smiled, "Oh, so you're a bookie and a cab driver." Mike Jordan raised his hands from the steering wheel for a second and said, "Whoa..whoa…a bookie? No what I mean to say, is that I might know a guy who could take such a bet. If you was interested in a random wager if you knows what I mean." Jack laughed, "Yeah, I **know** what you mean, you're a bookie. But no, I don't want to make a bet. I just want to have some dinner down at *Big Jim's*." Mike Jordan responded, "Yeah I hear they got some good burgers down there, and if anyone wanted to place a bet, they might be in the right place." Jack sat back in his seat. "Yeah, I'll try to remember that, since you're not a bookie." Mike Jordan continued driving, changing lanes, and stepping on and off the gas, all while humming the theme song to the *Godfather*. Jack thought to himself, "*only in New York*."

They arrived at Big Jim's and the driver turned around to Jack and said, "That's $12.50." Jack handed him a $20 and said, "Keep the change, Michael Jordan." Michael took the $20 bill and slipped it into an envelope and drove away.

Jack walked into *Big Jim's* and sat at the bar. Within about 20 seconds an ice-cold *Guinness* came sliding down the bar and stopped right in front of Jack. He looked down the bar and saw his friend at the other end. Jack yelled out "Teddy K. you still go it." Teddy came walking towards Jack with his bar rag over his shoulder and said, "Come on Jack, I never lost it." They both laughed. Jack said, "How are the fish and chips tonight?" Teddy said, "right off the boat Jack, right off the boat." Jack was nodding his head up and down. "Sounds good Teddy, I've been looking forward to some of your fish and chips all day." Teddy gave Jack a wink and went back towards the kitchen to put in his order. Jack sipped the creamy brown top off the *Guinness*. Then he looked up at the TV screen and the hockey game was just about to begin. The Bruins and the Islanders. He had no doubt the Bruins were going to win tonight. He yelled out at the TV, "*Let's go BRUINS!*" It got noticeably quiet in the bar for a moment and all eyes were on Jack. He raised his beer to the crowd and laughed. Jack enjoyed this competitive ribbing and for the most part, so did most of the New Yorkers at the bar. Teddy K came back over to Jack and said, "Hey Jack, I thought that I should warn you, Gumbati's boys, Sylvio and Jimmy have been around looking for you the last couple of nights." Jack nodded and made a brushing motion with his hand. "Yeah, I'm going to have to deal with those 2 Bozo's soon enough, but if they come in tonight, give me a high sign and I'll exit through the back, I don't want to tangle with them tonight." Teddy gave him a thumb's up and walked back to the cash register to ring up some drinks.

Jack continued to sip his beer as he watched the game on the wide-screen TV. It was 3 minutes into the game and the Bruins had already scored. He thought to himself "*Maybe I should have placed a bet with Michael Jordan after all.*" About 10 minutes went by and Teddy K came back with the fish and chips. He put the plate in front of Jack and a full bottle of *Hunt's* ketchup and said, "Enjoy!" Jack smothered the french fries with ketchup and sprinkled on enough salt that it looked like there had been a light snowstorm on top of the fries. He put a French fry into his mouth and closed his eyes. There was nothing better than the fries at *Big Jim's*." Crunchy but soft in the middle. He took a bite of the fish and there was just the right amount of flavor exchange between the fish, the batter, and the fries. The best fish and chips in the city. About halfway through the meal, another *Guinness* came sliding down the bar and stopped in front of Jack. He yelled out "Teddy K.!" Jack enjoyed his *Guinness*."

About 10 minutes later the fish was gone, the fries were gone, and Jack was at the bottom of his second *Guinness*. He was wiping his mouth with the napkin and he caught sight of 2 familiar figures coming through the door. It was the 2 men in the black suits, and they still had on their sunglasses. They walked directly up to Jack and stood behind where he was sitting. They both just had their arms crossed and were standing behind Jack's barstool. Jack turned and smiled and said, "If it isn't the blues brothers?" And then he laughed. The men in the black suits didn't laugh. One of them extended his hand towards Jack with his palm up. He stood with his hand extended for what seemed to be an uncomfortable 15 seconds. Jack pulled the key to the lockbox out of his pocket and placed it in the hand of one of the guys in the black suits. Jack said, "You know where to go right?" The 2 men in the black suits did not say a word. He put the key in his pocket and they both just turned and walked back out the door. Jack shook his head and said out loud "You get points for personality you know!" They were gone. Jack was hoping that they would be in Boston by the morning, and he would have his finder's fee by noon. Then he could deal with Tony Gumbati, Sylvio, and Jimmy on his own time. But things don't always go as planned.

Jack looked down the bar and Teddy K was giving Jack the high sign. Jack looked over towards the door and coming into the bar were Sylvio Donato and Jimmy Sissi. Sylvio had on a suit that was a baby blue color and Jimmy had on a black leather jacket. Jack knew that they were looking for him. It had been a long day and he didn't want to have to tangle with them tonight. Immediately he rose from his seat and walked towards Teddy K. His back was towards Sylvio and Jimmy, so they didn't recognize him. Teddy led Jack through the kitchen and out to the back door. Jack pulled out $50 and gave it to Teddy K. He said, "I owe you, Teddy." Teddy nodded his head, "Yeah, we'll settle up later. Now get out of here."

Jack went through the alley and came out on the street. He saw a taxi coming towards him, so he waved it down. The taxi pulled over and Jack got in. The driver was a tall thin man with short blond hair and a blond soul patch on his chin. The name tag over the visor said, “Victor Flamenco.” Jack said to him, “Hey buddy, are you some kind of a jazz musician?” He looked back at Jack with a half-smile and said, “Where to boss man?” There was a faint smell of marijuana lingering in the air. That was no surprise. Jack gave him the address of his apartment off 3rd Ave. The driver said, “No problem boss man, that’s where we’ll go.” He put the car in gear and almost immediately they were traveling at about 40 miles per hour. The driver didn’t say anything else; he just drove. He drove like he was being pursued by a squad of police cruisers. Probably a scenario that wasn’t too far removed from his past. Jack sat back in the seat and tried to think about how he was going to use the $100,000 that would be in his account tomorrow morning. Maybe he’d buy a boat or a washing machine for his apartment. Or maybe just a new hat. He was also thinking about how he was going to deal with Tony Gumbati when Gumbati found out that he wasn’t getting the watch. That part of the plan hadn’t been worked out yet, but he thought that the $100,000 would open up some options. The cab arrived at Jack’s apartment and pulled up in front of the apartment door. The cabbie turned around and said, “That will be $12.50 man.” Jack handed him a $20 and said, “Keep the change boss man.” The cabbie put the $20 in his shirt pocket and drove away.

Jack got out of the taxi and took a deep breath. It was cold, but the air in New York somehow seemed cleaner when there was a chill in the air. He went in through the front door and climbed the stairs to the second floor. He stood in front of the door to his apartment and looked down at the doorjamb. The matchstick was still there. He opened the door and went in. He reached over against the wall and flicked on the light switch. The room became illuminated, and Jack just looked around at the mess that his apartment had become over the past week. But this was the end of a long day. He had been shot at, been involved in a car chase, had lunch in Boston's north end, drove back to New York, had fish and chips and *Big Jim's*, handed off the key, and now he was ready for some solid sack time. He never went to bed without a shower, that was his rule. So even though he had just taken a shower a couple of hours ago, he needed a shower. He went into the bathroom and turned on the hot water in the shower and let it run for about 3 minutes to make sure it was hot. He reached into the shower to feel the stream of water to make sure that the temperature was right. He hated getting into a lukewarm shower. When the temperature was just right, he jumped into the shower, and just stood there letting the hot steaming water rain down on his head. It felt good. He felt the cares of the day leaving his body. He could have fallen asleep right there in the shower and he almost did. Jack always tried to act like a tough guy, but down deep, he really wasn't. The pink bar of *Caress* soap in the soap dish was a good indicator. It wasn't really a manly scent, but he liked the way it made his skin feel. He lathered up really good, then rinsed off all the suds and got out of the shower. He felt refreshed. He walked over to the sink and brushed his teeth. Now he was ready for a good night's sleep. He turned the light off in the bathroom and went over and turned off the lights in the rest of the apartment. Then he made his way towards the bed in the dark, and just fell onto the bed backwards. He got under the covers and within 3 minutes, he was fast asleep. When he first laid down, he was sure that this sleep would last until about 10:00 AM. He was wrong.

Jack was on a boat. The kind of boat that $100,000 would buy. He pulled a *Guinness* from the cooler and sat back behind the wheel and popped open the bottle. He could feel the wind in his face and the smell of the salt air. Then suddenly there was a ringing in his ears. It wouldn't stop. It got louder and louder. Jack opened his eyes and sat up in bed. His phone was ringing. Jack woke up from his dream. He shook his head, reached over, and picked up his cell phone. He looked at the caller ID. It was George Flax. Jack thought, "*He must be calling to thank me for doing such a great job.*" He answered the phone, "Hello George." The voice on the other end was loud and irritated. "All right Mr. Trane, what are you trying to pull? Is this some kind of joke? Where is the watch?" Jack thought that he still might be sleeping. He shook his head to get out the cobwebs. He said "George, what are you talking about? I gave the key to your 2 men last night." There was no pause in the conversation. George said, "Yeah, you gave them the key, but when they got to the lockbox at the Boston Mariotte, the lockbox was empty. NO WATCH!"

Jack was in disbelief, "That's impossible. I know that the watch was there. I put it there myself. I don't understand." George Flax responded, "I don't understand either Mr. Trane, but unless I get the watch, you don't get the $100,000." Jack was now standing up on the side of the bed. "Don't worry George, I'll get to the bottom of this. You'll have that watch by the end of the day." Jack was talking a good game, but he had no idea who had the watch or how he was going to get it back. Well, maybe he did have an idea. George Flax said, "I'm counting on you, Mr. Trane. Don't let me down." They both hung up the phones. Jack stood next to the bed just staring out the window. It was barely 8:00 AM and he was already sweating. He knew that the only one who had the key other than himself was Trudy. Trudy had the key in her possession while Jack was dealing with Hercules. His mind was racing as he contemplated the possibilities. He thought, "It couldn't be." Or could it?

CHAPTER 18

Jack sat back down on the bed. He thought long and hard about the key to the lockbox and then he shook his head. He couldn't believe that he had suspected Trudy of using the key to take the watch. He was ashamed of himself. He knew that Trudy was an honest person and would never do anything like that. She was loyal to a fault. He felt bad that he had even thought that Trudy could be a suspect. Then a light went off in his head. There was only one other explanation. The security guard at the hotel. He had a bad feeling about that guy from the beginning. Jack picked up his cell phone and dialed the number for Mr. Flax. It rang a couple of times and George Flax answered. "Hello, Mr. Trane. That was quick, do you have something for me? Jack sounded like he was out of breath, but he hadn't left the bed. He said, "Mr. Flax, are your men still in Boston?" Mr. Flax answered. "Yes, they are waiting for further instructions." Jack answered, "Good. There is a security guard at the Mariotte hotel, his first name is George. If your men can track him down, I'm sure that he will know where the watch is. He is the only other person who had access to the lockbox." Mr. Flax responded, "My associates will have some information within the hour. I will get back to you if I need you, Mr. Trane." Jack answered, "With all due respect Mr. Flax, you will indeed need me." They both hung up the phone.

Jack was confident that the men in the black suits would be able to track down George the security guard. There was no doubt in Jack's mind. The security guard was responsible for removing the watch from the lockbox. The question is, what did he do with it? There was nothing Jack could do at the moment, so he went into the bathroom to go through the morning ritual. He came out of the bathroom in 20 minutes all showered and shaved. He picked up the black pants from the floor and the green turtleneck that he had worn last night and put them back on. He had only worn them for a couple of hours. As he was putting on his pants, he stopped and thought for a minute about the watch. It seemed like the $100,000 finder's fee was slipping away. He pulled the turtleneck over his head and determined that he wasn't going to let that happen. Then he reached for his cell phone and it rang before he picked it up. He looked at the caller ID and it was George Flax. Jack answered, "Hello George, did your guys get any information?" George answered, "Indeed they did Mr. Trane. The security guard's full name is George McNulty, and it seems that he has a wall of keys in his apartment that fits all the lockboxes in the Mariotte. You know Mr. Trane; a hotel lockbox is not the most secure place to store valuable things." Jack was making a face, "Yeah, Yeah, I know. It was a dumb place to put the watch. What did George McNulty do with the watch?" Mr. Flax cleared his throat, "Well Mr. Trane, it appears that he sold it to a gentleman for a mere $10,000 just this morning." Jack was livid, "What? That idiot sold the watch for $10,000? Who did he sell it to? Did they get a name?" Mr. Flax spoke calmly, "Mr. Trane, it appears that George McNulty sold the watch to the same man that was in your room 2 nights ago. The man that entered your room with a gun." Jack was silent for a moment. He couldn't believe what he was hearing. "Mr. Flax, I know who has the watch. It's Harold Chumley. The security guard was supposed to turn him over to the police for breaking into my room, but obviously, he made a deal for the $10,000 instead." Jack didn't tell Flax, but when he had the watch in his possession, he had put a tracking device in the box, just under the watch. He knew this might come in handy if the watch fell into the wrong hands. Jack had a determined look on his face. He said, "Chumley won't get far. I'll have the watch back before the day is over." Mr. Flax laughed, "You're pretty sure of yourself aren't you Mr. Trane?" Jack gritted his teeth, "Let's just say that I've had about enough of Harold Chumley and today we'll settle the score. This time, he won't be expecting me. He won't even know what hit him." Mr. Flax responded to Jack, "Mr. Trane, my 2 associates are more than willing and able to assist in tracking down Harold Chumley, in fact, I would feel better if they did." Jack was shaking his head, "No Mr. Flax, Chumley is mine. I'm going to get the watch back and have it on your desk before the day is over. We'll talk later." Jack hung up the phone.

Jack walked over and sat on the couch and opened the app on his phone to track the box that the watch was in. He could see from the map that the box was just outside of Boston on Route 95 heading south. It appeared that Harold Chumley was headed back to New

York with the watch. That would make sense. Chumley had a buyer in New York the whole time. Chumley was headed back to New York to sell the watch. Jack was going to make sure that never happened.

After seeing that Chumley was about 4 hours from arriving in New York, Jack decided that he might as well get some breakfast. He put on his tan trench coat and his fedora hat and left his apartment and headed down to the Coffee Café. As he walked down the street, he had an unusual spring in his step. He didn't have the *Henry Graves Supercomplication* in his possession, but he knew for sure by the end of the day he would. He started whistling the song "*Build me up Buttercup*" As he strolled down the street. He stopped in at the newsstand and picked up the morning paper and threw a couple of bucks on the counter. Nicky gave him his usual morning grumble. Jack left the newsstand and continued whistling as he walked. He got to the Coffee Café and walked in. Immediately he heard Betty's voice, "Jack Trane, where have you been? I thought that you didn't like me anymore." Jack smiled, "Come on Betty, you know I always come back." Betty laughed, "Yeah, like an old family dog." They both laughed. Betty smiled, 'What can I get for you, Jack?" Jack smiled back, "How about something that will stick with me all day?" She smiled, "OK Jack, but I meant for breakfast." Jack raised one eyebrow, "How about those blueberry pancakes, Betty?" She showed him her pad. She already had the pancakes written down, along with the vanilla Latte and an orange juice. Jack opened his eyes wide. "I'm impressed. Either you can read my mind, or I'm so predictable you even know how much of a tip I'm going to give you." She smiled,

"Jack, every time you come in, you give me a $10 tip." He smiled, "Well maybe today I'll fool you and give you a $20 tip." She turned over her pad and showed Jack the page. It said, *$20 dollar tip*. Jack shook his head. He said, "You should be on TV Betty, *America's Got Talent*, you'd win for sure." They both laughed and she went back to place his order.

Jack opened the newspaper and scanned the headlines. There was nothing that qualified for news. Discord in the Middle East, Russian aggression, Flooding in the South, Fires out west. It seemed as though the front page never changed. He turned to the back of the paper, the sports page. On the top of the page, it read **ISLANDERS LOSE TO BRUINS 4 – 1.** Jack thought to himself, "*now that's newsworthy.*" Betty came back with Jack's Latte and put it down on the table. Jack took a sip and said, "Just right Betty, no one does it better than you." Betty tilted her head and smiled and went back towards the kitchen. He continued to scan through the meaningless drivel in the back pages of the paper. Then Betty came back with the pancakes. She put the plate on the table in front of Jack and then brought over a fresh bottle of natural organic maple syrup from Vermont. Betty said, "Enjoy Jack." He looked up and said, "Did you make these yourself Betty?" She smiled a sarcastic smile and said, "Yeah, and I tapped the tree in Vermont to get the syrup too." They both laughed and she went back to the counter. The pancakes were outstanding. They were cooked just right. A light brown on both sides with a little crispness to the edges and the insides had just the right amount of fluff. And there was a blueberry in every bite. As the syrup dripped from the top pancake down to the plate, he made sure to scoop up every drop with the pancake on his fork. Jack cleaned the plate of pancakes in about 5 minutes and by that time his Latte was gone as well. He picked up the small glass of orange juice and slugged it down. As he was picking up the napkin to wipe his mouth, Betty came back over. "How was it, Jack?" Jack smiled, "Simply the best Betty, simply the Best." She smiled, "Thanks Jack, but I meant the pancakes." He smiled, "It was worth at least a $20 tip." She smiled and put the bill down on the table and walked away. Jack picked up the bill and put a $20 tip down next to his plate, then he walked up to the counter to pay the bill. On his way out he could see Betty clearing his plates from the table and putting the tip in her apron. She yelled to him, "Don't be a stranger, Jack." He smiled and gave her a wave as he left the Café.

Once on the street, He checked his phone app to see how far Chumley had gotten with the watch. He was still about 3 hours away from the city. Jack was sure that he was headed to his apartment off West 52nd Street. A plan was developing in his head. He thought that the best way to get the watch back was to surprise Chumley as he entered his apartment building. But he knew that Chumley was carrying a handgun, so he would have to get him from behind, so he wouldn't know what hit him. He walked up to his garage and gave Fernando the attendant a wave as he walked in. He took the elevator to the second level and went to his car. He remembered that Chumley had put a tracking device on his rear bumper. Jack went to the rear of the car and reached under the bumper. He felt a little round tab and pulled it off. It was the tracking device. He dropped it on the floor and crushed it with his foot. He opened the car door and got in. He just sat in the driver's seat for a few minutes enjoying the custom leather feel and smell. This was turning out to be a really good day. He hoped that it would end that way too.

He spent about 30 minutes just sitting and thinking and then he was ready to put his plan into motion. He started the car and listened to the 500 horses under the hood. He put the car in gear and made his way down the ramp and through the exit onto the street. He passed by his apartment building, and as he did, he turned and looked at the entrance to the building and he saw Sylvio Donato and Jimmy Sissi coming out of the building. Sylvio was still wearing that same baby blue suit and Jimmy had on his leather jacket. Jack was glad that he missed them, but now he had to wonder if they got into his apartment and what kind of damage they could have done there. He thought to himself, "*I'll deal with them later.*" He drove towards West 52nd Street. Normally he would have called Trudy to let her know where he was going, but he had given her the day off. If everything went to plan, he would be calling her later anyway to confirm that the $100,000 had hit his account.

Jack weaved through the city streets like a serpent. Almost like he was part of the landscape. He arrived at Chumley's apartment building and pulled over to an open parking spot about 3 car lengths before the entrance to the building. He turned off the ignition and pulled out his cell phone to check Chumley's whereabouts. He was still about 2 full hours outside the city. That was fine with Jack. It had been a while since he'd been on a stakeout. He liked the solitude, the anticipation, and the butterflies in his stomach. He took his stun gun out of the glove box and put it into a holster on his left side. Then he just sat back and waited. He started to count people on the street. How many men, how many women? What color shoes were they wearing? How many blonds, brunettes, redheads? When you're on a 2-hour stakeout, you start to fill the time with just about any meaningless activity. The 2 hours passed quickly. Jack looked down at his phone and he could see that Chumley was now only about 2 blocks away from the apartment. He put his hand on his stun gun and got ready to make his move.

Jack looked out the driver's window and he saw Chumley's car pass by. He looked down at the app on the cell phone and tracked Chumley as he parked about a block past the building. Jack opened his car door and got out of the car. He walked up to the apartment building and there was an alley about 3 feet wide between the buildings. He crammed himself into the ally as he waited for Chumley to arrive. He put his cell phone on camera mode and reversed the picture so that when he held the phone out of the alley with his left hand, he could get a view of who was coming up the street. He could clearly see Chumley about 30 feet from the front door. He was carrying the box that contained the *Henry Graves Supercomplication* with 2 hands in front of him. As soon as Chumley started up the steps and approached the front door, Jack sprung out of the alley and shot the 2 electrodes from his stun gun towards Chumley. They landed in the base of his neck in the back of his head. Chumley started to shake violently and went to his knees. Jack pulled the electrodes out of his gun and stuck the taser on the side of Chumley's neck and Chumley went down face-first on the top step. He wasn't unconscious, but he was definitely incapacitated. As Chumley groaned and rolled around on the top step, Jack picked up the box with the watch and ran back towards his car. He got in, put the box on the passenger seat, and started the car, and drove off down West 52nd Street until Chumley was out of sight. After driving for about 5 minutes, he pulled over and took out his cell phone. He dialed the number for George Flax. The phone rang twice, and George Flax picked up. "Hello, Mr. Trane. So nice to hear from you. I trust that you have good news for me." Jack spoke slowly, "Mr. Flax, I have the watch and I'm going to deliver it to you. No more fooling around. I'm not going to your office or your apartment, but I'm bringing it directly to the main office for Amalgamated Insurance Company. I can be there in 25 minutes. I suggest that you do the same." Flax responded, "Yes Mr. Trane, that will be acceptable. I will be there." Jack smiled, "And we can make sure that you have my account number to wire the $100,000 finder's fee." Flax responded, "Of course Mr. Trane, that was the deal. When I get the watch, you get the $100,000." Jack was nodding his head, "I'll see you in 25 minutes, Mr. Flax." They both hung up the phones.

Jack had the box on the front seat, but he hadn't checked to see if the watch was actually in the box. He started to sweat just a little bit under the brim of his hat. He slowly reached over and opened the box. He breathed a heavy breath and a sigh of relief. There was the watch, still in the box. A beautiful sight for sure. He closed the box and drove towards the main office for Amalgamated Insurance, which was on Pearl Street in the financial district. As he drove, he was ever so careful not to stop quickly or do anything that would upset the $24,000,000 box on the passenger seat. About 25 minutes later he arrived at the Amalgamated Insurance company. There was a parking garage, so Jack pulled in and parked on the third level. He got out of the car with the box under his arm and got into the elevator. Two other men got into the elevator with Jack. One looked like he worked on Wall Street. He was tall with dark hair, sharply dressed in a dark gray suit, and he was carrying a briefcase. The other was a young man with dirty blond hair. He was carrying a skateboard under his arm and had so many holes in his pants, that you could see more skin than material. Jack was suspicious of both of them, but when you're carrying $24,000,000.00 under your arm, that's par for the course. The elevator descended to the first floor and Jack got out. As he left the elevator, he was suspicious of everyone. He couldn't wait to hand the box off to George Flax and put this case behind him.

He walked over to the skyscraper that Amalgamated Insurance was in. He walked into the building and there was a nice-looking receptionist sitting at a desk adjacent to the elevators. She was probably in her late 30's with short light brown hair. She was wearing white chunky hoop earrings and looked to be wearing a blush cashmere cable sweater. Jack went up to the desk and asked, "I'd like to see Mr. George Flax," The receptionist smiled as if she was expecting Jack. She said, "That would be the 12th floor, office 10B." He thanked her and got into the elevator. He pushed the button for the 12th floor and the elevator rose quickly. Within about 5 seconds, the door opened, and Jack walked out. He followed the signs to office 10B. As he was walking down the hallway, he could see 2 large men in black suits standing outside an office door. He assumed that was office 10B. He was correct. He walked up to the men in the black suits. He said, "Hello boys." They didn't answer. He walked into the office and at the far side of the room, George Flax was sitting behind a desk. George Flax saw Jack come in and he waved him over. Jack walked over and sat in a chair directly in front of Flax's desk.

Neither man said anything. Jack just lifted the box and put it squarely on the desk in front of George Flax. Jack sat back down in his chair and again neither man said anything. They both just sat there looking at the box. George Flax took a deep breath and reached for the box. His hands were shaking. He slowly opened the box, and his eyes grew wide, and his mouth was open, but nothing came out. Finally, Flax exclaimed, "Fabulous, just fabulous!" He looked up at Jack and said, "Mr. Trane, outstanding job. You did well. Your finder's fee will be in your account within the hour. It's been a pleasure doing business with you." Jack smiled a big smile. "Well Mr. Flax, if you ever need anyone to retrieve another $24,000,000.00 watch, you'll know who to call." George Flax was just staring down at the watch, he had nothing more to say. Jack got up and extended his hand to shake George Flax's hand. George Flax extended his hand to shake Jack's but continued to look at the watch. Jack shook George's hand and left the office. As he walked away, he turned and gave the thumbs-up sign to the two men in the black suits. They had no response.

Jack headed back to the garage and got into his car. He had a great sense of satisfaction in knowing that he had just closed this case, but it didn't last long. He knew that Tony Gumbati would be looking for him. He was still expecting the watch. Jack was going to have to use this to his advantage. This is the very reason that he had a 3D-printed watch in his safe. His plan was going to take care of Gumbati, Sylvio Donato, and Jimmy Sissi. At least that was the plan.

CHAPTER 19

Jack went back to his office. He was going to pick up the 3D-printed watch in his safe and bring it back to his apartment. As he opened the door to the office, he went slowly and listened for any sounds like footsteps or voices coming from within. It was silent so he closed the door behind him and went into his office. He sat down in his chair for a moment and contemplated what kind of improvements he could make with the $100,000 finder's fee. He thought that he might get a new file cabinet. The one that he had was an old upright forest green cabinet that weighed about 500 pounds. He thought that a nice tan horizontal file might give the impression of success. Or maybe he'd get one of those gold *Cross Townsend* pens to keep on his desk. He always wanted one of those. He thought that he would get a pen for Trudy too. Maybe one with her name on it. For Jack, those were major improvements. He never really had that much money, so he wasn't that good at spending it.

He was sure that the finder's fee would have hit his account by now, so he called Trudy at home from his desk phone. She answered, "Hello Jack, I thought that you gave me the day off?" Jack was leaning so far back in his chair that he could see the ceiling. He said, "Trudy, you know I never go back on my word. A day off is a day off.

But I just need you to go online and check my bank account. I need to know if the $100,000 finder's fee has cleared my account." Trudy breathed heavily, "Jack, why don't you just learn how to log into your account, then you could check it anytime you want." Jack laughed, "That's why I have you, Trudy." He hated online banking and figured that if someone else logged in, his information wouldn't be at risk. His internet skills were limited. Jack could hear Trudy snapping her gum and the clicking of a keyboard, then she came back on the line, "Yes Jack, the $100,000 has hit your account. You're a rich man. You know Jack, we could use some of this money to make some improvements around the office." Jack responded, "I'm way ahead of you Trudy, I already have some improvements in mind." Trudy had a skeptical look on her face, "Really, Jack? I can't wait to see what kind of ideas you have." She knew that her idea of improvements was much different than his. Trudy rolled her eyes towards the ceiling, "We'll talk about it tomorrow Jack," He was smiling and said, "No problem Trudy, I'm sure you have some good ideas too." They both hung up the phones.

Jack sat at his desk contemplating how things might be turning around for his PI business. This was the biggest payday that he had ever experienced, and so far, he had been able to stay clear of any bullets or cement overshoes. But things were about to change.

He heard the door to Trudy's office open. Then the sound of shoes walking across the floor. He looked up and standing in the archway of his door was Sylvio and standing right behind him was Jimmy. Sylvio smiled at Jack and said, "Hello Mr. Trane. We've been looking for you." Jimmy chimed in from behind, "Yeah, the boss wants to see you." Jack sat back in his chair and smiled back at Sylvio and said, "You boys must be tired from trying to track me down for the past couple of days. Why don't you come in and have a seat and we can all catch up?" While he was talking, he was also reaching down to the heels of his shoes and taking out the 2 knife blades. He held one in each hand and hid them in the cuff of his shirt. Sylvio yelled at Jack, "Quit stalling, Trane. The boss wants to see you right now and what the boss wants, the boss gets." Jimmy chimed in from behind, "Yeah, and you might want to bring an extra pair of shoes." Sylvio and Jimmy laughed out loud. Jack was still sitting in his chair. He said, "Look, are you guys still sore about that little train ride to Washington? That was just a little joke, nothing personal" Sylvio said, "Well Mr. Trane, now the joke is on you. And it's about to get very personal. Get up!" Jack got up from his chair and walked in front of Sylvio and Jimmy out the door. As they entered the hallway, Sylvio was on Jack's right and Jimmy was on his left. As they continued walking down the hallway, Jack knew that he had to make his move now, before they left the building. Just before they reached the top of the stairs Jack fell to his knees and took the knife blades in each hand and jammed it into the top of Sylvio and Jimmy's shoes. It pierced the leather and went deep into the top of their feet. They both went down on the floor screaming and holding their foot. As they were writhing in pain and rolling around on the floor at the top of the stairway, Jack sprung up and ran down the stairs. As he approached the door, he turned to look back. Sylvio had a gun in his hand and pieces of wood were flying in the air from a bullet that just hit the doorjamb to the right of the door. Jack ran out the door and onto the street. His car was parked about a block away. He got into his car, started it up, and stepped on the gas. Blue smoke rose into the air as the rubber from his tires burned as he entered traffic.

This was not part of Jack's plan. He was hoping to put off seeing Tony Gumbati until he met with Debra Thorn and Danny Watts. He wanted to make sure that when he exposed Gumbati as the person behind the plan to steal the watch, Thorn and Watts would be there to take him into custody. But now it looked like Gumbati had a plan of his own. From here on out, his office and his apartment were not going to be safe places to hang out. He needed a new plan. He needed someplace to crash temporarily until he could sort this all out. His good friend Detective Harry Soul came to mind. He was hoping that Harry would let him crash at his apartment for a couple of days. He pulled out his cell phone and dialed Harry Soul's number. The phone rang a couple of times and Harry answered, "Hello Jack, I haven't heard from you in a while. You must need something." Unfortunately, it seemed like every time Jack called Harry it was for some kind of favor. Harry was always ready to say no, but Jack usually persuaded him to say yes. Jack took a deep breath and said, "Harry, good buddy, how are you doing?" There were about 10 seconds of silence and Harry said, "Come on Jack, I know this is not a social call. What do you want?" Jack's voice was almost apologetic, "Look Harry, I need a favor." Harry broke in, "Gee, That's a surprise." Jack continued, "No, really Harry, I'm in a bit of a tight situation. Tony Gumbati is looking for me and I can't go back to my office or my apartment. I was hoping that I could stay at your place for a couple of days until this all blows over." Harry laughed, "Till what blows over? Your life?" Jack was serious, "Look Harry, I know that in the past I might have taken advantage of our friendship, but I'm really in a bind here. Can you help me out?" Harry thought for a minute and said, "Jack, is that cute secretary still working for you, Trudy?" Jack rolled his eyes; he knew what was coming. He said "Yeah, but we don't have to worry about Trudy, she'll be OK, Gumbati is not looking for her." Harry smiled and said, "Well Jack, I'll tell you what. If you can get me a date with Trudy, I'll let you sleep on my couch for a couple of days." Harry had been trying to weasel a date with Trudy forever, he really felt that this time it was going to work out. Jack said, "Now Harry, you know that I don't control Trudy's social life, and I think that she's seeing someone right now anyway. But I'll put a good word in for you." Harry raised one eyebrow and said, "Sorry Jack, that's not good enough. After all the favors that I do for you, I'm just asking you for this one little thing." Jack was now squinting as he responded, "Ok Harry, let's meet halfway. What if I take Trudy out to dinner, and you just happen to show up and join us at the table." Harry thought for a moment, "Ok, Jack, I think we can work with that. You can stay on my couch for a couple of days. When can we go out to dinner?" Jack responded, "As soon as I take care of Gumbati, I'll set something up for sure." In the back of Jack's mind, he knew this would never happen, but Harry Soul was so desperate to go on a date with Trudy, he bought it hook, line and sinker. Jack said, "See you later Harry." They both hung up the phone.

It was still early, about 2:30 PM and Jack had some thinking to do. He needed to come up with a new plan to trap Gumbati. There was a place under the Brooklyn Bridge near the water that he liked to go to when he needed time to reflect. So, he drove over the Brooklyn Bridge into Brooklyn and got on to Water Street. He found a parking spot and parked his car. Then he walked down to Empire-Fulton Ferry State Park. He found a bench overlooking the East River and he sat down. It was a clear day and the New York skyline along the financial district was inspiring. The November air was cold, especially when the wind came up from the East River. But he didn't mind. He liked the cool air. He sat there for about an hour, but he couldn't come up with a plan to trap Gumbati. He headed back to his car and the dark shadows were creeping across the city. It was approaching 4:00 PM and that's usually when the sun is low in the sky and the buildings all cast a dark grey shadow as a reminder that the darkness will soon overtake the city that never sleeps. Jack got back to his car and drove around the city for a couple of hours. He stopped to pick up a few things for his stay with Harry Soul and he also stopped at a McDonald's for a little fast food. By the time he was finished, it was about 7:00 PM and he headed over to Harry Soul's apartment which was over on West 157th street. It was usually so congested in this part of the city, it was not unusual to see cars double parked, but he found an open parking spot just 3 spaces before the front door to Harry's apartment building.

Jack went up to the building and rang the buzzer to Harry's apartment. The buzzer went off and Jack went in. Harry lived on the 3rd floor, so Jack climbed the stairs. He figured that after all the meals he had eaten over the past 3 days, he needed the exercise. He knocked on Harry's door and the door opened. Harry said, "Come on in Jack, make yourself at home." Harry was a bachelor. This was a no-frill's apartment. He had 4 rooms. A bedroom, a kitchen that turned into a living room, and a bathroom. It was decorated with a poor police detective theme. The furniture was old. There was a rip in the material on the couch. The table was an old Formica table from the '50s and the refrigerator was empty except for about 12 beers and a bottle of milk. Jack wasn't complaining, he was glad he had a place to stay for a couple of days. Harry asked Jack, "Would you like a beer?" Jack said, "You're playing my song, Harry." They both had a beer, they talked for a while about the case Jack had been working on and Harry warned Jack to stay clear of Tony Gumbati. Harry told Jack, "Jack, we've been trying to nail Gumbati for years. We can never get anything to stick. He always has an alibi, or he pays off some judge to clear the case, or the witness just conveniently disappears. The person who brings him down is going to get a medal." Jack laughed, "Remember that detective that used to be down at your precinct, Danny Watts?" Harry sounded disgusted, "Danny Watts? That punk was the definition of a train wreck." Jack smiled, "Yeah, well I'm thinking that He's going to bring down Tony Gumbati." Harry laughed and laughed until he coughed. "That will be the day Jack, that will be the day!" Jack agreed, "Yeah, Harry, that will be the day." After talking with Harry, Jack had started to formulate a plan, but he wasn't sharing it with Harry. It was getting late so both men decided to turn in for the night. Harry retired to his bedroom and Jack stretched out on the couch.

The mornings seemed to come fast. Jack opened his eyes, and he could hear Harry in the shower. Harry was an early riser. It was about 7:00 AM, Jack usually got up somewhere between 8 – 9. But beggars can't be choosers, so he sat up on the couch and rubbed his eyes. Everything was still a bit foggy, so he walked over to the window to get some sunlight. It was a clear day in the city, hopefully, this was a good sign. Harry came out of the bathroom and Jack went in. There was not much morning banter between them. Harry was not a morning person. While Jack was in the bathroom, Harry yelled at the door, "Jack, I'm heading into the office, make sure the door is locked when you leave." Harry left the apartment. Jack showered and shaved and came out of the bathroom and finished getting dressed. He had on the same black pants from yesterday, but since they were black, they still looked somewhat fresh. He had on the same dark green turtleneck too. He was starting to like the feel of a turtleneck. Every time he put it on, he pictured himself as *Steve McQueen*." Jack found some instant coffee in one of the cabinets on the wall, so he heated some water on Harry's ancient stove, and made a cup of coffee. He added some sugar and milk, but it was still a pretty bitter cup of coffee. He missed his morning Latte. Well, at least he was awake. The first thing he wanted to do today was to get in touch with Detectives Thorn and Watts to work out a plan to take down Tony Gumbati.

It was still early, about 8:00 AM, but he thought that he'd try to call the precinct and leave a message for Debra Thorn. He dialed the precinct from his cellphone. There was an answer, "28th precinct, how can I direct your call?" It was a man's voice, and it was all business. Jack said, "I'd like to speak to Detective Debra Thorn." The voice came back "Hold please." The phone rang and Debra Thorn picked up. "This is Detective Thorn." Jack smiled, "Detective Thorn, this is Jack Trane, I'm glad you answered. I really wanted to see you, um, I mean I'd like to meet with you and Danny Watts about something." There was an uncomfortable silence. "Mr. Trane, that's funny, because Detective Watts and I want to meet with you too. Can you come down to the precinct?" Jack thought for a moment. "You want to meet with me too? Why would you want to meet with me?" Detective Thorn answered, "Well, Mr. Trane, it's much better if we discuss these things face to face. Just come down and we'll explain everything." Jack was hesitant, "OK, I'll be there." Jack was taken by surprise. Why did they want to see him? He didn't mind seeing Debra Thorn again but seeing Danny Watts under these circumstances left him feeling very uneasy. He took the last sip of his coffee and left the apartment.

He got into his car and drove to 8th Ave and found the 28th precinct. He had to park on the street. He locked the doors to his car and went into the precinct building. He walked up to the main desk to ask for Detective Thorn but as he reached the desk, Debra Thorn and Danny Watts appeared through a side door and greeted Jack. Danny was dressed in a dark gray Armani suit and Debra was wearing dark slacks and a dark turtleneck sweater. The dim lights reflected off oh her reddish-blond hair. Jack looked at Danny and said, "So you still buying your suits at Walmart Danny?" Jack laughed and Danny gave Jack the snake eyes. Debra Thorn said, "Thanks for coming down Mr. Trane, we appreciate your cooperation." Jack was admiring how good Debra looked in a turtleneck, then he thought to himself, "Cooperation in what? What is really going on here?" Danny Watts chimed in, "Come with us Trane, we have some questions that we want you to answer." Now Jack was getting a little nervous. Danny Watts pointed towards the inside of the building, he said, "Let's go slick, don't make me use the cuffs." Jack responded, "What are you talking about? Cuffs for what? I'm here because I have some questions for you." Debra Thorn, chimed in, "Let's all just relax. Mr. Trane, can I get you a cup of coffee, a soda, maybe a donut?" Jack looked at her with a confused look and a smile. He said, "Yeah, maybe a cup of coffee and a donut would be good."

They led Jack into the precinct, down a dingy hallway with dirty walls and lights that were flickering overhead. Eventually, they reached the interrogation room and they all walked in. It was a typical interrogation room. There were 3 cinderblock walls and one wall with a full 2-way glass mirror. Jack sat down adjacent to the mirror. Danny Watts sat to his left. Debra Thorn left the room briefly to get the coffee and donuts. Danny Watts was all smug, he said to Jack, "Are you sweating yet Trane? You're going down for this. I always knew that you were just a 2-bit gumshoe, just a con artist in a bad suit." Jack looked at Danny Watts straight in the eyes and said, "Look you little punk, I have no idea what you're talking about, and unless you start making sense, I'm walking right out that door, after I wipe the floor with your face." Danny responded, "Oh I forgot, you're a tough guy." Jack was clenching his teeth and Debra came back in with the coffee and donuts. She put the box of donuts on the table in front of Jack and handed him a cup of coffee. She said, "I hope you two boys were playing nice." Danny stood up and began pacing the room at the far side of the table. Jack took a donut, a chocolate-covered one, and took a bite. He took a sip of his coffee and said, "Ok, now why am I here? What is it that you think I've done?" Detective Thorn said, "Mr. Trane, we know that you were working on a case involving the *Henry Graves Supercomplication*." Jack responded, "Yeah, that's right, I solved that case yesterday." Danny Watts chimed in, "Yeah you solved it alright." Jack looked confused. Debra said, "Mr. Trane, we got a call from George Flax, at the Amalgamated Insurance Company. He advised us that his 2 associates were killed on the way to deliver the watch to the rightful owners. The watch was stolen. It never made it to its destination." Jack still looked confused, "What does that have to do with me? I delivered the watch to George Flax; it was in his possession." Debra responded, "Yes Mr. Trane, we know. The problem is, you were the only one who knew that George Flax had the watch and that his 2 associates were going deliver the watch to the rightful owner. That makes you a person of interest." Danny Watts chimed in, "No! That makes you guilty. Admit it Trane you stole the watch and you're going to cash it in for millions." Jack stood up. Debra advised Jack, "Please sit down Mr. Trane." Jack sat back down. He said, "I did not steal the watch, I did not kill anyone, and I think that I'm being set up." Debra asked, "Set up by who Mr. Trane?" Jack breathed heavily, "I don't know." Jack thought for a minute and then he said, "When was the watch stolen?" Debra responded, "Sometime between 7:00 and 8:00 PM last night. Danny Watts looked at Jack with squinted eyes, "Let me guess, you were at the movies?" Jack smiled, "I have an alibi, one that you can't dispute. I was with Detective Harry Soul from 7 o'clock last night until 8 o'clock this morning." Danny Watts threw a pad of paper down on the table. He said, "We'll just see about that. You better not be trying to con us Trane. Remember, I know how you work." Jack now looked relaxed and calm, he said, "Keep your shirt on Danny, just call over to Harry Soul and he will back me up on this." Danny Watts and Debra Thorn left the interrogation room and left Jack alone while they went to make a phone call. Jack pulled another donut from the box, a Bavarian cream, and took a bite. He always liked the Bavarian cream ones, and this one was good. About 10 minutes later Debra and Danny came back into the room. Debra said, "Your alibi checked out Mr. Trane, you're free to go." Danny spoke up, "Yeah, but we'll be watching you." He put his index and middle fingers towards his eyes and then towards Jack.

Jack remained seated. He said, "Look, you two are obviously looking for someone who killed George Flax's 2 associates and then stole the watch. I think I can help. I've already logged a lot of hours on this case, and I know all the players. I think we can work together on this. What do you say?" Danny Watts responded, "No way Jose. You're nothing but trouble Trane." Jack looked at Danny and then at Debra, he said, "Hear me out. Danny, you want to get out of this bunko squad and get back to homicide, right?" Danny said, "Yeah, what of it?" Jack said, "The guy who solves this crime is going to get a huge commendation. And what if I were to say I can get you Tony Gumbati at the same time? What if the guy who brought him in was you, Danny? I think I can make that happen." Danny Watts was silent. Jack had given him something to think about. Debra spoke up, she said, "What about it, Danny? Every week you tell me you want to get back to homicide. This might be your chance." Debra disliked Danny. She disliked working with him. She disliked talking to him. She disliked looking at him. For her, it would be a win-win if Danny went back to homicide. Danny finally spoke up, "All right Trane, but I call all the shots, and don't get in my way, because if I have to, I'll take you down too." Jack smiled, "Sure Danny, whatever you say. Now let me fill you in on what I know, and my plan to catch a killer, a thief, and a mobster.

CHAPTER 20

Danny Watts wanted nothing to do with Jack's plan he resented working with Jack, he only agreed because there was something in it for him. But Debra on the other hand respected Jack and listened to what he had to say, and she was all in. Anything to get Danny Watts transferred out of her department sounded good to her. Jack said to Debra, "Detective Thorn, what if I told you that I could track the watch and we could recover it before the evening fell." Detective Thorn said to Jack, "Call me Debra. And I'd say I'd be pretty impressed if you could get the watch back period." Jack responded, "Thanks Debra, call me Jack, and rest assured we will have the watch back before the day is over. Let me set up a few things and when everything is in place, I'll give you a call. Then you and Danny can come in and take possession of the watch." She smiled, "OK Jack, you do what you have to do and let us know when you want us to come in." Jack smiled back, "Expect a call today Debra. I'm not sure what the circumstances will be or who has the watch, but I'll know more in a couple of hours. Stay tuned." Danny Watts came back into the room. He said, "Come on Debra, are we ready to roll or what? I think that I have some real leads on this case." Debra looked at Jack and smiled. She said to Danny, "Ok Danny, let's follow up on some of your hot leads." She rolled her eyes so only Jack could see, and she got up to leave with Danny. Jack got up and left the room too. They all walked out of the precinct together. Danny and Debra got into Debra's police charger. Jack got into his Shelby mustang, and they went their different ways.

Jack definitely had a plan in mind, but since he still didn't know who had the watch or where it was, things could change. And they did. Jack pulled over on 46th Street and pulled out his cell phone. He was hoping that the tracking device that he put in the box that contained the watch was still there and active. He opened up the app on his phone and the little red circle was still active. The little red dot was no more than 5 blocks from where he was parked. He put the car in gear and started in the direction of the little red dot. It led him right to the Port Authority Bus Terminal. The watch was somewhere inside the building. There was a parking garage right on 42nd street so Jack entered the garage and parked on the 3rd level. He got out of the car and headed across the street to the bus terminal. He was following the little red dot on his cell phone as if he were searching for buried treasure. There was heavy foot traffic around the terminal and several busses picking up and dropping off passengers. Jack walked into the building. The red dot on the phone app was coming from deep inside the building. The marble floors inside the terminal were littered with candy and gum wrappers and the sand crunched under his shoes. Jack followed the red dot. He walked down some stairs to a basement level and eventually ended up looking at a wall of red lockers. He put his phone near the lockers and inside locker

#B12 is where the box with the watch was resting. The lockers had little perforations in the doors so you could see inside. Jack looked into the locker through the holes, and he could see clearly, the box with the watch inside the locker. He tried to open the locker, but it was secured with a padlock. It was now obvious whoever took the watch and killed the 2 men in the black suits did not want to leave the watch in a bank lockbox. It would have been too easy to identify them by the security cameras. Whoever stole the watch was thinking. This was the perfect place to store the watch until he was ready to sell it. No one would ever suspect the watch in a bus terminal. However, whoever stole the watch was also unaware that Jack had the ability to track it. Jack stood in front of the locker with his arms crossed. Things were starting to come into focus.

Jack's plan was to get the watch to Debra and Danny so they could return it to the rightful owner. Then he was going to use his 3D printed watch to flush out the thief, the murderer, and the mobster. The details weren't all worked out, but Jack liked to work on the fly. The first thing he had to do was contact Debra Thorn. He got out his cell phone and called Debra. She answered, Hello, Detective Thorn." Jack smiled, "Debra, this is Jack. I have some good news. I've located the watch." She smiled and said, "Jack, I'm impressed. You work fast." She had a voice that was easy to listen to. Danny Watts could hear the conversation. He rolled his eyes and said, "Give me a break. Nobody could get the watch that fast. What did he have a tracking device on the watch or something?" Jack and Debra laughed. Jack said, "Of course I did Danny. If you would have stuck around to hear my plan you would have known that. Don't be such an idiot." Debra was laughing. Danny said, "Look Trane, why don't we just stick to the case and leave out the wisecracks." Jack made a pouty face, "Ohh..I didn't mean to hurt your feelings Danny boy." Danny's face was beet red. Debra broke in, "Ok Jack, tell us where you are, and we'll come and get the watch." Jack hadn't moved from in front of the lockers. He said, "OK Debra, I'm standing in front of the lockers in the ground level of the Port Authority Bus Terminal on 42nd Street. And when you come, bring a metal cutter, we need to cut off a padlock." Debra said, "Sit tight, Jack, we'll be there in 30 minutes."

Jack didn't move. He stayed right in front of the lockers for 30 minutes. He was tempted to walk over to the vending machine for a *Kit-Kat* bar, but he was determined that this watch was not going to fall into the wrong hands again. He made the sacrifice and stayed put. Debra and Danny came walking down the stairs and made their way over to the lockers where Jack was standing. "Jack said, "Nice to see you again Debra." Danny made a face, "Enough with the small talk. Where is the watch?" Jack pointed to locker B12. Danny had a pair of metal cutters at his side. He put the cutter on the padlock and clipped the top of the lock and the padlock fell to the floor and the small door of locker B12 slowly opened. Debra and Danny looked into the locker and Danny lifted out the Box with the watch. Jack raised one eyebrow and said to Danny, "Be careful with that Danny. There is a $24,000,000 watch in that box." Debra said, "Maybe I should carry it, Danny. This is more my area. When we get to the murder and mayhem part, I'll let you take the lead." Danny made a face and handed the box to Debra. She opened it up to look inside. The *Henry Graves Supercomplication* was still there. It "looked pristine. It looked new, even under the dim fluorescent lights of the Port Authority basement. Debra said, "It's really beautiful, isn't it?" Danny made a face, "Give me a break, it's just a watch." Jack said, "Yeah, and the Taj Mahal is just another timeshare." Danny said, "Whatever." Jack and Debra both shook their heads. Danny was such a punk; he had no appreciation for culture of any kind. He pretty much irritated anyone who worked with him or around him. Debra was motivated to make Danny look as good as possible. She wanted him to get promoted back to the homicide division and out of her hair. Debra turned to Jack and said, "We're going to take care of the watch, you keep digging and let us know what you find out on the robbery and murder. But don't take any chances, Jack. You're a private investigator, not a cop. There's a big difference." Danny spoke up, "Yeah, Trane, try to stay out of trouble. We don't want to have to bail you out." Jack just shook his head. Danny and Debra walked back up the stairs with the watch and left the building. Before Jack left the building, he placed a note inside locker B12. It read **6:00 PM, 281 W 53RD STREET PARKING GARAGE, 3RD LEVEL.** He was hoping to set a trap that would bring a thief and murderer to justice.

Jack headed back over to the parking garage. Now he needed a plan to take care of Tony Gumbati. It wouldn't be long before Gumbati had found Jack and fit him for cement overshoes. Jack wanted to find him first and set him up along with the murderer and the thief. In fact, for all Jack knew, Gumbati could be all three, but time would tell. He actually had 2 suspects in mind. One was Gumbati, the other was Harold Chumley, and it was time to set the trap. Jack left the garage and pulled over to the side of the road. He took out his cell phone and dialed the number for Tony Gumbati. The phone rang and Tony answered, "Hello Mr. Trane, good to hear from you. It seems like we keep missing each other." Jack smiled, "Yeah, but I seem to keep running into Sylvio and Jimmy. How are the boys?" Gumbati laughed, "Mr. Trane, I think Sylvio and Jimmy want to see you more than I do." Jack laughed, "Maybe they'll come to see me after they get a new pair of shoes. I hear their last ones have holes in them." Gumbati didn't laugh. He said, "I'm a businessman Mr. Trane, and we have some business to take care of." Jack leaned back in his seat and said, "I'm glad you mentioned that, Tony. Because, I have this watch in my possession and I'd like to get rid of it. So, we can do some business if you know what I mean." Gumbati got very serious. He said, "Mr. Trane, we have a deal. You deliver the watch and I give you $400,000." Jack was thoroughly enjoying this. He said, "Yeah, about that deal Tony. The price is now $1,000,000 and we need to make the deal tonight, or no deal." Gumbati coughed and said, "Mr. Trane be reasonable, I'm a businessman, not a bank. I can't come up with $1,000,000 in cash by tonight." Jack smiled, "Oh, that's too bad because that's the price and I'm holding a little auction tonight at 6:00 PM at 281 W 53rd Street Parking garage. The third level. Be there or be square. Good-bye Tony." Jack hung up the phone. He could only imagine the fury and rage on Tony Gumbati's face. He sat back and laughed.

He dialed again on his cell phone. This time he punched in the number for Harold Chumley. The phone rang and Chumley answered, "Hello, who is this?" Jack responded, "Harold Chumley, my old friend, how is that pain in your neck doing?" There were a few seconds of silence, then Chumley responded, "Trane, when I get a hold of you, I'm going to break you in half for what you did to me." Jack broke in, "Funny you should mention the word break, Chumley. Because that's just what I called you about." Chumley responded, "What are you talking about Trane?" Jack sat back in his seat again and said, "Well Chumley, I'm going to give you a break. I know that you still want the watch, and as it turns out, I have it. And if you want it back, it's going to cost you $1,000,000. Seeing that the watch is worth 24 million dollars, I guess that I'm giving you a break." Jack laughed. Chumley was gritting his teeth. "Look, Trane, I don't have a million dollars." Jack sounded disappointed, "Oh, that's too bad because you see, I'm auctioning off the watch to the highest bidder tonight and the bidding starts at a million dollars. If you're interested, and you're not doing anything tonight, and you can come up with some cash, the auction will take place tonight at 6:00 PM at 281 W 53rd Street Parking Garage, third level. Great talking to you Chumley." Jack hung up the phone on Chumley and then laughed out loud. He could picture Chumley banging his phone down on the table over and over again in a rage. Jack knew that no one was going to come up with a million dollars for the watch by 6:00 PM. But he also knew that Gumbati and Chumley would both be at the parking garage to get the watch. There was just too much money involved.

The plan was in place. The trap was set. Now he just had to make sure that Debra Thorn and Danny Watts would be there to back him up, otherwise, this could end badly.

Debra Thorn and Danny Watts were still in the process of returning the watch, so Jack gave them a little time before he let them in on the next part of his plan. He drove back to his office. He was pretty sure that Sylvio and Jimmy wouldn't be there after their last visit. He parked his car on the street about a block from his office. And he walked over to his building. He opened the outside door and went in. He climbed the stairs to the second floor. His knees creaked with every stair. After 49 years, he was glad that was all that was creaking. When he got to the top step, he could see little dried puddles of blood where he had stabbed Sylvio and Jimmy with the knives. Then towards the bottom molding on the wall, he found his 2 knife blades. He picked them up and wiped them against the side of his pants leg and put them back in his shoes. The way things were going, he thought that he might be needing them again, maybe at 6:00 PM.

He went into his office and headed directly for the wall safe behind the picture of Fenway Park. He turned the dial 10 left, 10 right, 10 left. The safe opened. Jack reached in and took out the box with the 3D-printed watch. He put it under his arm, closed the safe, replaced the picture, and sat down at this desk. He put the box on the desk. He dialed Trudy from his desk phone. The phone rang and Trudy answered, "Hello Jack, nice of you to keep in touch on my day off." Jack half-laughed, "Trudy, I just wanted to let you know that I have something big going down tonight and there are some really desperate people out there. I was hoping that you could stay with your friend Julie just for tonight. I don't want to scare you, but these people will stop at nothing to get what they want, and I don't want them to use you to get to me." Trudy was silent for a moment. She said, "Well I'm glad that you don't want to scare me, Jack. Why should I be frightened just because a bunch of hooligans are after me? I'll stay with Julie tonight. Should I come into the office in the morning, Jack? Or is someone going to be after you then too?" Jack made a face, "Very funny Trudy. But if all goes well tonight, everyone that's out to get me will be making license plates by tomorrow." Trudy said, "Ok, Jack, if you say so. I'll see you in the morning." Jack responded, "Thanks Trudy, see you about 9:30-10:00. I'll bring the donuts." He was still thinking of the donuts he had at the precinct this morning. Trudy said, "Good deal Jack, bring some chocolate covered." Jack said, "You read my mind, Trudy." They both laughed and they hung up.

Jack was still sitting behind his desk. He dialed the number for Debra Thorn. She answered, "Jack, what's up?" Jack said, "Plenty! I'm going to hand over Tony Gumbati and Harold Chumley to you and Danny tonight at 6:00 PM at the W 53rd Street Parking Garage. Can you guys be there and with some serious backup? There may be gunfire, so come prepared. I am going to get them to admit to the robbery and at least one murder, and there may be more. I won't know until it all unfolds in real-time. Debra answered, "Are you sure about this Jack? This seems to be put together a little too quickly for me."

Jack said, "Debra, this is what I do. No need to worry, I've got it under control." Danny chimed in, "Trane, you don't even carry a gun. How do you expect to come out of this alive?" Jack smiled, "Well Danny, that's what I have you for." Danny rolled his eyes. Debra asked Jack, "Ok, Jack, what's the plan?" Jack sat back in his chair so far, he could see the ceiling. He said, "Tony Gumbati and his 2 henchmen Sylvio Donato and Jimmy Sissi are going to meet me on the 3rd level of the parking garage on W 53rd Street at 6:00 PM. They will be heavily armed. Harold Chumley will arrive at 6:00 PM too and he too will be armed. They are both there thinking that they are going to get the *Henry Graves Supercomplication*, but what I have is the 3D printed watch that looks exactly like the *Henry Graves*. There may be another player that arrives too. I left a note in the locker at the bus station. We'll have to wait and see what happens. I am going to get them to admit exactly who committed what crimes before I hand over the watch. You guys will be there to hear everything. You might even want to record it. Then hopefully before the shooting starts, you can take them into custody. And Danny, you get the collar. How does that all sound?"

Debra took a deep breath. "Honestly, Jack, it sounds like a long shot. What's to prevent someone from just shooting you and taking the watch?" Jack smiled, "I have that all worked out. You'll see." Danny spoke up, "I say we do this. Sounds pretty low risk to me." Debra said, "Low risk for you Danny, not for Jack." Danny responded, "Yeah, that's what I meant." The back and forth, pros and cons went on for about 10 minutes, and then it was decided that they would go through with Jack's plan. Debra said, "We'll need about 10 uniformed policemen, to cover the perimeter of the garage and provide backup in case there is some action. And Jack do you have a flak jacket?" Jack answered, "Yes I do." She responded, "Then you better wear it." She continued "We'll have everyone in place by 5:00 PM, so Jack don't be late, and if anything goes sideways, say the word "**PICKLE**" that's the code word for us to come out and take over." Jack agreed, he said, "I like this plan, this is going to work." Danny spoke up, "It's go time." Debra said, "Ok, Jack, we'll be at the garage at 5:00 PM. See you there." They all hung up the phones. Jack was feeling good about his plan. He hadn't eaten anything since the donuts down at the precinct this morning, so he thought that he would get a bite to eat before he went over to the garage. He was craving a pickle.

Jack always kept a flak jacket in the closet in his office. He took it out and put it under his trench coat. It was bulky, but with the trench coat, you really couldn't tell that he had it on. It gave him a sense of security, even if it was a false one. He left the office and went down to the hot dog stand about 2 blocks up the street and he ordered 2 hot dogs with everything and 2 dill pickles. After Debra mentioned the pickles, he just couldn't get them off of his mind. He also ordered a Coke and a bag of *Sun Chips*. There was a bench nearby, so he sat down with the hot dogs. He put the box with the 3D watch next to him on a bench and he started eating. Sometimes, he enjoyed a couple of hot dogs just as much as a good steak. This was one of those times. He was going over the plan in his head as he was eating. There was so much that could go wrong with this plan that his head was spinning. He ended up eating the pickles before the hot dogs. He finished the meal and walked over to his car. He opened the door and got in. He placed the box with the 3D watch on the passenger seat and he just sat back in the custom leather seats. It always relaxed him to smell the custom leather and put his hands on the steering wheel. He sat there for about 45 minutes and then it was time to go. He reached back into the back seat and picked up his gray fedora and put it on. He started the car, put it in gear, let up on the clutch, and gently eased into traffic. In about 20 minutes he was parking his car on the 3rd level of the parking garage on W 53rd Street. Jack got out of the car and looked around. The place seemed empty except for the parked cars. Then he looked closer, and Debra was flashing a flashlight at him from behind one of the cars. That made Jack feel a little better, but he was still sweating from around the brim of his hat. Jack moved into position. He was standing towards the outside of the garage. There was an opening in the railing that would allow him to hold the watch out over the street below. This was part of his plan. It was about 5:30 PM. It was dark in the city and the lights in the parking garage gave off just about enough light so that you wouldn't bump into an oncoming car. The minutes passed slowly. Jack didn't usually suffer from anxiety, but he could hear the sound of his heart beating in his ears. There was a chill in the air and a stillness to the garage. Finally, it was 6:00 PM. Nothing seemed to be happening. Jack was wondering if he had overplayed his hand. Then a car rolled up the ramp. It was a black Lincoln Town car. It pulled into a parking space and 3 men got out. Tony Gumbati, Sylvio Donato, and Jimmy

Sissi. Sylvio and Jimmy were limping. Almost immediately another car pulled up the ramp. It was a late model Lexus. The car pulled into a parking space and Harold Chumley got out. All 4 men came walking in Jack's direction. Tony Gumbati yelled out, "Good Evening Mr. Trane." Chumley recognized Gumbati and said, "What's going on here Trane? Is this some kind of double-cross?" Then a 3rd man appeared in the dark recesses of the entrance to the 3rd-floor ramp. Jack couldn't believe his eyes. It was George Flax, and he had his gun drawn on Jack.

Jack stood with his back towards the railing and said, "Well it looks like the gang's all here." All 5 men stood in a semi-circle about 20 feet away from Jack. Flax spoke up, "That watch is mine Trane, give it here and there won't be any trouble." Gumbati responded, "That watch is mine, Flax. Back off!" Sylvio and Jimmy had taken their guns out now too. Chumley spoke up, "Why don't we just shoot Trane and take the watch?" Jack opened the box and took out the 3D watch. He dropped the box over the railing onto the road below. Jack said, "don't anyone come any closer, or I drop the watch 3 floors to the street below. Then this $24 million dollar watch becomes a piece of garbage." Jack smiled, "And by the way, if you shoot me the watch falls 3 floors to the street below as well and becomes a piece of garbage." Chumley spoke up, "Don't do anything stupid Trane, I'm sure we can all work out a deal." George Flax agreed, "Yes I'm sure we can work something out." Gumbati spoke up, "Yes Mr. Trane, I'm a businessman, we can work something out. I'm sure between the 3 of us we can come up with the million dollars that you requested."

Jack said, "All right, I'll work a deal with you bums, but before I let this watch go, I want the whole story. Flax, it appears to me now, that you were the ringleader in all this. Obviously, you found my note in the locker at the bus terminal. It was you that conspired with Tony Gumbati to steal the watch in the first place." Flax answered, "Very perceptive, Mr. Trane. I had the means; the motive and I created the opportunity. Tony had the connections." Jack spoke up, "Mr. Gumbati, it was you who employed Billy Bardsley to steal the watch from his armored car run. He was working for you. Why did you kill him?" Gumbati spoke up, "Mr. Trane I'm a businessman. Billy Bardsley wasn't good for business. He had to be eliminated." Jack spoke again, "I guess nobody expected the Valley's to steal the watch, and that's where you come in Chumley. Flax hired you to find the watch after the Valley's stole it. Then you came to me. You figured that I'd do all the dirty work for you. Then when Chumley went rogue and went after the watch for himself, Flax hired me to replace Chumley." There was silence for about 5 seconds then George Flax spoke. "Well, it looks like you have it all figured out, don't you Mr. Trane?" Jack said, "One more thing Flax, why did you kill the 2 men in the black suits? They were working with you." Flax laughed, "Mr. Trane, they were just employees. They knew too much. They became liabilities." Jack shook his head, "So once the watch was stolen from the armored truck, greed took over and it was every man for himself. Whoever gets the watch gets the spoils." Jack still had the watch dangling over the railing. Flax said, "Trane, the $100,000 that I paid you was just chump change. Why don't you bring that watch back in from over the railing, and we can all discuss how to split up the $24 million four ways? What do you say?" Jack smiled, he said, "I have a better idea, why don't we all just have some **PICKLES!**

It became silent very quickly and all you could hear was the sound of automatic rifles clicking their triggers ready. Danny Watts came out from behind a car and the 10 policemen came out from the shadows. Not a shot was fired. Flax, Gumbati, and Chumley all stood in shock and disbelief. They all looked at Jack as he held the watch outside the railing and let it fall to the street below. The look on their faces was priceless. There was actually a tear in George Flax's eye. Debra Thorn came out from behind the car. Gumbati, Flax, Chumley along with Sylvio and Jimmy were all put in had cuffs and Danny Watts got to read them their rights. Debra came over to Jack and gave him a big hug. Debra was a hugger. It was a firm, warm hug, and made Jack feel good. She said, "Congratulations Jack, for a minute there, I didn't know if we were going to get to the pickles." Debra and Jack laughed together. The 5 men were packed into police cruisers and taken off to the station. Danny Watts was close behind, he wanted to make sure that he got all the credit for the bust. Busting Tony Gumbati would surely get Dany his promotion back to homicide. Jack couldn't tell who was happier about that, Danny, or Debra.

When all was said and done, it was just Jack and Debra left standing on the 3rd level of the garage. Her reddish-blond hair even caught the dim lights of the parking garage. Jack looked at her and said, "You know, putting away punks and bad guys can really give you an appetite. Do you like fish and chips?" Debra responded,

"Funny you should ask Jack, I love fish and chips." Jack said, "Well I know a place not too far from here that has the best fish and chips in town. What do you say? My treat." She smiled, "I think I'd like that, Jack. I think I'd like that." He was right, things were finally starting to look up. He got to keep his $100,000 finder's fee, Tony Gumbati was finally off his back, and he was going to dinner with a redhead. It just doesn't get any better than that.